COLUMBUS NOIR

EDITED BY ANDREW WELSH-HUGGINS

BROOKLYN, NEW YORK, USA
BALLYDEHOB, CO. CORK, IRELAND

Published by Akashic Books
©2020 Akashic Books

Series concept by Tim McLoughlin and Johnny Temple
Columbus map by Sohrab Habibion

ISBN: 978-1-61775-765-5
Library of Congress Control Number: 2019935267

Akashic Books
Brooklyn, New York, USA
Ballydehob, Co. Cork, Ireland
Twitter: @AkashicBooks
Facebook: AkashicBooks
E-mail: info@akashicbooks.com
Website: www.akashicbooks.com

In memory of Mary Anne Huggins,
mother, motivator, lifelong mystery reader

ALSO IN THE AKASHIC NOIR SERIES

MUMBAI NOIR (INDIA), edited by ALTAF TYREWALA

NEW HAVEN NOIR, edited by AMY BLOOM

NEW JERSEY NOIR, edited by JOYCE CAROL OATES

NEW ORLEANS NOIR, edited by JULIE SMITH

NEW ORLEANS NOIR: THE CLASSICS,
edited by JULIE SMITH

OAKLAND NOIR, edited by JERRY THOMPSON
& EDDIE MULLER

ORANGE COUNTY NOIR, edited by GARY PHILLIPS

PARIS NOIR (FRANCE), edited by AURÉLIEN MASSON

PHILADELPHIA NOIR, edited by CARLIN ROMANO

PHOENIX NOIR, edited by PATRICK MILLIKIN

PITTSBURGH NOIR, edited by KATHLEEN GEORGE

PORTLAND NOIR, edited by KEVIN SAMPSELL

PRAGUE NOIR (CZECH REPUBLIC),
edited by PAVEL MANDYS

PRISON NOIR, edited by JOYCE CAROL OATES

PROVIDENCE NOIR, edited by ANN HOOD

QUEENS NOIR, edited by ROBERT KNIGHTLY

RICHMOND NOIR, edited by ANDREW BLOSSOM,
BRIAN CASTLEBERRY & TOM DE HAVEN

RIO NOIR (BRAZIL), edited by TONY BELLOTTO

ROME NOIR (ITALY), edited by CHIARA STANGALINO
& MAXIM JAKUBOWSKI

SAN DIEGO NOIR, edited by MARYELIZABETH HART

SAN FRANCISCO NOIR, edited by PETER MARAVELIS

SAN FRANCISCO NOIR 2: THE CLASSICS,
edited by PETER MARAVELIS

SAN JUAN NOIR (PUERTO RICO),
edited by MAYRA SANTOS-FEBRES

SANTA CRUZ NOIR, edited by SUSIE BRIGHT

SÃO PAULO NOIR (BRAZIL),
edited by TONY BELLOTTO

SEATTLE NOIR, edited by CURT COLBERT

SINGAPORE NOIR, edited by CHERYL LU-LIEN TAN

STATEN ISLAND NOIR, edited by PATRICIA SMITH

ST. LOUIS NOIR, edited by SCOTT PHILLIPS

STOCKHOLM NOIR (SWEDEN), edited by
NATHAN LARSON & CARL-MICHAEL EDENBORG

ST. PETERSBURG NOIR (RUSSIA), edited by
NATALIA SMIRNOVA & JULIA GOUMEN

SYDNEY NOIR (AUSTRALIA), edited by JOHN DALE

TEHRAN NOIR (IRAN), edited by SALAR ABDOH

TEL AVIV NOIR (ISRAEL), edited by ETGAR KERET
& ASSAF GAVRON

TORONTO NOIR (CANADA), edited by JANINE ARMIN
& NATHANIEL G. MOORE

TRINIDAD NOIR (TRINIDAD & TOBAGO), edited by
LISA ALLEN-AGOSTINI & JEANNE MASON

TRINIDAD NOIR: THE CLASSICS
(TRINIDAD & TOBAGO), edited by EARL LOVELACE
& ROBERT ANTONI

TWIN CITIES NOIR, edited by JULIE SCHAPER
& STEVEN HORWITZ

USA NOIR, edited by JOHNNY TEMPLE

VANCOUVER NOIR (CANADA), edited by SAM WIEBE

VENICE NOIR (ITALY), edited by MAXIM JAKUBOWSKI

WALL STREET NOIR, edited by PETER SPIEGELMAN

ZAGREB NOIR (CROATIA), edited by IVAN SRŠEN

FORTHCOMING

ACCRA NOIR (GHANA),
edited by NANA-AMA DANQUAH

ADDIS ABABA NOIR (ETHIOPIA),
edited by MAAZA MENGISTE

ALABAMA NOIR, edited by DON NOBLE

BELGRADE NOIR (SERBIA),
edited by MILORAD IVANOVIC

BERKELEY NOIR, edited by JERRY THOMPSON
& OWEN HILL

JERUSALEM NOIR, edited by DROR MISHANI

MIAMI NOIR: THE CLASSICS,
edited by LES STANDIFORD

NAIROBI NOIR (KENYA), edited by PETER KIMANI

PALM SPRINGS NOIR,
edited by BARBARA DeMARCO-BARRETT

PARIS NOIR: THE SUBURBS (FRANCE),
edited by HERVÉ DELOUCHE

SANTA FE NOIR, edited by ARIEL GORE

TAMPA BAY NOIR, edited by COLETTE BANCROFT

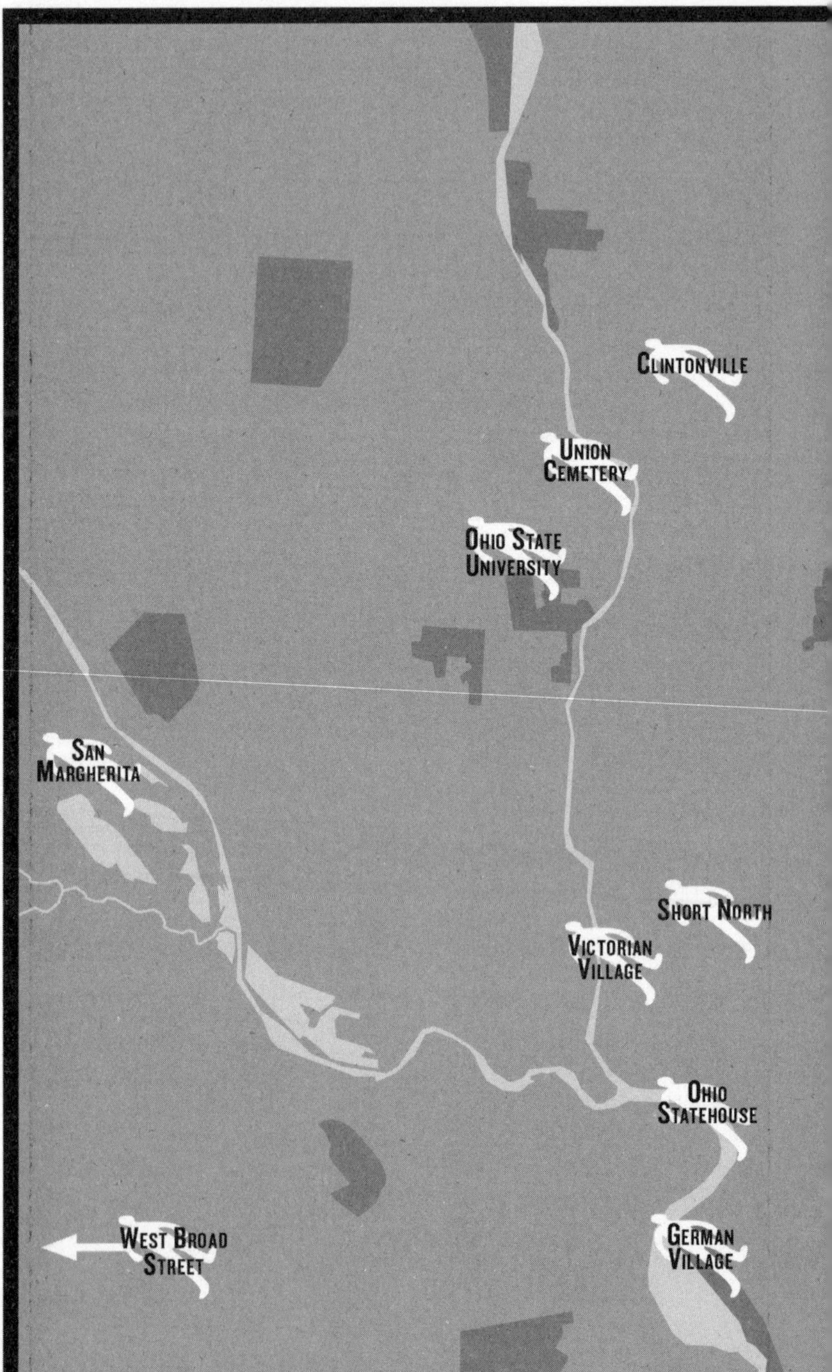
Clintonville
Union Cemetery
Ohio State University
San Margherita
Short North
Victorian Village
Ohio Statehouse
West Broad Street
German Village

COLUMBUS

NORTH SIDE

JOHN GLENN
COLUMBUS
INTERNATIONAL
AIRPORT

WHITEHALL

FRANKLIN PARK
CONSERVATORY
AND BOTANICAL
GARDENS

OLDE TOWNE
EAST

EASTMOOR

SOUTH END

TABLE OF CONTENTS

PART III: BUCKEYE BETRAYALS

INTRODUCTION
A CAPITAL PLACE FOR KILLING

You can kill a lot more than time in Columbus these days. Gang slayings, fentanyl poisoning, murder-suicide: we have it all, soup to nuts. Yet it's not like the older, supposedly kinder and gentler Columbus has completely disappeared. You can still take in a night of jazz at Dick's Den in Clintonville, visit the gardens at Franklin Park Conservatory on East Broad, stroll down the brick-lined sidewalks of German Village to the Book Loft, or admire the rows of muscle cars on display at the annual bean supper up on the Hilltop. And, as always, appreciate the sea of red that swarms Ohio Stadium on Saturday home games. Old Columbus is no farther than these still-vibrant city hallmarks, fondly pondered by residents as they do a slow burn sitting in traffic on 315 and 270 and 670 at the beginning and end of each day, wondering where in the hell all these cars came from.

Old Columbus, an afterthought burg that came with a silly nickname: Cowtown. The state capital dismissed as a sleepy Midwestern backwater, a bland center of state government and insurance workers and mindless football fans where the most exciting thing each summer was the Sale of Champions at the Ohio State Fair. The city unable to shake that annoying modifier—Columbus, *Ohio*. The Columbus recalled by former *New York Times* food writer Molly O'Neill in her memoir about growing up here, *Mostly True:* "Being average is considered a civic virtue in Columbus. 'We tend to do everything in this city at about a B-grade level,' Mayor Tom Moody once told the *Chicago Tribune* proudly." A locale considered a slice of white bread compared to the ethnic smorgasbord of Cleveland or the power lunch of Cincinnati and its Fortune 500 pedigree.

But the Cowtown moniker was a delusion, even way back when. The city's detractors, including some who called Columbus home, overlooked the legacy of the Ohio State Penitentiary that sprawled just north of downtown, where thousands of prisoners served their time in increasingly brutal conditions, and where not a few met their deaths at the end of a noose or from a jolt of electricity. They forgot the terror of the .22 Caliber Killers, whose slayings gripped the area in the 1970s. They've turned the page on Dr. Michael Swango, a serial killer believed responsible for at least thirty-five deaths of patients under suspicious circumstances in hospitals in the United States and Africa, including five deaths of otherwise healthy patients at the Ohio State University Medical Center in the early 1980s. And they gloss over the capital's long and shameful history of segregation. Those who consider the old Columbus a comfy couch conveniently ignore the guns and knives that were hidden just under the pillows.

Today, the city is experiencing the kind of growth spurt you associate with the chugging of steroid-laden Muscle Milk. We're creeping toward a million residents, the most of any city in the state, far outnumbering our few remaining bovine. More people live inside the city limits than in Boston, Denver, or Nashville. Developers are reshaping the region with thousands of new condos and apartments. And while it doesn't seem possible to squeeze in a single more brewpub or microdistillery, it appears that a new one is announced almost every week. A city built by Irish and German immigrants 150 years ago is experiencing new waves of visitors, with large populations of Somalis, Mexicans, Bhutanese-Nepalis, and many more pouring into town, even as a company called Amazon took notice and put us in the running for its second headquarters. These days, Columbus—"Cbus" to the hipsters—is a place millennials are moving to. Food, arts, LGBT friendliness: it took awhile, but we're finally as list-worthy as any big American city.

Of course, tall buildings cast long shadows. Columbus is also an epicenter of the opioid epidemic, awash in heroin and the even deadlier fentanyl as dealers flood the city with their wares. More than six hundred people died of fatal overdoses in central Ohio in 2017, a nearly 50 percent increase from the year before. On the streets, homicide rates have soared, with 143 deaths in 2017, surpassing a record set in 1991—old Columbus, remember?—at the height of the crack cocaine epidemic. The wealth gap in the city is growing, and Columbus is now one of the deadliest places in the state for babies trying to make it to their first birthday, even more so if their mothers are African American. These days, Columbus is a place forensic investigators are moving to. Overdoses, homicides, infant mortality: at long last, we're finally as lethal as any big American city.

In that light (and darkness) I'm pleased to present *Columbus Noir*, a collection of shadowy tales from the city's best storytellers set in neighborhoods across the metropolis. Sexual passion drives many of the stories, appropriate for a genre marked by protagonists striving for things out of their reach. Racism makes an appearance or two, as do those twin pillars of noir, greed and pride. Still, a deep appreciation of Columbus runs through the book as forcefully as the swath cut by the Olentangy after a couple of days of hard rain. In the end, it's my hope that this volume will stick a dagger in the heart of Cowtown once and for all, and instead reveal a robust, modern, exciting-as-hell city with opportunity, but also danger, lurking around most corners.

Opioids feature prominently in the stories, beginning with Robin Yocum's yarn of police corruption and desire, "The Satin Fox," set in Victorian Village, and which opens the first section, "Sin in CBus." The dark side of the city's booming housing market takes center stage in two stories set in very different neighborhoods, Kristen Lepionka's "Gun People," about home renovation gone awry in always-up-and-coming Olde Towne East, and Craig McDonald's "Curb Appeal," which explores the real estate gold rush in German Village. Finally, a city police detective struggles with a painful past in Chris Bournea's Eastmoor-set story, "My Name Is Not Susan."

Starting off the section titled "Capital Offenses," I draw on my reporting days covering shenanigans at the Ohio Statehouse for a glimpse into the darkest secrets of someone sworn to protect and serve in "Going Places." Tom Barlow uses Clintonville to tell a veteran's story of service, and fatalistic impatience with changes to his neighborhood, in "Honor Guard." For decades, the path to prosperity for many in Appalachian Kentucky was the trip up US 23 to Columbus. In "An Agreeable Wife for a Suitable Husband," Mercedes King goes back in time to the city's gritty South End in the 1970s to look at the aftermath of one family's northward journey. In "Take the Wheel," Daniel Best plumbs the limits of friendships and the dark side of gentrification in his Short North tale. Concluding the section, Laura Bickle, best known for her urban fantasy fiction, brings a touch of the Gothic to the relationship between a down-and-out young woman and a hoary homeless man who meet in Union Cemetery in "The Dead and the Quiet."

Starting off part three, "Buckeye Betrayals," Lee Martin looks at another chance encounter between an older man and a young woman, each reflecting an aura of death, in "The Luckiest Man Alive," set around San Margherita on the West Side. In "The Valley," based in Whitehall, Yolonda Tonette Sanders reveals how psychological lacerations suffered as a child drive a broken woman's quest for justice years later. Julia Keller lines up academia in her sights in "All That Burns the Mind," as she lays bare the evil side of good prose at Ohio State University. In "Long Ears," the volume's penultimate story, Khalid Moalim examines the impact of gossip on a North Side Somali family's attempts to both preserve its norms and mores and assimilate with modern America. Cities are enlivened and enriched by immigrants but don't always welcome them, as Nancy Zafris elucidates in our concluding story, "Foreign Study," about the inadvertent journey to the Hilltop neighborhood by a newly arrived Chinese scholar.

Head north out of Columbus on Riverside Drive a few miles, and not long after crossing under the I-270 Outerbelt you'll come to another old Columbus landmark—the limestone slab sculpture known as the Chief Leatherlips monument. The display, honoring a chief of the area's native Wyandots, is just this side of roadside kitsch, and is nonetheless—or perhaps because of that—a popular tourist destination. It also underscores the blood at the roots of the region even at the beginning: fellow Wyandots executed Leatherlips by tomahawk in 1810 for befriending whites. Like many a character in a tale of noir, he tried to rise above his station only to suffer a fatal setback. From time immemorial, it's a common problem in Cowtown—in Columbus—and beyond.

Andrew Welsh-Huggins
Columbus, Ohio
November 2019

PART I

Sin in Cbus

THE SATIN FOX

BY ROBIN YOCUM

Victorian Village

I was half in the bag, my forearms leaning against a sticky bar in a jiggle joint wedged hard behind the plasma bank on High Street. It was Christmas night. The girl on the stage was gyrating against the brass pole and had stripped down to a pair of knee-high black boots and a Santa hat. A dancer named Rochelle was sitting on the stool next to me, a pair of store-bought breasts pressing against my arm, her lips inches from my ear, her breath like a blowtorch. She said I was the most handsome man she had ever seen and, in the same sentence, asked if I had any cocaine.

I didn't, and sensed that I had immediately become much less attractive to her. I was going to tell her that vice cops didn't usually carry cocaine, but I thought that tidbit of information could wait until later.

"I'll buy you a drink," I said.

She looked over one shoulder, then the other. "How many sad sacks are sitting in here on Christmas night?"

Without looking, I said, "All of them."

"Yep, and every one of them will buy me a drink. I need a little flake. Can you get some?"

"Maybe."

She leaned away from me and frowned. "You're not a cop, are you?"

"Why would you think I'm a cop?"

"You look like a cop."

"That's extremely unfortunate."

"If you're a cop, you have to tell me. If I ask, you have to tell me the truth. That's the law."

It isn't the law; it's a myth perpetuated by cops to get people like Rochelle to say and do things that will eventually put them behind bars. Cops lie all the time—more than the perps, probably. "I'm not a cop," I said. "How many undercover cops work Christmas night?"

Although I was a cop, I wasn't on duty. Sadly, this is how I decided to spend Christmas. My daughter had invited me to dinner at her home in Minerva Park on the northeast side of town, but the ex and her new husband would be there, so I passed. He sold chemical fertilizer to farmers, and I didn't want to be subjected to more conversations about the importance of optimum nitrogen levels for soybean production, or listen to the ex blather on about how, in the world of agro-chemicals, he was a god. Good for you, Mr. Green Jeans. Take the ex and the cow shit on your boots and have a nice life. I told my daughter I was spending the day with my new girlfriend, which was only partially a lie. Rochelle wasn't my girlfriend, but I was leaning hard that way.

The girl onstage swung her Santa hat like a lasso and threw it into the crowd before walking off in nothing but her knee-highs. As she did, a stripper wearing a two-piece buckskin costume with fringe and beads, her straight black hair down to her waist, tapped Rochelle on the shoulder. "You're up, Buttercup," said Pocahontas.

Rochelle said, "When can you get the stuff?"

"I didn't say I could. It's Christmas, you know. Even drug dealers take time off."

"Uh-huh. Got to go, sugar." She pressed an index finger

to the tip of my nose, kissed the air, and climbed onstage. A moment later, she was peeling off her clothes, occasionally glancing my way and winking.

I could get her some cocaine. It was an asinine thought, but no less a reality.

It also meant that, by any barometer, my life was not heading in a positive direction.

There was a placard on the wall of the vice squad room that clearly spelled out the three most important rules for an undercover cop.

1) *Don't fall in love with a stripper.*
2) *Don't fall in love with a stripper who also is a junkie.*
3) *If you cannot determine if she is a junkie, see Rule No. 1.*

Vice cops violated these tenets on a regular basis. At least four cops I know married strippers. One of them, not having learned his lesson the first time, married another one. Only one of the marriages lasted more than a year.

In my fourteen years in the unit, I had steadfastly obeyed these rules—until the night I first saw Rochelle. Cops don't succumb to the temptation of the streets because we are weak. We succumb to the temptation because we want to. All that stuff you hear about the job being tough on families and causing divorces is a bunch of bunk. Cops are tough on their families and cause divorces because we have a difficult time keeping it in our shorts.

We all make bad decisions in life. Sometimes, we make terrible decisions, and we do so with full knowledge that they are terrible decisions. That was the case with Rochelle. Why was I so attracted to a woman who I knew was bad for me?

Because I'm an idiot?

That's certainly part of the equation. But mostly because I thought I could save her. It made no sense. How many cops had I told, *You can't save them, and you can't change them?* If it was fewer than fifty, it wasn't by much. Cops think they can walk into the lives of damaged human beings and suddenly it's all sunshine and kittens, all the ills and addictions and psychoses that afflicted them suddenly cured because a cop showed up with a pressed white shirt and badge. Every cop I know—apparently me included—thinks he's the smartest street psychologist in the world.

But here's the rub, bub. Most of them don't want to be saved. The myth that strippers are single moms trying to put food on the table is just that, a myth. For the most part, they're addicts, damaged goods, who have inserted them-selves into an environment where drugs are readily accessible. They want drugs and money, and an easy way to get both is to work in a jiggle joint. Semierect men will shove bills down their G-strings with uncanny rapidity.

Rochelle's performance was lackluster. She went through the motions without enthusiasm. Still, I felt a sting of jealously that she was naked and shaking the most perfectly rounded ass I had ever seen in front of a roomful of strangers. Yes, I see the irony in this. But, again, it was no less a reality.

When she finished, she went backstage to dress. She re-turned wearing a gold-sequined outfit with breastplates that reminded me of something a Viking shield-maiden might have worn.

"Nice outfit," I said.

"So, are you getting some stuff?"

"Maybe. I gotta go. Are you here tomorrow?"

"I'm here three sixty-five, sweetie."

As I got up to leave, Rochelle was already walking across

the room in search of someone with access to cocaine. A bouncer, a three-hundred-pound mouth-breather with more hair in his nostrils than on his head, was sitting on a stool that was groaning for mercy as I walked out. He looked me over, trying to recall how he knew me. I remembered. He had worked at several of Danny Bilbo's clubs, and I had arrested him years earlier during a raid at the Satin Kitten on Bryden Road. I remembered because I'm good at filing away the faces of dumbasses I've arrested. We were going to let him walk that night, but he lipped off and we arrested him for "contempt of cop," a catch-all charge for people not smart enough to keep their mouths shut. The official charges were interference and resisting arrest. He was so big we couldn't get our handcuffs around his wrists and had to use fourteen-inch cable ties instead.

My shoulders were hunched into the wind as I walked south on Neil Avenue toward Fifth Avenue and my apartment on the third floor of a Victorian home that had been restored to perfection by a couple of aging queens named Nick and Aldo. Sleet stung my face. I pondered the series of events that were about to put me on a path that could send me to prison.

Forty years earlier, a bunch of do-gooders—liberals and gays, mostly—decided that a section of Columbus north of downtown was ripe for gentrification. They started with Flytown, the working-class neighborhood where I grew up. They added a section of the nearby Short North and transformed both into the more egalitarian Victorian Village Historic District. We like doing that in Columbus—taking a dumpy part of town and renovating it into a trendy neighborhood of over-priced houses and chichi coffee shops that charge nine bucks for a mochachokachino, or whatever. We have Olde Towne

East, Old Oaks, German Village, Hungarian Village, Italian Village, Merion Village, and so on. At the department, we refer to this as "moving the trash," as it simply displaces a problem in one area and moves it to another.

When I started on the force, the Short North was derisively known as Little Appalachia. It was a neighborhood of enormous Victorian-era homes that had been butchered into apartments and leased to low-income tenants who escaped the hill country to the south. In those days, the Three Rs in Little Appalachia were Readin', 'Ritin', and Route 23 to Columbus as a steady caravan from southern Ohio and Kentucky made its way north in search of opportunity. The Short North became a haven for runaways and teenage prostitutes, and it was commonly said that the only virgins in the area were those who could outrun their brothers and stepdaddies. No one had a problem with the strip joints and shooting galleries in those days. It was fine to relegate them to one part of town, as long as no one of importance lived there. But now that money was flowing into the area, the old vice was an affront to the sensibilities of the new gentry.

As best I knew, the daughter of one of the mayor's major supporters moved into a house in Victorian Village and woke up one morning to find a derelict sleeping on her back stoop. She called Daddy, who called the mayor, who called the chief of police. As shit rolls downhill in the department, the order eventually ended up on my desk: *Clean up Victorian Village.*

The Satin Fox was one of the establishments on the hit list. I went in undercover in mid-November. That's when I first saw Rochelle. She was in her midthirties, but without the hardened look of the other girls. She was beautiful, and I was smitten. I saw her at the Giant Eagle on Neil Avenue one Saturday morning not long afterward. Even in the light of day, without the black lights and heavy makeup most of the girls use to mask a hard life, she was stunning.

I began going back to the club when I was off duty. And I began stealing cocaine from the property room.

It's not as difficult as you might think. You just need to be smart about it. There is always evidence for dozens of drug cases in boxes on the shelves. I would walk in under the pretense of double-checking evidence in some cases I had pending. While I was there, I opened a few boxes containing cocaine from arrests made by the narcotics boys. The coke, which had already been sent to the lab for testing and returned, was in plastic bags labeled by the narcs. I slipped them into my pocket and took them home, where I emptied the contents into a sandwich bag and refilled the bags with vitamin B powder. The next day, I returned and replaced the bags. Simple as that.

The key is, don't get greedy, and target the low-level busts that are likely to get pled out. Once that occurs, the confiscated drugs are incinerated, and no one is the wiser.

It was not unusual for me to be in the evidence room, and since I have a stellar record with several commendations for valor, no one suspected anything was amiss.

I returned to the Satin Fox with a small amount of cocaine. Rochelle saw me sitting in a corner and came over. "It's my handsome friend," she said. "What's your name again?"

"I didn't give you my name."

"Oh." She looked a little stung.

"I've got something for you."

Her brows arched. "Really? Something good?"

I nodded.

"When can I have it?"

"It's not free, you know?"

"It never is. What do you want?"

"Dinner, breakfast, whatever you call it when you go out to eat at three a.m."

The fine-dining options available around Victorian Village at that hour of the morning are limited to a couple of White Castles. I arranged to meet her at the Waffle House on Wilson Road on the West Side. The black man at the grill was One-Eyed Jerry Jack, a former Columbus middleweight who had been ranked eighth in the world in the late sixties before unleashing his famed left hook on the temple of his wife, putting her in a coma for two months and him in the Ohio Penitentiary for six years. The waitress was Delores McCool, who was pushing seventy, had varicose veins the size of mooring lines, a sprinkling of teeth, and three grandchildren she was raising for two meth-head daughters. I knew them both because the Waffle House was a regular stop for the vice boys after we got off our shift at two a.m. As we entered, I shook my head once and broke eye contact, and neither greeted me. They knew what I did.

We sat in a booth next to the jukebox and in full view of Wilson Road and a Speedway gas station, which is as intimate as it gets at the Waffle House. She said, "So, are you going to try to rescue me from the life?"

I shook my head. "Why would you think that?"

"I've gone out with some guys I've met at the club. They all come there because they like the excitement, the tease, the possibilities. Then, the first thing they want to do is fix you, make it all better, like I'm damaged goods."

She was describing every cop in the bureau. I said, "My experience has been you can only rescue people who want to be rescued."

"It's not a disease," Rochelle said. "It's a choice."

Delores walked up to our booth, pad and pen in hand. We both ordered coffee. I had scrambled eggs with cheese, and raisin toast; she had waffles with pecans.

"If you don't mind me saying, you speak pretty intelligently for someone who . . ." My words trailed off.

"For someone who takes off her clothes and shakes her junk at a roomful of men who would still be virgins if it wasn't for hookers?"

I swallowed hard. "Yeah, that."

"You might be surprised."

"Why's that?"

She told me she had earned a degree in musical theater from Otterbein, and once had a nice job in the development department with the Columbus Symphony Orchestra. She had belonged to a book club, run two marathons, and volunteered a couple of times a month at Children's Hospital.

"I had a pretty normal life—a good life," she said. "I'm one of the girls who should've known better. But once you're hooked on the dust, it's hard to get unhooked."

"How'd you get started?"

"Dancing or drugs?"

"Either."

"The same way just about every girl in the club got started. I made the mistake of going out with Danny Bilbo."

"You were Danny's girl?"

She shrugged and sipped her coffee. "As much as anyone can be Danny's girl."

"How'd you meet him?"

"I was with some coworkers at the Charity Newsies gala."

"How did a slimeball like Danny Bilbo get invited to the Newsies gala?"

"He's considered very respectable these days. He bought some of those quickie car lube franchises, some car washes, real estate. He's up front with that, but you can't find his name anywhere on his clubs or porno shops. In all honesty, I didn't even know who he was when I met him. He was charming. We flew to Florida on his private jet. He bought me nice jewelry and took me to nice restaurants. He bought me these." She glanced down at an impressive pair of breasts. "I thought things were getting serious, so when he told me I didn't need to work anymore, I quit my job. That's when he introduced me to cocaine. He set the hook. After a while, if I wanted more, I had to pay for it. He started giving me all the cocaine I wanted and running a tab. Of course, I couldn't pay for any of it because I'd quit my job. He tells me I can work it off in the clubs. I knew the love had gone out of the relationship. He has me right where he wants me. I'm his property. That's how I ended up at the Satin Fox. I'd like to tell you my story is unique, but it's not. All his old punches end up in the club, hooked on the junk, desperate for a way to get more."

Daniel Dominick Bilbo was a scumbag of the first degree and had been as long as I'd known him, which was all my life. He grew up in a duplex down the street from me in Flytown. His mother cleaned houses for people in the affluent suburb of Bexley, and his father was a drunk who beat the kids with a leather strap. They played in the street with welts and bruises on their backs and arms. The old man was found shot to death in 1969 in an alley behind the Columbus Buggy Company buildings; it was never solved. I looked at the file once and got the impression that no one put much effort into the investigation. It wouldn't surprise me in the least if Danny was the one who pulled the trigger.

Danny grew up wild and was just sixteen when he started

working as a bouncer in Benny Cassio's titty bar. He was a quick study. It wasn't long before he had a string of jiggle joints and adult bookstores all over Columbus. He had been at it for thirty years and had built an empire of human flesh with tentacles that reached out from central Ohio for hundreds of miles. The cops and the IRS were always poking at Danny, but he had loaded up with enough attorneys and accountants to keep trouble at bay. At least one business partner and three of his strippers had ended up in abandoned lots with holes from .22 caliber slugs behind their ears, but nothing ever connected Danny to their deaths.

He was a millionaire many times over and lived in a sprawling mansion in southern Delaware County, raised horses, and drove a Mercedes worth more than I make in three years. The corporation papers for his clubs were filed in different states using the names of different lawyers to place a nice buffer between Danny and the skin trade, so he could portray himself as a respectable businessman.

Yeah, in case you're wondering, I'm a little salty about our respective lots in life. I went to Catholic schools, got slapped around by the nuns, kept my nose clean, and followed the old man and three uncles onto the police force. After twenty-five years of dealing with pimps and whores, being spat on and cursed at, I'm living in a small apartment on the western edge of Victorian Village with a beautiful view of the parking lot of Battelle Memorial Institute, a mammoth research facility.

"What do you do?" Rochelle asked.

"This and that. I keep busy."

"I still think you're a cop."

I smiled. "Then why would you come out with me?"

She shrugged, ran a finger around the lip of her coffee mug, and told me why. It was exactly the answer I wanted to hear. I'm not going to tell you about the rest of the conversation. It's personal. Suffice it to say, I'd stepped out of an airplane at thirty thousand feet without a chute. I was falling hard.

We walked into the parking lot, passing a drunk couple talking too loud, and stood outside her car.

"I want to see you again—someplace other than the Satin Fox or Waffle House," I said.

"You seem like a really nice guy. Maybe you should find someone with a more promising future."

I leaned down and kissed her softly on the lips, caressing her face with my left hand. As I did, I reached into the pocket of my sports coat with my right, grabbed the baggie of cocaine, and dropped it into her purse.

She glanced down. "You never told me your name."

"It's Joe."

She started laughing. "Is that the best you can come up with? Joe?" She laughed again. "Okay, *Joe*, see you around."

I stood in the parking lot and watched until her taillights disappeared beyond the overpass, and she turned east on I-70.

My name really is Joe.

My instincts told me to listen to Rochelle and put her and the Satin Fox in my rearview. Of course I didn't. I went back the very next night. I supplied her with more cocaine and tried to come up with a plan of how to get her out of that club and off the bump. There was also going to be the uncomfortable conversation about my real job, but that could wait.

She was vague about her debt to Bilbo, but said it was crushing, and she couldn't afford to take time off. On one rare night away, we went to a nice restaurant in Springfield, about an hour west of Columbus, where I figured there was virtually no chance of being seen. We met for breakfast a couple of times, and twice she came to my apartment after her shift. I continued to steal cocaine and was confident that no one was looking at me. I was feeding a habit that I desperately wanted her to break. I had decided to find out exactly how far in hock she was to Bilbo and buy her freedom.

On Monday of the third week of February, I went to the Satin Fox just before midnight. I had bought her a peridot necklace and matching earrings for Valentine's Day. I was going to take her back to the apartment to give them to her. I also was going to present my plan to get her free of Danny Bilbo.

She wasn't there.

My gut seized up. A little Asian girl walked up to my table and leaned in, her breasts clearly exposed beneath her kimono. "All by yourself tonight?" she asked.

"Where's Rochelle?"

"I haven't seen her." And that quickly, she clutched the top of the robe with one hand and walked away.

I went straight to the mouth-breather at the door. "Where is she?"

Without comment, he reached into his shirt pocket and produced a business card. He said, "Mr. Bilbo said to stop by in the morning. You don't need no appointment."

The card read, *Daniel D. Bilbo, President, Bilbo Enterprises*, and listed his Delaware County address.

I was at his forty-acre spread at eight fifteen. He was leaning against a white fence that encircled a meadow where three quarter-horses were grazing; his eyes were focused on the animals, even as I pulled into the circular driveway. When I approached, he said, "Well, Sergeant Cullen. How's my old Flytown buddy?"

"I don't recall us ever being particularly close, Bilbo, and they bulldozed most of Flytown years ago. I-670 goes through where my bedroom used to be."

"Times change." He turned, one arm resting on a fence railing; he made no offer to shake hands. "We've got a little problem, Sergeant. You've been sniffing around one of my ladies."

The heat moving up my neck was like a gas fire. "Is there a law against that?"

"Of course not. You've got good taste. Rochelle's a doll baby."

"I hear you would know."

"One of the benefits of the job," he said, chuckling, enjoying my torment. "Rochelle's a good girl, but she talks too much. She told one of the other girls she had an admirer who was getting her all the cocaine she wanted. Of course, word got back to me because my clubs are like little Peyton Places. They can't wait to rat out one another. I wondered who would be giving her all that cocaine." He pulled his cell phone from his pants pocket, tapped a few buttons, and held the screen toward me. "So I looked at the security tape and, lo and behold, it was Vice Sergeant Joe Cullen."

"You've got nothing on that tape showing me giving anyone cocaine."

"No, but my understanding is that internal affairs doesn't have that high of a standard for conviction. My bet is you stole it from the property room. I send them a copy of the tape with you snuggling up to the stripper and tell them to check the property room for missing dope. There are probably records of you making too many trips there. You know how it works with those pricks in IA. You'd be a handsome trophy, Cullen."

I fought the urge to reach into my ankle holster, pull my service revolver, and pump six rounds into his heart. "Where is she?" I asked.

"I decided it was in Rochelle's best interests to get her away from the bad influence of a dishonest cop. She's on the rotation."

"Where?"

He smirked.

Bilbo had strip joints in Detroit, Buffalo, Fort Wayne, Pittsburgh, Cincinnati, Louisville, and Indianapolis. "On rotation" meant transferring the girls from club to club. It was a good way to keep the talent fresh, hide their felony warrants, and keep them from getting too close to the clientele, like me.

"If you hurt her, Bilbo, I swear to Jesus—"

"Why would I hurt her, Cullen? She makes me a lot of money. Do you think you're the only swinging dick who comes to the club looking for Rochelle? She's going to make me money somewhere else for a while. Let's just talk about your dilemma for a minute, shall we? The way I see it, you're in no position to be issuing threats."

"Bring her back to Columbus."

"We can talk about that. Everything's negotiable. I can bring Rochelle back and forget that you've been a naughty cop . . . for the right price, of course."

"What do you want?"

"Your narcotics boys busted Jimmy Meli last month."

"And . . ."

"He was carrying eight pounds of high-grade snow for Fat Joe Mangano. Half of that was my investment."

"So?"

"I want it back."

"I'm sure you do. That's impossible."

Bilbo held up the image on his phone. "Apparently, it isn't."

"Sneaking out a baggie or two is one thing. I can't walk out of there with four pounds of coke from the biggest bust in five years."

"Then we have a problem. You need to figure a way to get me the stuff. You do that, maybe you get your girl back."

"Maybe?"

"Let's remember, Cullen, you're the one with his dick in a wringer."

I turned and started back to my car. "I'll be in touch," I said.

"When?"

"This doesn't happen overnight."

"The clock is running, and I'm very impatient." I had taken a few more steps when he added, "Hey, Cullen, do you remember your nickname for me, the one you and all your necktie-wearing Catholic school chums thought was so funny?"

"That was a long time ago, Bilbo."

"I know, but certainly you remember Bilbo the Dildo. How could you forget?"

"Like I said, it's been a long time."

"Just so you know, I remember it with great clarity."

It was personal; I got it.

I drove back through Victorian Village to the Grandview Heights duplex where Rochelle lived. It was dark. I rang the doorbell once and knocked twice before I heard stirring inside. Pocahontas finally answered the door. Her real hair was a brassy blond, and it was matted to her forehead; she was barely dressed, if at all, and spoke from behind the door.

"Where's Rochelle?" I asked.

"I don't know."

I pulled out my badge. "Detective Cullen, Columbus vice. Do you want to rethink that answer?"

She swallowed. "I really don't. She left here yesterday morning with one of Danny's men. That's all I know."

I believed her.

She said, "These things happen sometimes, you know? I don't want to be next."

I handed her my business card. "If you see her, give her this and tell her to call me immediately."

She took the card, nodded once, then closed the door.

Two mornings later, I drove back to the Delaware County compound of Danny Bilbo. There were obviously security cameras everywhere, because Bilbo was already on the front porch as I was driving up the long lane. He pointed toward the horse barn, and I nosed my car up to the front doors. We walked inside, where a scrawny Latino was mucking out stalls. He set his fork against a stall wall and left without comment.

I handed Bilbo a paper bag, in which was a pound of high-grade cocaine in a ziplock baggie.

"Step into my office," he said, walking to a tack room at the rear of the stables. He pulled a sheet of paper from a battered desk and carefully drew out a line of cocaine. He pulled a crisp fifty-dollar bill from his money clip, rolled it tight, then leaned down, pinched off a nostril, and inhaled the line. It disappeared like dust into a shop vac. His eyes watered, and he smiled. "That's the stuff, Cullen. You may get your girl back yet." He swiped at his nose with the back of a hand. "When are you going to get the rest of it?"

I headed for the door. "I'll be in touch, Bilbo."

* * *

It was three days later before I called him again. "Bring it up," he said.

"No. I can't be seen at your compound anymore. It's too dangerous."

"Fine. Where?"

"There's a Mexican restaurant in the little strip mall across from the Lennox Town Center on Olentangy River Road. Meet me behind there at eleven o'clock tonight."

"How much have you got?"

"All of it."

"All three pounds?"

"No, all of it."

"Seven pounds?"

"I want Rochelle back, Bilbo."

It was overcast when Bilbo pulled behind the strip mall. He had the good sense to drive a nondescript Ford sedan. No sooner had he parked the car than I walked out of the shadows. "Pop the trunk," I said.

The trunk lid lifted, and I dropped a grocery bag inside. It hit with a thud.

I jumped into the passenger side and handed him a small baggie of cocaine. "Here. I peeled some off the top so you didn't have to open the entire package."

Bilbo said, "What are you so nervous about?"

"Oh, I don't know, maybe because I'm a decorated cop carrying around seven pounds of cocaine that I stole from the property room, and I'm sitting behind a Mexican restaurant with a guy who runs peeler bars."

"I'm a respectable businessman, Cullen."

"Uh-huh, keep telling yourself that, Bilbo. Test it, and let's get out of here."

"You worry like an old woman. You've gotten soft."

"Try it."

"I trust you."

"You shouldn't. Try it. You're not coming back at me later, claiming it was bad dust. We're done tonight."

Bilbo spread a long line of cocaine on the middle console. "Looks good," he said.

I held out my hand. "Let me use your cell phone."

"What? Hell no."

"Let me use it, goddamnit. I've got to make a call, and I didn't bring mine. It's got a GPS in it, and the department monitors every place I go."

Bilbo punched in his security code and handed me the phone. "You know, if you have access to this kind of stuff, we could make a lot of money."

I watched as he rolled up a bill and leaned into the line. The look on his face was orgasmic. He leaned back in his seat and smiled. But only for an instant. He had been doing cocaine for years, and he knew he was in trouble. "What was that?" he asked.

"Some stuff that's making its way into Columbus from southern Ohio. The cops down there call it Gray Death."

"Gray Death?"

"It's killing people left and right in Appalachia. I mixed up that batch especially for you, Bilbo. I put extra carfentanil in it for good measure. Do you know what that is?"

Danny's eyes seemed to be losing their focus. "No."

"It's an elephant tranquilizer."

"Elephant what?" Bilbo slowly reached into his jacket pocket for his phone, then realized his error. "My phone . . ."

"It's right here."

"Call 911. I'm in trouble."

"I know."

I went to his photos and erased everything. He made a gurgling noise as his lungs filled with fluid and his breathing slowed. His face went ashen, and beads of sweat appeared on his forehead and lips. I pulled a syringe out of my jacket pocket and held it in my palm. "The squad will never get here in time, but I've got what you need right here, Bilbo—naloxone. It'll fix you right up."

He nodded rapidly. "Give it to me." His speech was slurred and barely audible.

"Where is she?"

"Please, Cullen. Help me."

I removed the cap from the syringe. A tiny bubble of fluid mounded at the opening. "I'll spray it right up your nose, but first things first. Rochelle. Where is she?"

He swallowed twice, gasping for air. Bits of white foam were forming at the corners of his mouth and along the edges of his nostrils. "The Satin Mink. Fort Wayne."

I pointed the syringe toward him. "You better not be lying."

"I swear. Fort Wayne. Please, help me."

I looked at Bilbo, turned the needle toward the floor, then squirted the contents of the syringe onto the floor mat.

He stared at me. His eyes held a look of confusion, or perhaps resignation, as though struggling to comprehend the finality of the moment. He was Danny Bilbo. He had more money than God. He had a private jet and controlled businesses and women. This couldn't be the end—not behind a Mexican restaurant in a beater Ford.

But it was.

I stepped out of the car and walked down a path toward the Olentangy River. As I did, I heard him throw up. I threw Bilbo's phone far into the river. I took out my handkerchief and wiped off the syringe before dropping it in the water too.

It had held only tap water. I'd had no intention of saving his sorry ass.

I walked out of the weeds. Bilbo was slouched against his steering wheel, a "foam cone" spilling from his mouth and nostrils. If he wasn't dead, he wasn't far off. I walked away from him and the bag of sand I had thrown in the trunk.

It was eleven twenty when I walked through the door of the Johnny Rockets in the Lennox Town Center. I ordered a large coffee—black. Ten minutes later, I was heading north on Riverside Drive—Route 33—hoping to make Fort Wayne before the last dance.

GUN PEOPLE

BY KristEN LEPIONKA

Olde Towne East

I t turned out that Anya had zero aptitude for home improvement. The mess of it, the dry chemical stink, the two thousand hexagonal shower tiles that had to be placed with such exhausting precision—it was nothing like the HGTV shows she loved, edited as they were into palatable chunks. The real-life version was noisy and full of loose nails and cracked plaster and, even three months into the process, their beautiful ruin of a house still resembled a *before* photo of itself more than any kind of *after*.

Her husband, calm, patient Eli, was in his element, his mathematical brain perfectly suited to tedious tasks. He reveled in a job well done, in straight lines and right angles. He was surprisingly adept with tools for a rangy, bookish accountant. But it had all been her idea. Joining the ranks of the Olde Towne East gentrifiers, rescuing a condemned Queen Anne on Bryden Road and restoring the house to its nineteenth-century glory—why had she ever thought this was a good plan?

She was sick of it after the two-month mark. The part that Anya was interested in, the selection of paint colors and furniture and the right style of curtains, was ages away. It embarrassed her that after all this, what she actually wanted was to go shopping. But by the time she realized it, what was there to do? Suggest they abandon everything and move back to the suburbs? Her friends had been telling her she'd made a mistake, a series of mistakes, really, and she wasn't about to prove them right.

They'd met in the jewelry store where she worked after college—her fashion design degree collecting dust—when he came in to buy a gift for his niece. He wasn't her type; he was a good ten years older than her, she guessed at the time— fifteen, it turned out—with tortoise-shell glasses and hair threaded with gray. But he radiated a calm, solid confidence that she found unexpectedly charming. He returned the next week to ask her to dinner. She liked that he didn't come in with a pretense, didn't ask her without actually asking, the way men did sometimes—*What are you doing later?* or a direc- tive instead of an invitation, *Get dinner with me*—or couch the invitation in self-deprecation to make her say yes out of pity.

She fell for him fast—or maybe with the way he made her feel, with the version of her that he saw: sophisticated, smarter, more interesting than she really was. He didn't play games or make things unnecessarily complicated, and she always knew where she stood with him. And the sex was good; it was. So sometimes he could be a little too careful with her, like he was polishing a violin, and he was fast asleep by ten o'clock most nights, and he subscribed to three different newspapers and read them all, every day. But in the interest of finally deciding what kind of life she was going to lead, she could deal with that. He wanted her to have everything she wanted, and in that way they were perfect for each other.

The problem was, she had never really known what she wanted herself.

The trouble really started in February. She dropped a hammer on her right foot, fracturing two metatarsals. The doctor in the emergency room at Grant Hospital gave her the big blue shoe and said she was to avoid putting any weight on it for six to eight weeks. That meant six to eight weeks more in the half-done house, or longer; tax season was ramping up for Eli, and his longer hours at the office meant less progress anyway.

And now this.

She became slightly hysterical at the thought.

Eli rubbed her back while she cried, the first time she had done so in his presence in the two years they had been together. He said, "Listen, I know we said we wanted to do all of the renovation work ourselves. But maybe we can bring some contractors in. Just to keep the ball rolling while you're laid up."

"You won't be disappointed?"

"Nah." He kissed her temple. He was so decent that it could irritate her a little. "The important thing is that we're in this together."

That was her last chance, she realized after what happened, to tell him the truth. But instead she nodded and tucked her head into his shoulder and just let him take care of things.

Eli hired a crew called Wel/bilt to take over. There were four of them: two college-age kids always plugged into their headphones, a grizzled old guy who chewed tobacco like gum, and the foreman of the crew, Steve. The energy drinks they consumed each day left an alarming quantity of crushed cans in the trash, which Anya moved to the recycling bin each evening. She emptied the coffee mug they used as an ashtray. Otherwise she avoided the men, holing up in her "office" which, while small and plain, was the most intact room in the entire house. She was creating pattern flats for Abercrombie, freelance—a boring process that made her brain itch, restlessly, for a creative outlet. The renovation was supposed to be that outlet. But it wasn't. Sometimes she took a break on the clock and tried to sketch something new, a dress she might wear at the open house they would throw once this nightmare was completed, but nothing came to her. There was a blank white square in the center of her imagination, like she'd stared directly at an eclipse.

It was during one of these breaks when Steve knocked on her office door. "'Scuse me, miss, the power's going to flick off for a minute here, just wanted to let you know." As he spoke, the door slowly ticked open from the force of his knock. "Oh," he said, taking in the blue foam shoe. She'd been behind a sewing table the few times he had seen her before.

"Okay, thanks," she said.

Steve stayed where he was and nodded at her foot. "Let me guess," he said. "It happened when you fell from heaven?"

It was the most ridiculous thing anyone had ever said to her, and she laughed out loud, a harsh, sudden cackle that seemed to startle both of them. Then she felt bad, even as she struggled to keep from laughing again. "You nailed it."

"Thought so," Steve said, doubling down instead of melting into the hallway from embarrassment. He was short, not much taller than Anya, but sturdy and muscular, his features almost entirely hidden under a baseball cap and behind a neat dark beard. Then he winked, like maybe he was in on the joke after all, and pulled the door closed behind him.

After that, he started stopping by her room to tell her something each day—they were turning the boiler off for a while so it might get cold upstairs; they were ordering Jimmy John's for lunch and did she want anything.

It became a welcome distraction from the blank white square.

* * *

Her friends would not come to visit her here, citing the street crime. Indeed, her college roommate Leslie had her car broken into the one and only time she did venture into Olde Towne, but that was mostly her own fault for leaving an iPad sitting on the passenger seat in full view—a bad idea in any neighborhood. And, sure, there were occasionally muttering strangers in the alley behind the house, and every so often a series of pops that might have been gunshots *or* a car backfiring. It was impossible to say. The area felt safe enough to Anya; no one had ever bothered her on the street, not like when she lived in the Short North and she was accosted at least twice a day by panhandlers. But she hadn't gone outside in a week; she wasn't allowed to drive yet and the city was frozen in snowy gridlock, Bryden Road seemingly one of the last streets to get plowed for some reason. Eli had cleared their sidewalk but the houses on either side of theirs had not. Where would she go? The porch? Eventually she tried it, bundled herself up in two coats and a quilt she made in high school.

"What on earth are you doing out here, hon?" Steve said when he found her there. "It's fifteen degrees." Though he wore nothing but a T-shirt and didn't seem to be cold.

"I just needed a change of scenery. Cabin fever. I've been stuck in there for too long."

He looked up at the house, its towering three stories. "Castle fever, more like. I'm actually gonna run over to the Ace Hardware on Parsons, if you want to come. Just to get out for a bit."

"That would be great, actually."

She was able to hobble down the steps on her crutches, but when it came to hoisting herself up into his massive truck, she required assistance, unable to stand on her right foot long enough to step up into the cab with her left, unable to do the opposite, either.

"Here, um," Steve said, "just, here." He grabbed her by the hips and lifted her as easily as placing a dish on a shelf.

Anya was a little shocked—that he was that strong, that he'd touched her like that without asking if it was okay. He tucked her crutches into the backseat and slammed her door closed. The inside of the truck smelled of smoke and paint.

She stared straight ahead as he got in and drove away from the house. Her face was hot but she didn't know why.

Then he said, "So how come your dad doesn't take you places?"

Anya cringed. Oh God, this had been a mistake. "My dad? No. No. He's my husband."

Steve raised an eyebrow. "How'd a guy like him land a fox like you?"

"This is inappropriate, I think." Had she encouraged him by letting him flirt with her out of boredom? Had she accidentally flirted back?

"I'm just messing with you," he said, shooting her a wink.

"Oh."

"Really."

"Okay."

"I mean, you *are* a fox."

She laughed. "Stop."

"I'm speaking the truth. You got those big Eastern European blue eyes. Am I right?"

She nodded. "Polish."

"Ah, you know how to cook that good shit? Pierogi and, whatsit? Halushki?"

"I do."

"Damn. Eli's lucky in every way."

"Not if you ask him," Anya said. "He's not a fan of pierogi."

Steve flicked his turn signal on. "That," he said, "is not right. The next time you make it, save me some."

"Finish my kitchen and I will."

He laughed. "Deal."

She waited in the truck while he went into the store, pressing her cold hands to her cheeks to cool them. She was embarrassed on his behalf but also—just barely—she felt a tug of desire. Was this what happened when she spent too much time on her own?

When they returned to the house, he hopped out first and came around to her side and scooped her up. "My crutches," she said.

"Oh, right."

Still balancing her against him, he reached easily into the backseat to grab them. Anya gasped when she felt a sudden hardness pressing into her thigh. "What—oh my," she said, grateful when the crutches were in hand and she could step away from him. But then she saw what she'd felt—a gun, holstered to his hip, just the bottom of it sticking out from under his T-shirt, and some small part of her was disappointed, and she was ashamed, and then profoundly intrigued.

Steve saw her looking and lifted up the hem of the shirt. "What did you think it was?"

"I didn't . . . nothing. But why? Why do you have a gun?"

"This isn't a good neighborhood, darlin'," he said. "A bunch of rich people trying to fix up these old mansions doesn't change that."

That night, eating Chinese takeout from the place on Broad Street, she asked Eli, "Have you ever fired a gun?"

He twirled a noodle around his chopsticks. "I can't say that I have. Why?"

"I was just wondering."

He shrugged and went back to the *Wall Street Journal*.

"I was wondering," Anya went on, "if we should get a gun. For in the house."

He put down his newspaper in surprise. "I don't think you and I are gun people, are we?"

"Not for fun. Like, for safety."

"Safety?" He stared at her, eyes growing concerned behind his glasses. "Do you . . . are you . . . you feel unsafe here? Anya—"

"Well, no."

"A gun doesn't make anyone safer."

"No. Never mind. I was just asking. I think a lot of people around here do. Have guns."

"What people? If anything, more guns mean *less* safety. Percentage-wise . . ."

He continued but she tuned him out, realizing she didn't have the vocabulary for what she was trying to say.

It was after five when Steve tapped on her office door and just stood there. The other members of the Wel/bilt crew were gone for the day. It had been a week since the awkward trip to the hardware store.

He said, "I've been thinking about you."

"That's nice."

"Have you been thinking about me?"

"Steve," she said. In truth, she had been. His lack of self-awareness for how embarrassing their last conversation had been repelled her, but also drew her in. Ditto for the smell of him—beer and dust and smoke and sweat. Was there a word for that? Both a thing and its opposite?

He stepped closer, touched the edge of her desk with his hands—rough, with perennially dirty nails. "I'm going to kiss you."

He wasn't asking, but she didn't say no.

They fucked on her drafting table, urgently, only removing the mandatory items of clothing. He was the opposite of Eli in every way, his body compact and rock-hard with the kind of muscle that came from manual labor, not a gym, his chest blanketed with thick dark hair. He held her wrists above her head, both in one hand, the other hand clamped at her hip to keep her from sliding off the table as he thrust into her, hurried and starving. A lamp tipped onto the floor, the bulb shattering on impact and spraying their legs with fine shards of glass. They came in unison, something Anya never thought possible, and as soon as it was over, she was repulsed again, by him, by herself, by the endless series of mistakes she seemed so determined to keep making.

"Jesus, that was good," Steve said, patting her on the ass like she was a dressage horse. "Whew. Baby. *Baby.*"

"Please don't call me that." Anya buttoned her jeans, smoothed down her shirt. What had just happened? It already felt like it had involved someone else entirely.

"Okay," Steve said, "baby."

"Antilogy," Eli said, later, behind his newspaper. "When a word has multiple meanings, including its own opposite."

Anya probed a sliver of glass still lodged in the blue Velcro of her stupid foam shoe. Once she had teased it out, she pressed the point of it into her index finger until it bled. "I knew you would know," she said.

Although she insisted that it could not—would not—continue,

it continued. Her resolve, weakened to nothing by boredom. That's all it was: boredom sex. For both of them. There was no seduction; he presented himself at her office door, sometimes already in the process of removing his shirt. Sometimes with it already off. She assumed he had a girlfriend from the way he licked her collarbones, right and then left, right and then left, quickly, a move so specific it had to be the desire of someone else. He brought her things—flowers, an old bottle of Gallo wine he claimed to have been given by another one of his customers along with a papasan chair, which he was keeping. She tried to imagine what his home looked like, but couldn't. Didn't want to. She always told him it was the last time, and he always nodded, yes, of course it was.

"The last time till tomorrow," he added sometimes, winking.

"Do you think we should take the guys out for a drink, once everything's done?" Eli said from behind his newspaper. "They've done such a good job."

"They have. But I think a gift card, maybe," Anya said. "I think that would be better."

As the renovation work began to wind down, Steve started to drop hints. Places he'd like to take her. "Ever been to the fair? They have deep-fried Kool-Aid."

Briefly, she was caught up in wondering what that meant. "A deep-fried liquid?"

"Well, it's solid. Like donut holes. They do a Coke one too."

"Never mind," she said. "We're not going to the fair. This is just a . . . temporary thing."

"Well, yeah. Clearly. I was just making conversation."

It got harder and harder to make him leave, after.

Sometimes he asked questions that made her nervous. One afternoon he said, "Does your husband have life insurance?"

She stared at him.

"Just wondering, in case the geezer should drop dead."

"That's not even funny."

"Does he know about this? About us?"

"No, of course not," she said quickly. Maybe too quickly—should she have said yes? "Why?"

"Just wondering. Thought maybe you had one of them, you know, modern-type arrangements."

"There is no *us*, Steve."

"Yeah, no. Clearly."

But *clearly* he didn't understand what she meant.

Clearly neither did she.

She and Eli picked out paint swatches for the kitchen. Warm Buff, Raw Cotton, Milk Tea. Those were the ones he liked. Anya was partial to the darker shades: Grape Vines, Bison Brown, Dormouse. The little gradient strips littered the floor like betting slips at a racetrack.

"What kind of a name is that for a paint color? For the kitchen?"

Anya hung on to the Dormouse. "No one will know what it's called," she said.

"We'll know," her husband said. "I'll know. Think of the *House Beautiful* article. *Lovely dormouse-colored walls.*"

"What, and milk tea is better?"

"Than a dormouse? Much."

She suggested they go with Travertine because neither especially liked or disliked it. This was the only way it could be totally fair.

"I love you, you know that?" Eli said before giving in.

She focused on the Dormouse swatch until the letters blurred together.

Once she was freed from the blue shoe and pronounced fully healed, driving privileges reinstated, she told Steve things would be different. It had to end. She had an entire city to see now, furniture to buy. She wouldn't be home all day. "I might not be home at all."

"Right, yeah." He winked.

"No," Anya said, "I'm telling you, I might not be. So this is probably the last time."

Steve nodded, pulled his hat back on. That was that.

Within a few weeks, she felt entirely cured of whatever had possessed her in the first place. The desperate boredom, the blank white square in her imagination. Who had that person been? She was grateful—to who? The universe? The god of bad affairs?—that it ended without incident. She didn't deserve the good fortune she'd gotten.

He started calling, though. Twice a day, then five times a day. Anya put her phone on silent and hoped he wouldn't start showing up at random.

Sometimes Eli lowered his newspaper and stared out at the street. "What was that sound?"

"What sound?"

"That."

"I don't hear anything."

"You don't hear that?"

Anya listened. The house was creakily expressive. Its silence wasn't silence, but filled with coughs and sighs, a tone of mild exasperation. "No," she said, "I don't know." But sometimes she could smell smoke curling into the room through the open window, and in the mornings she found piles of cigarette butts just off the porch.

The last time she saw him, it was May, early evening. The tax rush was over and Eli's Audi was already in the driveway when she returned home after a trip to the fabric store. Then she saw Steve's truck on the street as if he, too, were waiting for her to get home, and she gasped out loud.

He *was* waiting for her. He saw her pull in and slipped quietly out of the truck and came to stand next to her passenger-side window. Finally she rolled it down; he reached in and unlocked the door and climbed in.

"I need to go inside," she said, her heart hammering in her ears. "Please, get out of the car."

"Where were you all afternoon?"

"I was buying fabric for a project."

"Is that all?"

"I was—I went shopping for a while—"

"I'm just messing with you," Steve said.

It occurred to her that this was something he said only when he was definitely not messing with you.

"I just want you so bad, baby."

"We talked about this. I'm going inside."

"Just—"

"No—"

He grabbed her hand and pulled it to his crotch. "It'll just take a minute."

"Jesus, Steve—"

"Come on, please?" he said, squeezing her hand, preventing her from pulling away.

Anya closed her eyes. *This* was what she deserved. "One time," she said as she unzipped his fly.

Eli was at the stove frying pancetta when she went inside. She kissed him hello and discreetly ducked into the half-bath to wash her hands. Her face in the mirror above the sink was that of a stranger. No, not a stranger. A person she knew and didn't like.

She began to weep.

"Hey, what's the matter?" Eli suddenly in the doorway, pulling her into him. "Aren't things starting to look up now? You're going to have everything you wanted."

She nodded into his chest, shame rising to the surface of her skin in pinpricks of sweat. "I'm just so happy," she said.

But he kept calling and calling and calling and calling and calling and calling and calling and calling and calling and calling and calling and calling and calling and calling and calling and calling and calling and calling and calling and calling until she took her phone and dropped it into the toilet, watching it shudder one final vibration before the screen went black.

She told Eli she was enjoying the unplugged life, might not replace the phone at all.

"That's a good idea," he said. "Maybe we both should."

"None of my ideas are good," she said.

He laughed; funny her.

It was the wrong time to give up cell phones. The following week she came home from drinks with Leslie to a pair of police cars and an ambulance parked in front of the house, lights swirling.

Her stomach twisted as she swerved into her parking spot and jumped out. Eli was sitting in the back of the ambulance while a paramedic bandaged his hand; he also had a deep gash on his cheekbone.

"Oh my God," she said, reaching out for his free hand, instantly certain that Steve had been behind this. *Does your husband have life insurance?* Nausea bubbled inside her. "What happened?"

"It's okay, really—"

"Eli—"

"We've been seeing a lot of break-ins lately," one of the cops said. "Every year. Like clockwork. As soon as the weather gets nice."

"I guess thieves have seasonal affective disorder like the rest of us," Eli said.

After things settled down, he told her the story. He was in the first-floor laundry, heard the crackle of breaking glass, went into the kitchen for the landline, and there he was, a guy in a ski mask, a gun in one hand.

"I don't know what came over me," Eli said, "but I just yelled at him, *Get the fuck out of my house!* And he did."

"He just left."

"Well, I was standing between him and the door. So he ran toward me and"—he gestured at his face—"pushed me into the doorframe as he ran out."

The injury to Eli's hand occurred when he tried to clean up the broken glass while waiting for the police.

"It's not a very good story," he said. "But I'm fine, everything's fine. He didn't even get anything."

Anya was shaken, deeply. Physically. Eli made her eat a few crackers, to keep her body from going into shock.

"It's really okay. I mean, I'm just glad it wasn't you here alone."

"Maybe we should move," she whispered.

But he didn't hear her. "I do wonder," he said. "If we'd had a gun in the house. I mean, not that I wanted to shoot the guy just for breaking a window, but imagine if he was determined not to leave empty-handed? Christ, Anya, maybe we should."

She nibbled a cracker, nodding. "Maybe. Yeah."

She couldn't sleep and she couldn't sleep and she couldn't sleep and she couldn't sleep and she couldn't sleep and she couldn't sleep and she couldn't sleep and she couldn't sleep and she couldn't sleep and she couldn't sleep but finally it was morning, so she must have slept. Somehow, it always got to morning. When she saw her doctor for a checkup on her foot, she tried to explain. "It's like, it feels like I stay awake all night. Every night. Even when I sleep, it still feels like I'm awake."

The doctor wasn't concerned. He was already writing out a script for Rozerem. "This is what I take. Nothing like it. One pill, lights out."

She left thinking that she wouldn't fill the prescription, but then she did.

The guy working at the gun store had on a hat that said, *Guns don't kill people. Guns kill dinner.* "I don't know about this," Anya said, clutching her husband's arm. "It's like you said. We're not gun people."

Eli kissed the top of her head. "We'll just go through the class and see what we think. If we hate it, we leave. It'll be okay. The important thing is that we're doing this together."

Anya fought back tears through the entire workshop and demonstration, a cloying panic in her throat. When it was her turn, she squeezed off six shots with her eyes barely open.

"Damn, girl," the guy with the hat said, "and you told me you've never done this before?"

He pressed a button to bring her paper target up to the

booth and she saw that all six bullets had passed through the ring next to the bull's-eye.

Eli said, "She's one of those women who's just good at everything."

He put in motion-sensor lights in both the front and back of the house but they flicked on and off all the time. "Possums," Eli said. "Apparently they run rampant around here."

Anya knew the possums weren't to blame, though she had seen them barreling through the backyard. Something about them made her feel sick—the long furless tail, like a skeletal, pointed finger. "Maybe we should shoot them."

Eli raised his eyebrows. "Okay, Belle Starr. That's not why we got the gun."

"I know," she said. She thought about the weapon, upstairs in its little black case. Nestled in a dense gray foam that reminded her of a mattress topper. "I'm just messing with you." The words falling right out of her mouth.

When Eli went to Indiana for a two-day conference that summer, the first thing Anya did was unscrew the motion-sensor bulbs. At the sketchy carryout at the corner of Wilson and Franklin, she bought a new phone. A *burner*, is what they would say on crime shows, a clunky old thing in a dusty clamshell package that she had to use a can opener to unseal. Then she drove to the other side of town to send the text, thinking of the cell towers, triangulation.

I really need you tonight. 10 p.m.

She waited in the living room, the window open, lights off.

Just after ten, she heard a vehicle pull up, park at the curb. Door open, engine off. She'd been sitting in the dark for so long she had started to see sounds—a flutter of ions as he walked up the sidewalk, slowly, cautiously, into the driveway. She wasn't hallucinating—she was achieving a deeper level of consciousness, of eerie calm.

She fired just like she had at the gun range, *pop pop pop pop pop pop*. Out in the open, ears unmuffled by those airport headphones, the sound was devastatingly loud. How did people mistake a car backfiring for gunshots? The last shot hit him and he gave a soft, stunned cry as he fell.

"Anya, help," he said.

But it wasn't Steve's voice. It was Eli's.

She sprang out of the house and found him struggling to a crouch there in the driveway, one hand over his midsection. "Anya," he said again. "Go . . . inside. Someone's shooting."

She eased him down into the grass, pressing both palms over the spurting blood at his belly. "Someone, please call 911!" she screamed at the street. "Please!"

Eli's breath was jagged and wet. A familiar truck cruised around the corner and slowed, and the front yard flashed under its too-bright headlights as it lingered a moment, sped up, and was gone.

"I wanted to surprise you," Eli whispered, ". . . came back on an earlier flight . . ."

"Shhh, don't talk." In the distance, the wail of sirens.

". . . happy to see me?"

"Yes," she said. "No. You weren't supposed to be here."

"Antilogy," he murmured, and he nodded, like he understood.

CURB APPEAL
BY CRAIG MCDONALD
German Village

i
The Home Stager

Samantha, a pretty but presently frustrated interior designer, stared fascinated at the man next door restoring the ornate porch railings of the rambling house overshadowing the one she was spending so much time whipping into shape.

The man was exceptionally good with his hands; clearly truly knew his stuff regarding custom woodworking and period-appropriate restoration. Sam thought more about that yawning living room corner she couldn't find the perfect decorative shelving unit to fill, the piece critical to bringing balance to the otherwise exquisitely adorned room.

Yeah, she thought, *this guy is very, very good.*

And if this expertise she was witnessing extended to custom cabinetry?

Settling back to her own work, Sam thought about how to maybe best break the ice with the woodworker.

ii
Ms. Falk

He watched the pretty stranger arranging furniture on the front porch next door. A *For Sale* sign teased a looming open house.

From a distance, Jacob thought the stranger hot: blue-black hair, tall but curvy. Also oddly familiar, though he couldn't place her as a neighborhood regular.

And *never* the type to show interest in *his* type, Jacob rued, watching her position a porch chair, *just so*.

She hadn't seemed to notice him. And even if she had?

Jacob Zimmermann: seen from any distance, he painfully knew it was obvious he was under six feet tall and *big-boned*. That last was his recently passed mother's gentle euphemism for *stocky*, before she arrived at the even kinder *husky*. But in his mind, big-boned had stuck. That was Mom—always smilingly undermining him.

Jacob was also tragically solitary and never one to make first moves in a potentially platonic relationship or—*as if*—otherwise.

The big, old, adjacent homes of German Village overlooked the eastern edge of Schiller Park. Proximity to the park made all Jaeger Street properties infinitely more desirable in a resurgent Columbus real estate market.

The generic *For Sale* sign next door touted a hot-shot, upstart realty company lately dominating within Columbus' gentrifying historic neighborhoods.

For his part, Jacob was passing the brisk December Saturday morning replacing the dry-rotting spindles and railings of his recently inherited family home's front porch. Rather, he was trying to do that in the time not lost ogling the stranger's figure, fetchingly defined by the curve-clinging, second-skin sheen of her black leggings.

Wind-driven leaves rustled across weathered porch planks as both worked and Jake undressed the stranger with his eyes.

She suddenly paused in her positioning of a white wicker settee. She turned to face him. Jesus, maybe she'd caught him sneaking peeks. He figured she was going to call him on it. *Goddamnit!*

Still, even if she *was* about to declare him a creeper, Jacob thought the view was even better from in front. She wore knee-high black leather boots over her distracting leggings. Her fleece black jacket was almost as tightly fitted over a black turtleneck.

Jacob found himself imagining her as some kind of combination dominatrix and interior designer. He thought he'd maybe just invented a new smut genre. Call it Real Estate Porn?

But she shot him a smile. Shielding her eyes against the setting sun, she said, "God, you're *good*. Are you a master woodworker? It looks to me like you must do that professionally."

Immediately all butterflies in his gut, Jacob shrugged, called back, "Custom cabinetry professionally, yeah. Mostly bookcases. Some dining room and end tables. But *this*? I don't do much of this. But wood is wood, you know? And a master? I'm pretty much self-taught."

Wood is wood, you know?

Moron.

Like *that*, he wanted to turn his Craftsman drill loose on his goddamn forehead—drive that sucker right between his eyes and down to the chuck at full torque, fitted with the biggest-bore drill bit he owned.

But she shook off a chill, said, "Really? You taught yourself to do that? Honestly? Those spindles are, like, amazing. You can't even hire for that kind of detail work anymore. Not even close. Not for money that makes sense for a flip, anyway."

Jacob almost said, *Just takes a pattern and a lathe,* but stayed silent this once.

His father had been a career carpenter, so Jacob had

served an informal but lifetime apprenticeship, he supposed. The more he thought about it, the more he agreed with her. Hell, he *was* a master, in his way. *Sure.* And even better to be declared so from this stranger's pretty mouth.

Grinning, he said, "Yep. Taught myself, I mean. Yep. I did that."

She scowled at him and Jake freshly died inside. But then he realized she was probably thinking about something else.

She smiled again, said, "Cabinetry. Very cool. And very lucky for me. I've got an issue in this place and hardly any time to fix it. Very tricky cubbyhole. It's vexing me. You ever make a Lawrence drawer étagère?"

Afraid to bluff, but even more scared to end their connection, Jacob said, "Not even sure how to spell that. But I might have already made one. Could you draw it for me?"

She beamed, held up her iPhone. "This is better." Another smile and a finger, beckoning. She ordered, "Come here, you." One more smile. "I'm Samantha Falk, by the way."

For the next few minutes at least, she was Ms. *Falk.*

iii
Samantha

As he peered over her shoulder at Pinterest-pinned images of *étagères*, she became *Samantha,* and he quickly went from no-name "master carpenter" to Jacob Zimmermann, and soon after, unique in his lonely life, just *Jake.* He seized on that version of his name. Savored it. For the first time, he started calling himself *Jake* in his mind.

Jake: It opened . . . avenues. Stoked notions.

Looking at the pictures of the shelving piece she wanted, he said, "Tough to say, and tougher to spell, but easy enough to build. I could knock this out in a couple hours. If you or I stained it right away, it would work fine for a Sunday showing. You could always seal it later."

As she ushered him inside to examine that vexing, tricky "cubbyhole" in person and take exact measurements, they small-talked.

Soon, they were commiserating over still-fresh losses. Quite recently, Jake's parents had died peacefully together in their sleep, victims of a faulty furnace their stoically grieving son had since replaced.

What had happened to his folks was tragic, sure. He missed his father most acutely. But when he let himself think about it, he was also enjoying the freedom of having a house—one that was paid for—and now he had a stunning woman *admiring* that house. No, admiring *his* house.

For the first time, maybe ever, Jake thought he scented possibilities. It was like he finally had something rolling his way. Call it luck?

Samantha observed, "That's a lot of house for one person. How many bedrooms?"

"Five, but there was still only ever me and my folks," he said. "Some dogs, but years back. Folks each kept their own den or home office. I had the attic too, with all those dormers on four sides. Pretty much, it's like an open-plan third floor. Full basement too."

"Sounds fantastic. You've got to promise to give me a tour after this."

Then, after expressing her condolences for his parents' deaths, Samantha spoke of her mother's recent passing after a short but fierce battle with cancer. "Just me and my brother now," she said.

He told her he was very sorry for her loss too. He did that, he realized, in almost exactly the same comforting words she'd offered him. That made him freshly want to kick himself.

The scent of her shampoo and her musky perfume were almost overwhelming. He'd never stood so close to such an attractive woman of about his own age—presently just north of thirty—let alone sustained a dialogue of this length with someone like Samantha.

And yet?

And yet, there was something almost familiar about her.

He couldn't quite put his finger on it, but he felt like he already knew her face somehow. At least, knew that smile.

As she walked him through the rest of the place, all the while quizzing him more on his just-inherited home, it became clear that Samantha was not just sexy and deliciously snarky, but also possessed of a world-class interior-design aesthetic of the kind critical to moving high-ticket properties.

They were each home decor savants in their own way, he decided on the spot.

What he could do with wood, Samantha could do with furniture, swatches of fabric, and throw pillows. With shabby-chic custom cabinetry and distressed runs of shiplap.

Her skills seemed particularly in demand in the Village, as she described recent jobs closer to Livingston Avenue and farther south, nearer Parsons Avenue. And she had bigger, even more lucrative projects on the horizon, ones also ringing the park, she confided. Maybe she would have more work for him, and really soon, *if* he was game? Maybe, *if* this rush-job étagère met muster?

The raw smile on her face as her voice trailed off reached him in ways he couldn't define. She let it hang there—as if he'd actually say no to *anything* she might ask of him.

She was good at her job, and she thought he was good at his work. Jake began to think about some kind of *significant* partnership. Then he began to fantasize about even more between them. This woman could be his foot in a very heady door, he let himself think.

"It's all about curb appeal from the jump, of course," she said. "Like books and covers, you know? But then it's more like with people, and how you can't really know what's what until you get *inside*."

The next day, he handed over a fully finished cherry étagère that left her beaming and freshly gushing about his skills as a craftsman. He was over the moon from her reaction. *Sure*, he thought, *we make a hell of a team.*

They immediately embarked on an informal partnership as she commissioned another piece. This creation was for a home on the same block. She wanted a massive dining room table to be crafted from Samantha-supplied recovered Amish barn wood, and a matching custom armoire adorned with rusting salvaged hinges, ringed handles, and chains. The project freshly stoked his Real Estate Porn fantasies with a barely clothed Samantha standing center stage in his basement workshop.

They shook hands and Jake's knees nearly quaked at her touch. She shook hands like a man, he thought, firm and hard.

She said, "Call me Sam, please. All my friends do."

Less than a week after that, the ragged end of a long Friday of frenzied staging subsided into a drowsy late-night dinner at Lindey's.

That was chased by two bottles of South African red wine picked up at Hausfrau Haven—vino downed in his recently Sam-redecorated living room after they returned from the restaurant.

That same night, to Jake's deep dismay but dizzy delight, they became lovers.

iv

Sam

The next night, while they ate a Spanish dinner at Barcelona (her treat), freezing rain shellacked the street and sidewalk pavers. Those brick streets and walkways were German Village's hallmark—picturesque and *so* not-Midwestern in their European texture and atmosphere. Lovely. At least until they became coated with ice or covered with snow that thwarted road salt, city snowplows, and shovels. Heavy snows could strand Villagers on their streets for days during a particularly harsh winter, which this one was shaping up to be.

Arms linked, walking carefully over slippery, glinting bricks, they took a meandering path back to his house to ogle Christmas lights.

His house: its first and second floors had recently been re-imagined and raised in aesthetic appeal by Sam's considerable skills. It was still his place, of course, but it looked a world away from the house he grew up in. Hell, it looked like a million dollars now, every room in his pad a vision—practically an image ripped from some glossy interior-design magazine. As a creative design team, he thought—and not for the first time—they truly clicked, elevating one another's work through mutual inspiration.

Their plans for this evening called for a couple more postdinner bottles of wine from Hausfrau. Sam was on a dry red Spanish wine kick—vino headily sublime and thick and ruby red as bull's blood, followed by some serious TV binge-ing. Jake's evening TV fare since she'd entered his life had abruptly shifted from gorging on his preferred fare: Netflix original series heavy on violence, nudity, and gratuitous sex. Instead, they devoured HGTV shows hosted by quippy spouses, vaguely creepy twin brothers, or this snarky Canadian Realtor pitted against a European interior designer to see who would triumph in a challenge to remake a home. Jake missed his own shows, but viewed such programs as an investment in their shared business future. Ideas seen on TV sparked better, bigger ideas in his imagination—that's what he told himself.

Around one a.m. each Saturday-night-into-Sunday-morning, the TV would finally go dark and there followed fleeting and boozy sex in a frustratingly (to Jake at least) pitch-black bedroom.

Sunday morning meant brunch at the Old Mohawk with turtle soup and Long Islands, or maybe the weekend lunch buffet at Schmidt's, the servers in kitschy lederhosen and dirndls, German oompah and accordion music buried beneath the buzz of diners' chatter; where the sugary aroma of generous cream puffs somehow overpowered even the strong scent of metric tons of sizzling sausages and vinegary German potato salad.

And Sunday night? Repeat Saturday night.

Oh, they might have dinner during the work week, but there was never any physical intimacy Monday through Friday night, not even kisses or hand-holding.

But Jake was hardly given to complaining about any of that.

Saturday and Sundays on the couch, and then in bed with Sam?

Well, those days were still a dazzling gift, or so Jake had convinced himself.

Besides, weekdays were *work* days. They were, on those days, he reminded himself, building something important together, building a future, personally and professionally.

Passing St. Mary of the Assumption Catholic Church, Jake

nodded at the chain-link fence barring entrance inside. A lightning strike had compromised the church's sharply slanting roof and placed the house of worship in an enduring financial struggle to repair and reopen.

Jake had attended school there. He was also an altar server. He confided all that to Sam as they passed by with careful steps on the ice, describing an exceptionally cloistered childhood: home, school, church . . . playing with a solitary friend and a succession of family dogs at Schiller Park.

He pointed across the street to the Book Loft, where Jake had secured his first true woodworking job, building simple but sturdy bookcases. His father built the first one; Jake replicated it, then gradually improved on that model, building at least fifteen more.

He confided that he missed the church bells that used to ring at St. Mary's each afternoon, the sound reaching all the way down Third Street and across the park to his family home, fully audible in his bedroom during springs and summers with the windows open. The lightning bolt had changed all that too, silencing the bells.

His memory unleashed, Jake continued talking about the German Village of his youth, people and places already fading into dust. As they cut diagonally across the park with their fresh bottles of wine, sticking to the grass to avoid slipping on the pavement, he was going on about two dead local legends named Fred and Howard, but Sam looked like she'd lost the thread; like her thoughts were very much elsewhere. Then she proved it.

"Your neighbor—the one to the south of your house," she said, cutting him off midsentence. "What do you know about him? Seems to me he's alone in that giant place." This half smile he couldn't read. "You know, kind of like you."

Jake said carefully, suddenly jealous, "Doug Lentz is his name. Yeah, he's kind of in my same boat. Inherited the place. Just him in there."

Sam asked, "Think Doug might be interested in selling?"

Ah. Jake's spark of jealousy was already ebbing.

Between the two of them, Jake figured, they could surely make Doug's careworn place a gem. But Doug was dug in pretty deep there. He might be a hard sell, so to speak.

Focused squarely on Sam's interest in Doug's house, Jake started thinking about possible angles. Maybe he could dupe Doug; make the poor bastard think his place had termites . . . a compromised foundation? Convince him that his pricey slate roof was long past needing replacement? Some catastrophic failure just waiting to happen in the next big snow or hard rain?

Yeah, maybe something like that.

Hell, it wasn't like they were friends. And it wasn't like it was really illegal what he was thinking about doing. Just . . . gray.

Later that night: more HGTV out the ears.

Despite Jake's greater body mass, he'd drunk perhaps only the equivalent of a quarter bottle of the rioja. Sam, with her lithe and fit personal trainer–style body, had put away infinitely more liquor. But somehow she appeared more focused and far sharper than Jake felt at the moment. At least it seemed so in his admittedly fogged perception.

He felt profoundly numb. When he closed his eyes, the room began to spin, and he put his feet flat to the floor and his white-knuckled hand gripped the sofa arm to try to set things straight, or really, set them *still*, if only for fleeting seconds.

Smiling with sloe eyes, Sam said, "I know this is supposed

to run the other way, but I don't want to wait or hope any-more, Jake."

Then she began to talk of a future together, in this house. *His* house.

Through a drunken fog, he realized Sam was proposing marriage.

He didn't need to think about it. He said yes before she closed her pitch.

She took off his glasses, then kissed him hard with the lights on for the first time since their first brush of lips.

Then she handed him a pen and a sheaf of papers. He reached for his glasses.

Sam clasped his hand and squeezed. "I'll show you where to sign," she said. "It's a lot of paper, because we're going to do this right." As she said that, she pointed to the first of numer-ous Xs that he dutifully scribbled his name alongside.

Beaming, she said, "No family, either side, other than my brother who won't care, so I say we're getting married in Lon-don." Another hard kiss. "We'll do it in Kensington," she added with a cunning smile, "just like Meghan and Prince Harry. How romantic is that?"

Jake signed on the final line. Then he suggested going to bed. He felt desperate to do that before he got drunker from more wine and maybe shamed himself during this watershed night of his life.

But Sam conjured a fresh bottle of champagne. "Sure, bed. Soon. But a toast to our future first!"

Jake wouldn't remember the cork popping, let alone a sin-gle sip of the cheap spumante. He wouldn't even remember if they'd ever really made it to bed together.

In the morning, he awoke to a titanic hangover and Sam's announcement that they were off to a storage facility just outside the Village to meet a Craigslist seller about an antique cabinet the dude was trying to unload, super cheap. Sam handed Jake coffee. "Gotta sober you up, Tiger."

Despite the caffeine, he immediately nodded off in her rented U-Haul truck.

Some hours later, somewhere east of Parsons Avenue, Jake awakened gagged and tied to a metal chair.

v
Samantha Falk

Sam tilted her head and smiled sadly at Jake. "Up at last. You know, it's too bad you're not really attractive. Or at least just buff. Then we might have continued this partnership. Even become power flippers. You know, like the Joanna and Chip Gaines of central Ohio?"

Groggily, it occurred to him that he thought that was exactly what they were on their way to becoming. If he could just tell her that, get his mouth to open properly . . .

Wide-eyed, he jerked at his bonds, tried to upset the chair, but the tubular steel legs of the vintage lawn chair were duct-taped firmly to the floor of the storage locker. His eyes began to adjust to the storage space, dimly illuminated by the buzzing overhead of fluorescent tube lighting. Just in view, about a dozen real estate signs leaned against a battered old armoire. The topmost sign showcased a beaming Sam and read, *Falk Homes: Sell It with Sam!*

Finally. Jake remembered why he'd felt he thought he had known her face; knew her *smile*. He'd seen her image on the same kind of sign next door to a client's place for several days as he was installing custom cabinetry. Each time, after freshly spying Sam smiling back at him from the sign, he'd thought, *She's hot.*

Sam, still looking sad, said, "Really sorry you ever woke up. My brother, my real partner"—she gestured at the signs— "was going to wrap it up while you were still out. You know, do it humanely. But these idiots in the storage unit next door are unloading tons of crap. Seems like no end of sorry shit to shove into the unit over there. And so . . . ?"

She hardly needed to finish that sentence. Jake broke out in a fresh, cold sweat.

Sam said, "You're all questions, I know. See, home staging is good business, and there's some real money there, sure. But the best money comes from controlling the whole product, top to bottom. So, I got my real estate license about a year ago and started branching out. Learning the ropes and building some word-of-mouth. Now, the housing market's finally moving again after eight years of *meh.* Gotta love the Trump Bump!"

Sam disappeared from view and out of the range of the overhead light. He could still hear her voice plenty fine, as well as the much noisier jostling from those folks in the adjacent storage unit.

If he could only make some noise of his own . . .

But there was a swatch of duct tape over the gag in his mouth and the chair he was tied to still wouldn't budge.

Sam said from the darkness, "Those papers you signed weren't for a London wedding, of course." She returned to the light, gripping a bottle of Jack Daniel's by the neck. Sam hoisted, took a fiery sip, then, voice husky from the whiskey, she growled, "They were for your house. It's got such great *curb* appeal." A sly smile played on her bee-stung lips.

"Now I'm going to sell it," she continued. "I already have

some nibblers. The other day, when you were out picking up pizza? Someone even actually cold-knocked. A nice young couple, Marcus and Jason. Seem crazy wealthy. They just adopted their first child and dug the fact that they could sit on the front porch and see their daughter on all that Schiller playground equipment, just across the street."

She suddenly stepped toward Jake, all whiskey and wrath: "Don't you dare look at me like that!" She followed his gaze to the bottle of Jack. "You know, I wasn't much of a drinker until the past few weeks. Not at all. All those no-touch weekdays, and all that wine before bed on weekends? Truth is, I had to be hammered to do you. I *had* to be that way, every goddamn time, and that's on you!"

She took another swig and said, "And if I had to be at least half in-the-bag to have sex with you—eight goddamn times—I figure I'm going to need to be fully trashed to see you put down."

She backed away from him, a little unsteady on her feet from the fresh hit of booze. "I'd been working on that place next to yours for a time, you know. Got to know your mom a little. She talked about you, a lot. Just *blah blah blah*, on and on and on."

Sam slid into a recognizable approximation of his mother's voice: "*Jacob, our poor only lonely child. Jacob, who will someday inherit this house. It's much too big for one, really . . .*" Switching back to her own voice, Sam went on, "Jacob, who has no girlfriend. No friends. And now Jacob, the grieving orphan, who clearly won't be missed ultimately, when he just disappears."

Sam took another look at the whiskey bottle, then searched his eyes. "Oh, about that orphan stuff. Yeah, that's on me, unfortunately. Your mom mentioned there was some furnace thing going on. It had your folks fretting. She wondered if I maybe didn't know someone who wouldn't cost an arm and a leg to take a look?

"Big brother is kind of a Renaissance man. Handy with things. And he's even a licensed CPA, which will be *so* helpful with our recent paperwork. Dale did a job on their furnace. Timed it to that motorcycle trip you took solo. Your folks, living on fixed incomes and having growing health issues? They couldn't turn down a same-as-free, off-the-books furnace fix."

Another gut punch: he finally got some distance from his folks and it got them killed. Jacob—his name for himself again, suddenly—felt freshly stricken.

Sam's smile turned mean. "Afterward, it was all just cozy-up to poor lonely Jake. And now, Jake honey, you *are* just going to disappear, but not really. I know you don't keep up with the news, but you must have heard on the radio at least. Columbus is on pace to set a new record for homicides this year. Bunches of them are still unsolved. So, the cops aren't going to spend much time chasing after a misfit of a missing person with no family or friends and who, let's face it, isn't going to even be reported missing. Jesus, Jake, we're just getting to the holidays. You don't even have any customers right now to get pissed off because you've suddenly gone missing. Perfect timing, yeah? Yay me!"

It was too true: over the past few weeks, Sam had become his only customer. Pop had warned him against just that thing—putting all your eggs in one basket. That always invited disaster, Pops had insisted.

He flinched at the stench of his own sweat: it tickled under his arms and trickled in a cold stream toward his tailbone, despite the chill of the hardly heated storage unit.

"About that so-called disappearance," Sam said, voice slurring from more of the whiskey. "Big brother Dale's official day job is hauling trash. For now, anyway. So he has full and easy access to the county landfill out on Route 665. It's not the worst place to end up. All those seagulls always out there, hovering? It's almost like the beach. Just no water. But don't worry. It won't be the fall that kills you. 'Cause we're not monsters."

A shaft of light momentarily blinded Jake as the door to the storage unit rattled open, then closed again, bringing back the dark. The sound of a lock being turned.

A male voice said, "I don't think those sons of bitches next door are leaving anytime soon, sis."

Dale stepped into the light. He had some of his sister's coloring, but Sam had gotten all the looks. Dale's chin was undershot, his black hair thinning at twentysomething. "So I don't think we wait anymore," he said.

He took the gun from his waistband and Jake's eyes somehow got even bigger. "Not going to be able to use this because of those idiots next door." Dale stowed his gun and picked up a rag and a can of starting fluid. "You go out in the truck and wait while I take care of business, sis. Cab's warm and the radio's set to that shitty station you keep your car radio parked on. I've got a dolly, but I'll need your help getting it all up and into the back of the truck."

Dutifully following her brother's orders, Sam picked up her bottle of Jack and took another sip before she sealed it. She granted Jake a last, pitying look, then said, "You're not such a bad guy, really, *Jacob*. You're just . . . unlucky. Believe me, I don't mean to keep doing this to guys like you. I just needed a toehold in the neighborhood and your house is my golden ticket."

Then Sam turned sharply, vanishing in a blinding flash of late-afternoon winter sunlight as the storage unit garage door again opened, then closed.

"Don't squirm and don't fight it, Ace," Dale said, closing the ether-soaked rag tightly over Jacob's nose. "Just breathe it in, brother, nice and deep."

vi
ABC
(Always Be Closing)

Sam positioned the *For Sale* sign graced with her smiling face in Jake Zimmermann's front yard. She pressed the toe of her *do-me* heels into the sign's bottom rung to drive it deeper into the winter-hardened sod. Then she set a two-by-four across its top, hoisted a small, rubber-headed mallet, and drove the sign deeper into the ground with short, sharp blows.

In her head, she was already writing the ad copy: *Location, location, location! Beautiful, sprawling Jaeger Street, German Village home. All brick, with glorious Schiller Park playground view. Fantastic curb appeal. Just call Sam at 614 . . .*

Her copywriting exercise trailed off as she realized she was being watched.

The man next door, the one Jake called Doug Lentz, was eying her.

Sam gave him a little show as she bent to adjust the sign once more, then made her way carefully to her Mustang parked curbside to slip her materials into its trunk. She turned and looked at Doug, pretending to at last register his presence.

Awkwardly, he smiled and waved at her, then called out, "Figured old Jake would pack it in after his folks passed. That's way too much house for just one person." He glanced around his own cavernous front porch and added, "Trust me. I know."

Thank God this one was at least attractive. Sam gave him her best smile, mounted the curb, and said, "Hey there, you! And funny you should say." Then she carefully made her way closer to Doug's front porch. Gripping the handrail, she beamed up at him. "What a great place you have here." Smiling, she asked, "Ever thought of selling?"

MY NAME IS NOT SUSAN

BY CHRIS BOURNEA

Eastmoor

Lynda Carnes sat at her computer in her home office, scrolling through a spreadsheet. When she got to the end of the last row, she realized nothing she'd just read made any sense. She took off her reading glasses and tossed them aside. She got up and walked across the room, looking out over the backyard.

Her eyes fixed on the swing set she played on as a child. Everything about the surroundings was familiar, including the neighborhood on the East Side of Columbus. She had always imagined herself as a big-city attorney, handling high-profile cases in New York, Chicago, or Los Angeles. But eking out a living as a tax attorney in her hometown in Ohio was where she ended up.

Lynda's gaze drifted from the swing set to the rusting slide. She could almost feel her mother's hands on the small of her back. Lynda always hesitated, but it was her mom who would give her that little push she needed, sending her squealing down the slide into the arms of her father waiting below.

Reflecting on the memory, a faint smile flickered on Lynda's face as she looked at her parents' photo on the wall. Even as they aged, her mother remained regal and dressed in the latest fashions, her father dapper in three-piece suits. It was clear that Lynda got her tawny coloring through the union of Lydell, a handsome dark-skinned man, and Barbara, a beautiful light-skinned woman. Lynda's family represented the diversity of the African American community, and she was used to people asking if she was Latina.

Lynda turned from her parents' portrait, glancing at her framed Howard University School of Law degree hanging above her desk. That degree had been hard-won. But her undergraduate degree in communications had been even more difficult because she missed so many classes in her senior year shuttling from DC to Columbus to care for her ailing parents. Mom and Dad were inseparable—even unto death, as it turned out.

When Lynda finally graduated a couple of semesters late after making up all the missed work, she moved back into the modest two-story brick-and-stucco house on Eastmoor Boulevard. And once her parents passed away within months of each other, she never left. Her childhood home served as a security blanket, providing her with comfort and stability in their absence. New York, Chicago, and Los Angeles just weren't meant to be, it turned out.

Lynda sat back in her father's leather recliner and stared at the blinking cursor on the computer. She retrieved her reading glasses and, with a deep sigh, returned to proofing the spreadsheet. A moment later she was startled by the ping of an instant message popping up on her screen: *We need to talk.*

Heart pounding, Lynda swiveled in her chair and looked out again over the yard, reflecting on the request. And more importantly, the identity of the sender: Susan.

The name dredged up a tangle of mixed emotions. Lynda once again caught sight of the swing they took turns pushing each other on as children. They had so much in common, so many shared experiences. They even resembled each other, so much so that people often mistook them for sisters.

Lynda again fixed her sights on her Howard degree. She recalled with fondness her undergrad days there with Susan, giggling over boys and comforting each other over heartbreaks. But she also couldn't forget the competitive streak between her and her one-time "bestie." A competitive streak that changed from friendly one-upping to outright warfare after Lynda's parents died. Realizing that it was now her against the world, Lynda's grief morphed into ruthless ambition. Sleeping in, skipping class, and helping herself to Susan's notes—as well as her boyfriends—offered cold comfort for such a devastating loss. But it was comfort nonetheless.

Lynda felt an uncharacteristic ripple of fear at the thought of getting together with Susan. It wasn't hard to guess what she wanted to discuss. One more thing they'd competed over. It was unfortunate that their mutual interests extended to Susan's husband.

Lynda turned back to her computer monitor and placed her hands on the keyboard, hesitating like she did as a child at the prospect of going down the slide. *About what?* she typed, stalling, a tactic that worked in throwing adversaries off their game in legal negotiations.

But Susan's reply called her bluff: *I think you know.*

Lynda sat back, staring at the screen, hesitating again. She had known for months that this confrontation was coming and she might as well get it over with.

Where do you want to meet? she responded after a long moment.

Lynda made a note of the time and place Susan suggested. She opened a desk drawer and retrieved the watch she'd been meaning to return to Morris since she'd broken it off with him a few weeks ago. She ran her finger over the screen and the high-tech device clicked on, beckoning the user to enter the number of steps, calories, or laps to be expended throughout the day. Lynda ran her tongue over her upper lip, thinking of the day she'd presented the watch to Morris as a gift. She knew the ex-football-star-turned-fitness-trainer would love it, and he had, expressing his gratitude in bed.

Lynda closed her eyes, remembering those forbidden encounters with Morris, running her hands over his ripped chest, his smooth ebony skin caressing hers, the taste of his full lips. She shuddered, recalling those delicious liaisons in her bed, on the living room sofa, in this very chair, straddling him.

Lynda glanced again at Susan's message and a stab of resentment shot through her. Because let's face it—this situation was Susan's fault. It was she who had referred her husband to Lynda. Morris's sloppy record-keeping had landed him in trouble with the IRS and Susan had leaned on Lynda to help him out—at a discounted "friends and family" rate, of course.

As it turned out, working on Morris's tangled business affairs wasn't the drudgery Lynda assumed it would be. In fact, he made it fun, regaling her with tales from his days on the road with the Cleveland Browns. His endearing laugh, his charisma, and above all his good looks hadn't faded since his days as the Howard Bison's star running back, when Lynda and Susan sat side by side in the stands cheering him on.

Those late nights working with Morris turned into something more than an old friend helping out another. One evening, he stopped by her home office after a training session at his gym. With a grin, he asked if he could jump in the shower and, before Lynda could object, began taking off his clothes.

Lynda couldn't help but eye Morris's chiseled physique, and the fact that the legendarily conceited athlete seemed to be stripping for her benefit. She should have told him to put his clothes on, reminded him that his wife was her best friend.

But loneliness got the best of her, all those years of isolation as she tended to her sickly parents and then buried herself in work to avoid human interaction and all of its messiness. She had to admit that she enjoyed the attention. Morris had a way of making a woman feel like she was the only one in the world. And after all—this was Susan's fault, anyway, wasn't it? Just like it was her fault for keeping her notes in the open in their dorm room, and not giving her boyfriends everything they wanted, which drove them so naturally into Lynda's bed.

During Morris's striptease in her office that night, Lynda at first just observed. But no longer able to contain herself, she then made the fateful decision to go from spectator to participant.

"You look like you could use some help," she said, slipping her fingers into the waistband of his briefs.

Still, once they wrapped the case and successfully contested the IRS's judgment, Lynda broke it off. Even by her standards, the guilt became overwhelming and Lynda hoped Susan would never find out. But Lynda should have known that a man who was careless enough to jeopardize the brand and livelihood he'd built was also reckless enough to risk his marriage. Though Lynda had cautioned him time and again to delete e-mails and destroy any exchanges between them that didn't pertain to his tax case, Morris never listened—refusing even to set security controls on his phone. And what spouse, especially a woman with instincts as keen as Susan's, could resist scrolling through her husband's call history and texts?

Lynda picked up her phone and shot Morris one last text, keeping it short and to the point, all business: *I need to see you. I have something of yours.*

Lynda looked up to see a woman entering the coffee shop

on East Broad the next day, right on time. She shifted in her seat in nervous anticipation of the showdown. When the woman seated herself, Lynda realized this wasn't Susan, but a near-perfect facsimile of her former friend.

"I'm—I'm sorry," Lynda fumbled. "Do I know you?"

The woman smiled, taunting Lynda with a mischievous gleam in her eye—just like Susan. "You should."

Lynda grappled for a response, but was interrupted by the barista.

"Sorry this took so long, ma'am," said the young, nose-ringed blonde, setting the coffee in front of the stranger.

Lynda raised her index finger, the way she did in court when trying to get the judge's attention. "Actually, that's my order."

"No worries," the strange woman said, sliding the coffee across the table to Lynda.

The mishap was too familiar to upset Lynda. She had lost count of the number of times someone had told her they'd seen her browsing at the mall or jogging in the park, only to learn upon Lynda correcting them that it had been Susan.

"Thank you, miss," Lynda said, dismissing the barista in an authoritative fashion that mimicked a judge releasing an alternate juror whose presence was unneeded. The barista looked from Lynda to the other woman, as if noticing the similarity in their appearances, then turned on the heels of her Crocs and plodded away.

Once alone again at the table with the stranger, Lynda said, "I'm sorry, ma'am, but I'm meeting someone here." She nodded at the chair where the woman sat, indicating that she should vacate it. As much as Lynda was intrigued by this woman who so closely resembled Susan, she needed to make way for Susan herself. The practical attorney in her took over once again, just wanting to get these proceedings concluded.

"Oh. My apologies." The woman lingered for a moment, seeming to challenge Lynda to a staring contest, then rose and made her way to the door.

At the exit, a man held the door open for her.

"Hey, Detective Perez," the blonde called out from behind the counter. "Right on time."

Lynda watched the man wave back with a friendly smile. With his swarthy complexion and mop of thick black hair, he exuded ethnic—downright *exotic*—male beauty. She allowed her eyes to scan his muscular physique and noted that he had the athletic build she preferred. Picking up her phone, she reminded herself to stay focused on the task at hand. She checked the time. Susan was running late, but hadn't bothered to call or text. That wasn't like her.

Eddie Perez turned off East Main, hung a right onto South Ashburton Road, and a moment later pulled into his driveway. Once again, he suppressed irrational pride at his manicured lawn and the palette of colors from his spring flower plantings. This place was supposed to be the starter house for the family he and Rosario hoped for. He damn well was going to keep it looking nice—for her, if not for him.

Getting out of the car, he waved to his neighbor. Even at dusk, Jose was tending to his yard, mulching around tree beds and trimming weeds.

"Congratulations on your promotion," Jose called out over his weed trimmer. "But I miss you driving the squad car home. Keeps the bad element away."

Eddie nodded, appreciating Jose's shared goal of keeping the neighborhood safe. There were advantages to living in the area Eddie had protected as he worked his way up through the ranks at the Columbus Division of Police. Eddie's continual presence in the neighborhood not only built trust and made witnesses more forthcoming, but also fostered an overarching sense of community.

Eddie waved to Jose's kids, who kicked a soccer ball around the yard as their father worked. It was cool that this street was becoming a little brown enclave in this mostly vanilla Midwestern city. Eddie just wished Jose would move his pickup truck off of his front lawn. Eddie hated to admit it, but he was embarrassed every time one of his own people confirmed stereotypes about Mexican Americans. It was hard enough proving yourself in an environment in which people with Hispanic surnames were still viewed as the mysterious "other."

Once inside, Eddie poured a glass of Scotch and retreated to his bedroom. Flicking on the bedside lamp, he unbuttoned his shirt and gazed at the wedding photo on the nightstand. Remnants of his late wife permeated the house, including the closet where he hung his shirt next to her clothes. The one and only fight he'd had with Jose was when, over a few too many drinks, Jose suggested his neighbor was maintaining a shrine for Rosario and should think about moving on. "Lot of pretty girls out there with a lot of empty beds," Jose teased. They'd almost come to blows. He just couldn't bring himself to seal the lid on the life he and Rosario had envisioned together.

Eddie sometimes still caught himself expecting to hear the familiar sound of her opening the front door after a late night at work. He half expected her to come bounding into their room in her nurse's scrubs, still full of energy after a double shift at Grant, the downtown hospital. It was a cruel coincidence that she'd been rushed to that very emergency room after a drunk driver plowed into her.

Losing Rosario so suddenly and inexplicably made Eddie question whether there really was any justice in the world. But he had to push down any doubts he harbored about such things if he was going to continue in his line of work.

In an attempt to drown out the thoughts that began to rush through his head, Eddie took a big gulp of Scotch and turned on the TV. He had to turn the set on manually, having misplaced the remote again.

"Where is that goddamn thing?" Eddie muttered, ransacking the nightstand drawer. Changing the channel away from the nightly news became an urgent mission, lest he be reminded of some stress-inducing case at work that would keep him up at night.

When he finally located the remote, it was too late. The anchorman began narrating a story about the case that had just come across Eddie's desk. "*Police are still searching for leads in the murder of former NFL star Morris Johnson and his wife Susan. The department's spokesman said several potential suspects will be questioned in the coming days.*"

Eddie clicked off the TV, massaged his forehead, and sank to the bed. Any chance he had of getting a good night's sleep was gone, so he figured he may as well work on the case. He'd had a long day today and would have an even longer one tomorrow, making his way through the list of the popular Johnson's friends, clients, and—to judge by the tips pouring in—multiple girlfriends. He opened his briefcase and removed the file for the Johnson double homicide. Eddie took another swig of Scotch, viewing the gruesome crime-scene photos of the couple side by side in bed, covered in blood from gunshot wounds.

Eddie rubbed his eyes and, upon opening them, glimpsed his wedding photo again. He thought once more of Rosario, and then, unexpectedly, of the woman in the coffee shop earlier that day. *Lots of pretty girls* . . . At some point much later he awoke, papers strewn across the bed. He turned off the light and tried to get another couple of hours of shut-eye before the day and new duties dawned.

"Is there something I can help you with, officers?" Lynda said, answering a knock at the front door. She took a step back at the sight of the handsome police detective from the coffee shop a couple of days ago.

Judging from the detective's expression, he also recognized her. But he flashed his ID nonetheless. "Detective Perez, CPD. Sorry to disturb you, ma'am, but we're investigating the murder of Morris and Susan Johnson and we're here to ask you a few questions."

Lynda twitched at the mention of her dead former lover and best friend. She had been doing her best to forget them, but Morris and Susan haunted her once more.

"*We?*" Lynda said.

Perez moved aside, revealing a balding, portly African American man. "This is my partner, Detective Carter," Perez said, prompting the man to nod at Lynda with a guarded expression.

Lynda returned the nod, attempting to disguise her disappointment at the discovery that she and the good-looking Latino detective were not alone. "Come in." She led the detectives to the living room and gestured for them to have a seat on the couch.

"What did the Johnsons say to you when you last saw them?" Perez asked, and Lynda noticed his eyes rove her body. And not in an official, evidence-gathering way.

"Did they mention an argument with anyone, someone

who might do them harm?" Carter interjected. "You were, by all accounts, the last person to see them alive."

Lynda shifted in the love seat, choosing her words carefully. "I did meet with Morris that afternoon. He was a former client," she said, adopting her lawyerly demeanor. "He left a personal item in my office and I returned it to him."

"Personal item?" Perez said. "What was it?"

"A watch. He took it off one evening to get more comfortable when we were working late on his tax case."

"More comfortable?" Carter said.

"You heard me."

"And what about his wife Susan?" Carter continued after a moment. "What did she say when you met with her at the coffee shop?"

"That woman at the coffee shop wasn't Susan," Lynda said firmly, resuming her businesslike tone. "I don't know who she was."

"I don't understand," Perez said. "I was there. I saw you two sitting together."

Lynda held his gaze for a moment before responding. His expression reflected genuine confusion.

"That woman sat down at my table without my invitation. Like I said, I don't know who she was. I was supposed to meet with Susan that day, but she never showed up."

"The woman sitting at your table matched the victim's description," Carter insisted. "And witnesses reported seeing you and Mr. Johnson in a hotel lobby later that afternoon. Are you saying it was a mere coincidence that you were spotted with both victims on the day they died?"

Lynda remained silent, treating his question as rhetorical. Thought back to her and Morris's final meeting, where she returned his Fitbit. She knew better than to respond to such a question, as any answer she gave could be misinterpreted and used against her.

Carter scooted forward, not backing down. "Tell me, Ms. Carnes, was Morris Johnson more than a client to you?"

Lynda cocked her head, signaling that she didn't understand Carter's question, although she knew full well what he was getting at. "I beg your pardon?"

"Were you sleeping with Johnson?"

Lynda looked at the older man, staring him down. "I don't think I should say anything else without my attorney."

The two detectives exchanged a glance. Lynda tried to read their expressions, but the partners seemed to have a silent shorthand she couldn't decipher despite her legal training.

"I'm sure your time is valuable, so that's all for now," Carter said in his gruff manner.

Perez reached into his wallet. "This is my card, in case you, uh . . . think of anything."

When Lynda accepted the card, her hands brushed his and their eyes locked. If she wasn't mistaken, a surge of attraction passed between them. Perez backed up, following Carter to the door.

Glancing over his shoulder at her on his way out the door, Perez said, "We'll be in touch."

In Eddie's office at the downtown headquarters, he and Carter discussed the interview with Lynda while going over the Johnson case file.

"She's lying," Carter said.

"Or at least not telling us everything she knows," Eddie said. "But she was so adamant that the woman in the coffee shop wasn't Susan Johnson."

Carter shrugged. "She'd say anything to try to throw off

CHRIS BOURNEA // 89

suspicion." With a smirk, he added, "She is a lawyer, after all."

Eddie obliged him with a half smile. "It is possible that the woman at the coffee shop wasn't Johnson's wife," he said, thumbing through the photos of the dead athlete's girlfriends that forensics had retrieved from his cell phone. "Maybe one of Johnson's women thought he was having an affair with Lynda and went up to the coffee shop to confront her."

"Oh, there's no question the lawyer was banging her client," Carter said, reclining and tucking his palms behind his head. "But it's just too convenient that one of Johnson's other women showed up to have it out with Lynda at the same time she was supposed to meet with the wife. How would the woman have known Lynda and Susan were going to be there?"

"Whoever that woman was, she obviously wanted to be seen with Lynda," Eddie said. "I just don't know why."

Eddie shuffled through the photos of Johnson's girlfriends again. "Looks like our man Morris was quite prolific."

"Yup. This guy was a real player, in every sense of the word," Carter said. "Apparently, he used his gym to hook up with lonely women."

Eddie rubbed his forehead, indulging the habit that did nothing to alleviate the massive headache he felt coming on. "Seems he had a type: light-skinned black girls with long hair. Heck—that attorney and the lady in the coffee shop, whoever she was, could have been twins. Some of them look familiar. I probably saw them around the neighborhood back when I was working the beat."

"This certainly makes the case more complicated. Any one of those women he bedded could have killed him and his wife in a jealous rage."

When Eddie came to a photo of Lynda, he fixated on it. There was something about her, something that made him not only want to believe her but made his mind wander to thoughts he knew he shouldn't be having about a potential suspect.

That night, coming home from another long day, Eddie went through his nightly ritual: fixing a drink, emptying his pockets, checking messages. Relieved no one had called or texted during the drive home, he set his cell phone next to his bed. He picked up his wedding photo and brushed his hand over his late wife's face.

"Goddamnit, Rosario," he whispered. "I miss you. I miss you so damn much."

He returned the photo to its place and picked up the remote, quickly flipping through the channels and landing on ESPN. He'd dozed off watching the Reds game when he was awakened by the ring of his phone. Fumbling for it, he knocked the wedding photo off the nightstand, nearly shattering the glass.

"Perez."

"It's Lynda Carnes—we met earlier—"

"I remember. Do you know what time it is? Is everything all right?"

"There's something I'd like to talk to you about."

"Now?"

"I'm sorry. I know it's late."

"It's okay. I'm listening."

"I'd really rather not do this over the phone."

"Okay," he said. "Where would you like to meet?"

"Can you come by?"

Eddie paused, clutching the phone. "I'll be right over," he said.

* * *

"Thank you for doing this," Lynda said, opening her front door thirty minutes later. She eyed the detective standing there, trim and handsome in a polo shirt and khakis, a stark contrast to his earlier buttoned-up look.

"No problem. So what is it that you have to tell me?"

"It's a bit complicated." She beckoned him inside and motioned for him to have a seat on the couch in the living room. She sat across from him, then rose and sat next to him on the couch. She crossed her legs, uncrossed them, and crossed them again.

"Look," she said finally, "I know you've probably figured it out, but Morris Johnson was more than an old school friend and client."

"Oh?"

"I represented him on a tax case and one thing led to another and, well . . ."

"I see." Perez looked down at the floor. "How long did it go on—your relationship with Morris?"

"A couple of months. But I swear, I broke it off with him." She touched Perez's hand to underscore her sincerity. "I broke it off with Morris way before . . ." She paused, her voice cracking. She buried her face in her hands.

"It's okay." He touched her back.

Lynda looked up at Perez. "You know, I called you here to tell you about my affair with Morris." She scooted closer to him. "To remove any suspicion."

"I understand, Lynda."

She leaned in and put her hand on his chest. She saw the surprise in his eyes and the tension in his body as he tried to inch away.

"I'm sorry," she whispered, removing her hand.

"Don't be," Perez said a moment later, wrapping his arm

around her waist and pulling her closer. She closed her eyes and felt his lips grazing hers. She pulled away. She gazed at him and recognized the look in his eyes, the same look she saw in the mirror every morning. Hunger for human connection.

She kissed him again, pressing against him with a force that communicated that she never wanted him to let her go. As if anticipating her desires, he moved his lips to her neck and slipped his hand under her blouse, caressing her breasts.

Lynda leaned away from Perez and looked into his eyes again. Without another word passing between them, she took his hand and led him upstairs and down the darkened hallway. In the doorway of her bedroom, they lingered, kissing. He unbuttoned her blouse and she slid her hands underneath his shirt, running her hands over his chest. Any memory of Morris faded away.

Eddie sat in his office the next morning, staring at Lynda's photo. She had made him feel something he hadn't felt since he'd lost Rosario: alive.

When the office door swung open, Eddie tucked Lynda's photo back into a file. He had promised to protect her, and he couldn't do that if he were removed from the case for getting involved with a suspect.

"What's up?" Eddie said as Carter approached his desk.

Carter set a stack of papers before him. "Transcripts of all the e-mails, texts, and messages from the Johnsons' devices."

Eddie scanned the transcripts, struggling not to reveal the pangs of jealousy that gripped him at seeing the exchanges between Lynda and Morris, arranging liaisons and expressing their desire for one another. The last few texts corroborated Lynda's claim that she had broken it off with Morris weeks before the murders.

Eddie spread the transcripts across his desk and fanned out the photos from the case file to get a bird's-eye view of the evidence and discern any clues he may have missed. One of the transcripts caught his eye, an instant message from Susan to Lynda the day before the murders: *Meet me at Eastmoor Bagels and Coffee tomorrow morning at 8.* He plucked two of the photos from the stack and held them up side by side: Susan Johnson and one of the doppelgänger girlfriends.

"Oh shit," Eddie said.

"What's wrong?" Carter said.

"It's her. The woman I saw with Lynda Carnes at the coffee shop."

Suddenly, it became clear to Eddie: Lynda was indeed telling the truth. And she was in danger.

"Where are you going?" Carter asked as Eddie stood and grabbed his keys.

"I have to take care of something."

"You've reached Lynda Carnes. Please leave a message and I'll get back to you at my earliest convenience."

Frustrated at getting her voice mail once again, Eddie tossed his cell phone on the passenger seat of his car. He returned his attention to the road, careening down Eastmoor Boulevard. Driving to Lynda's house, he pieced it together. That woman in the coffee shop was, in fact, one of Morris's jilted girlfriends and he was now certain she had orchestrated this whole thing. Resentful at being tossed aside, she plotted to kill Morris and his wife when he didn't make good on his promise to leave Susan Johnson and drop Lynda and his other "side tricks."

The woman had found the exchanges between Morris and the other women in his phone and zeroed in on Lynda. Why?

Because Lynda was Susan's best friend, and who better to pin the murders on? Lynda and Susan had a long, complicated history and it would be easy for investigators to find a motive.

He recalled Lynda's confession about her and Morris as they lay entwined the night before, unable to stop holding each other. Her resentment that Morris never locked his phone—that his arrogance was as boundless as his physical prowess. There seemed to be something sadistic in his carelessness, his willingness to allow his wife to catch him and flaunt the fact that she wasn't enough to satisfy him. Using passwords she'd swiped from Morris, the woman must have hacked into the Johnsons' computer and literally stole Susan's identity. She lured Lynda to the coffee shop, figuring witnesses would identify her as Susan and offer evidence that Lynda was the last to see her alive.

With her cunning, the woman had efficiently disposed of the no-good Morris Johnson and his long-suffering wife. But, as Eddie suspected, the woman not only planned to make Lynda the scapegoat, but also her next victim. It would be all too easy to murder Lynda and make it look like a suicide. The killer figured the police would deduce that Lynda was overcome with the guilt for sleeping with her best friend's husband and then murdering them both. Lynda was blind with envy over the life the Johnsons had, the life she so desperately wanted. Based on their well-documented feuds, Lynda Carnes wanted to *be* Susan Johnson. And when she realized that wasn't possible, she snapped. The workaholic attorney had no family and few, if any, friends who could dispute that scenario.

There was no telling when the woman would carry out the final phase of her plot. Eddie had to warn Lynda, tell her to get out of town or go anywhere and lie low before this vengeful woman struck again.

When Eddie pulled up at Lynda's house, he found the front door standing open. Drawing his gun, he dashed into the house, calling Lynda's name but getting no answer. He bounded up the stairs and went straight to her bedroom. And it was there that he found her, still looking as peaceful as he'd left her that morning after one final, heated round of love-making. Except that she was now drenched in the blood that oozed from a gunshot to her temple.

Eddie sat next to her and checked for a pulse. It was too late.

He called for an ambulance and backup. He stood and stepped away from the bed. He thought of their encounter the previous night. What had he been doing? That could cost him his badge. He'd betrayed his job and Rosario. He thought again of his late wife, in the emergency room. He—

A sound. A familiar sound. He turned, too late.

She stood behind him, gun leveled at his head. "Figured out my plan, huh?"

Eddie held up his hands in a gesture of surrender. "I understand why you did it. Morris Johnson was a liar and a cheat and he deserved what he got. If you explain that, I'm sure the jury will understand. If you come with me—"

"Shut up." She waved the gun at him. "You're Perez, right? I recognize you from the news. So listen, *Detective* Perez. The only place I'm going is over the border to Canada."

He backed up. "Please. Put the gun down. You don't have to do this, Susan."

Eddie winced, realizing his error at the woman's sharp intake of breath. He had spent so much time going over the case and reviewing the photos of Morris Johnson's women that they all blurred together.

"My name is not—"

"I'm sorry," he said. "I didn't mean—"

"Didn't mean what?" She took another step forward.

"Your name—"

"My name is not Susan," she said, pistol aimed straight between his eyes.

PART II

CAPITAL OFFENSES

GOING PLACES

BY ANDREW WELSH-HUGGINS

Ohio Statehouse

I'm in the atrium, a late afternoon in early September, worrying for reasons I can't explain. It's the conclusion of lobbying day for the Association of Digital Marketing Professionals. Something like that. My boss the final speaker, relegated to the end thanks to his already full day of meetings with legislators, meetings with cabinet members, meetings with members of the national press corps writing the latest profile. The Honorable Bradley Pendleton. Governor of the great state of Ohio. A successful second-termer with a reputation for bipartisanship that has people whispering *Lincoln-esque* as they tout his accomplishments: factories buzzing again; state rivers and streams healthier than ever; reforms shrinking the prison population by the day. Little surprise he's on the short list of veep candidates for the presidential election a mere fourteen months away.

After his speech—witty, warm, and above all, brief—I stand beside him while a gaggle of Statehouse reporters lob questions at him. What about the charter school bill? What about the gun purchase background check bill? What about the payday lending bill? Late-afternoon sunlight filters through the atrium's floor-to-ceiling windows, striping the gathered lobbyists and other guests as they migrate postevent toward steaming pans of hors d'oeuvres, trays of vegetables, glass stands of cookies and brownies. Black-clad servers circulate with trays of complimentary chardonnay and pinot noir—from Ohio vineyards, naturally, which boosts their favorability for a Statehouse event, if not their actual taste. Standing just behind Pendleton, I turn and eye the stuffed pigeon sitting high above the crowd in a small alcove over the entrance to the Senate annex. The fixture a reminder of the days when the space we stand in was open to the elements and the rain of bird shit so constant that umbrellas sat in canisters on either side to assist those making their way across. "Perfect metaphor for this place," goes the punch line my boss has delivered often, and which always kills.

His five minutes with the press corps concluded, the governor shifts toward the middle of the atrium and the line of people waiting to greet him. I shift with him, keeping an eye on the crowd but not overly concerned about danger to my boss right at the moment, despite whatever it is that's worrying me. After all, the Statehouse bristles with state troopers from top to bottom. I should know. I'm one of them.

"Amanda Purnell," she says, stepping forward, next in line. They shake hands and she presses a business card into his palm. "I really enjoyed your speech. But I wonder if you're aware of the broadband issues with—" and here her voice lowers a bit as she leans forward revealing a hint—just a hint—of cleavage.

Pendleton responds in kind and I lose the gist of their conversation. Not that it matters; I've already caught the gleam in his eye. Now it's just a question of seeing whether he follows an all-too-familiar script. The signs are not good. Digital marketing appears to be largely a woman's game, to judge by those milling about the atrium, and attractive women at that. But even among these Purnell stands out—tall, raven-haired, dark designer glass frames, wearing a red ruffle sleeve sheath dress that stops just above the knees. In hindsight, this should have been a warning signal, since my routine-bound boss prefers a certain type—blond, buxom, hippie, and never, ever his height. Purnell is none of those things, starting with her ability to look Pendleton directly in the eyes. But she's a ten, no question, regardless of her type.

"I see what you mean," he says after a long minute, pulling himself up out of their conversation. "Let's be in touch."

"I really appreciate that, governor," she says, flashing a smile as she moves aside to permit the next well-wisher to step forward.

I watch my boss, waiting to see how the scene concludes— selfishly, since the outcome will affect me directly. Ninety-nine times out of a hundred, the governor turns and hands me the latest business card, leaving it up to me to place it on the desk of the most appropriate aide—or not, depending on my read of the presenter. But not today. Today, as the buzz of a well-fed and well-lubricated crowd grows in the atrium, Pendleton slips Amanda Purnell's card into the left pocket of his suit coat jacket as he turns without missing a beat to greet the next woman in line. The nagging feeling of something wrong fades slightly as the reality of the situation sinks in.

In other words: here we go again.

Before Purnell, here are the three that stood out over the years.

The scheduler. Two years out of Denison, back home after an obligatory policy stint in DC. To repeat: blond, to her shoulders, not natural but not tarty either; buxom—*Eyes up* my mantra whenever I spied her; and curvy but in a gym-after-work kind of way. Her desk just around the corner from Pendleton's on the thirty-first floor of the Riffe building—Riffe rhymes with *knife*—at State and High across from the Statehouse. To my surprise—my surprise then—she showed up at an all-day Appalachian economic forum at Hocking College our first March in office. During a break between morning meetings and Pendleton's lunchtime keynote, he signaled me to follow him through the convention hall to a room in the small attached hotel. I caught a glimpse of the scheduler sitting on the end of the bed as the door opened and closed. And that was that, for the next several weeks.

The professor. They met in a wood-paneled antechamber outside my boss's ceremonial Statehouse office two years in. Brief, private introductions ahead of Pendleton's commissioning of a blue-ribbon task force studying connections between school funding and urban academic performance. She was a much-published education policy expert, although ironically what I recall them discussing in that moment was Mrs. Pendleton's love of hot yoga, an enthusiasm the professor apparently shared. Into his pocket went her business card. And there went my lunch breaks the next six months.

The lawmaker. Impossible to say when they met, since both were in politics in the same party for years. But easy to say when it began. At that time, she was vice-chair of the House Health Care Committee, where in weekly meetings in the Harding hearing room she grilled hospital executives hoping to water down price-control bills. The week after the inauguration launching Pendleton's second four-year term, he held a Saturday-afternoon Medicaid policy retreat at the governor's residence exactly 3.7 miles east in Bexley. Mrs. Pendleton—Beth—and the children conveniently away in Youngstown visiting her parents. After drinks and a concluding dinner, guests gathered in small groups in the library, the collection heavy on Ohio authors, for final conversations before drifting off into the evening. At the end of the night I was leaning over a coffee table to retrieve an errant copy of Louis Bromfield's *Pleasant Valley* when I was interrupted by a cough. I looked up to catch the eye of my boss as he and the lawmaker drifted away themselves—up the stairs to the private residence. I replaced the book on the shelf and positioned myself at the base of the staircase.

In obvious ways, she was the riskiest of them all. Despite what you see on TV, it's hard as hell for two high-profile individuals to copulate secretly on a regular basis. More often than not, they ended up in her condo in Dublin, which helped some. But sometimes—talk about hazardous—they hooked up in the Statehouse itself, giggling like teenagers going at it with Mom and Dad in the next room. Begging Pendleton to be careful, I entrusted him with a ring of spare keys to rooms people rarely went, rooms outside the web of security camera coverage. You can imagine my relief when term limits kicked in and she decided to return home to Cincinnati to take over her ailing father's law practice. A serious danger to my boss's reputation had passed.

Until Amanda Purnell came along.

I know what you're thinking. How was all this possible in the #metoo age, not to mention the era of smartphones and social media? I asked myself the same thing constantly. By my count we were always one tit pic away from disaster. The short answer, I think, is that for all his faults, my boss was not a pig. He respected women deeply. He was the first Ohio governor to have a majority of female cabinet members. He never pressured anyone; it was guaranteed that when the business card went into his pocket instead of my hand, it was because of a mutual spark. He was Bill Clinton without the cigars and the fake flattery; Henry Hyde without the "youthful indiscre-tions" hypocrisy. As a result, his partners were both lovers and partisans: they knew the risk to the good government he rep-resented if word of their liaisons leaked out. Of course my boss knew this too, and used it to his advantage when selecting paramours. With that kind of calculation at work, was it any surprise he was on the veep short list?

"What are you staring at?"

I start, and stand to attention. "Nothing, ma'am."

"Bullshit. You were looking at me. Why?"

"I apologize, Mrs. Pendleton. I didn't mean—"

"Didn't mean what?"

"Nothing, ma'am."

We're in the kitchen at the residence. I'm in my civvies—Rockports, chinos, button-down shirt, sports coat. The First Lady perched on a stool at the island in the middle, half-consumed slice of toast on a plate beside her, reading today's *Columbus Dispatch*. Back from this morning's hot yoga workout. "Veep Announcement Soon; All Eyes on Pendle-ton," screams the above-the-fold headline. You'd have to be blind to miss the tiny smile that crossed Beth's face when she saw the news. But that's not the reason I'd been staring at her.

She stands and circles the island, a piece of paper in her hand. I keep my eyes trained on the clock on the wall, pol-ished oak face in the shape of Ohio. Try my best to ignore the fit of her yoga tights, the press of her bosom through her green workout shirt, the sheen of perspiration on her brow. Blond hair pulled into a ponytail with a pink scrunchie.

"What is this?" she says.

"Ma'am?"

"*This*." She thrusts the paper toward me. A printout of

Pendleton's calendar, a document to rival a Spielberg daily shot list, nearly every fifteen-minute interval accounted for. She points at the entry for ten a.m. The longest of the day, at exactly one hour. It says: *WFD**.

I keep my eyes glued to the clock. It's 9:05 a.m. The Pendletons' stair-step kids—son eleven, daughter nine, daughter seven—already at school. The boss upstairs, making calls. Down soon.

"I believe that's an economic development meeting. Short for Work Force Development. The single asterisk signifies the level of—"

"I know what it means. Ground level, barely in the door, not a big deal yet, but could be. I mean, who's it with? And where?"

"In, ah, Upper Arlington. I'm not entirely sure who the principal is."

"You're not?" Voice sharp as a school teacher's batting down a homework excuse.

I shake my head. I regret the white lie, but what can I do? I know perfectly well that by five minutes after ten my boss will be fucking Amanda Purnell on her Dakota Jackson bed beneath 300–thread count cotton sheets in a condo across the street from the Upper Arlington Public Library. He might even do it twice if he has time before his next event, a ribbon-cutting at a state-funded opioid treatment center.

Dissatisfied, she stalks back to her stool. "Sometimes I wonder if you realize what's at stake here." She taps the *Dispatch*, drawing her finger across the headline about her husband.

"I believe I do, Mrs. Pendleton."

"Would you please call me Beth? I've asked you a thousand times."

"Yes . . . Beth," I say, almost unable to voice her name.

"That's better, barely," she says, throwing me the smallest of smiles.

But bigger than the one triggered by the headline.

Which means a lot, given how madly I'm in love with her.

I'd known her almost exactly ten years. Her and Pendleton both. I landed his security gig during his last two years as House speaker, the stint that cinched his power base and convinced him to run for governor. The job wasn't as time-intensive as now, consisting mainly of daytime bodyguard duties around Capitol Square and late-night chauffeuring when a power dinner at Mitchell's Steakhouse on Third or the Capital Club adjoining the DoubleTree on Front went long. Not as many extracurricular outings in those days either. I first laid eyes on Beth dropping him home one day after an afternoon House session went late. She greeted him in the driveway of their Westerville split-level, toddler son perched on her hip, and then shook my hand firmly.

"My husband's going places; keep him safe, all right?" she said, all smiles.

"Yes ma'am," I said.

In hindsight, I was smitten on the spot, though my painful divorce proceedings kept me from seeing it clearly then.

The smile that Mrs. Pendleton—Beth—favored me with that day faded in the months and years that followed. As discreet as my boss was, and as careful as I was preserving that discretion, she must have had her suspicions. She must also have known I was the one enabling him. Cordiality turned to coolness turned to contempt. And all the while, like the man hungering for the meal he can never afford, I fell deeper and deeper in love.

* * *

"I have a favor to ask. Can you run Beth home? I'm going up to the office for a bit."

I don't move from my post at Pendleton's shoulder, and to my credit, don't change expressions.

"The office?"

It's September 16. The anniversary of Abraham Lincoln's 1859 visit to the Statehouse as he sought the Republican nomination for president. First of three visits in total the president made to the Greek Revival capitol. An anniversary Pendleton has ignored seven of his eight years in office. But with the way things stand now, a chance to make a few more headlines outside the gritty work of state government. An opportunity to emphasize his statesmanship. *Lincolnesque*, after all. We stand in the rotunda in the center of the building, the salmon-colored dome soaring overhead. Behind us, the marble frieze of Lincoln and his Civil War generals commemorating the Union victory in the Battle of Vicksburg. Opposite us, the west side alcove with its portrait of the Wright Brothers, those favored sons of Ohio, and two walkways leading to private offices, the second one nearly forty feet off the ground. Perfect place for a shooter, I remind myself as I glance upward. Probably imagining things, but I can't afford to take chances. After all, I'm the one guarding Lincoln, as it were.

The assembled crowd of dignitaries invited for Pendleton's speech mingles after the conclusion of the event. Among them Beth, chatting with Pendleton's Medicaid director and her wife.

"I've got some West Coast calls to make," the governor tells me. "Bunch of Silicon Valley types. I won't be long, maybe two hours. No need for you to come back—one of the troopers can run me home."

I study him. "Just the office?"

"Office and then home. Promise."

"Does the First Lady know?"

"She knows I have to work late. It'll be fine."

It doesn't seem fine, not at first. Beth strides along in silence as I walk her to my Tahoe on the first level of the underground parking garage. She climbs into the passenger seat without speaking and stays quiet as I drive us into the early evening dusk and down Broad Street toward the residence.

We're passing Franklin Park, the peak of the conservatory's greenhouse just visible through the trees, when Beth says, "Why do you hate me so much?"

I swallow hard. "I'm sorry?"

"Did I do something to you to cause you to act this way?"

"I—I don't hate you, Mrs.—"

"It's Beth, goddamnit. Don't you ever listen?"

I keep my eyes on the street, face burning. "I'm not sure I know what you're talking about. Beth."

"You sure as shit do. Turn here."

"What?"

"You heard me. Turn here!"

I signal at the last second and make a hard right into Wolfe Park. I drive through the parking lot to the far end. Glancing at Beth, I nose the Tahoe into the last space, facing Alum Creek. Behind us the *pock . . . pock . . . pock* of a tennis match. To our left, a jogger passes a woman walking a pair of corgis on the exercise trail running south of the parking lot. Early-evening shadows lengthen around us.

I say, "Is everything okay?"

She sighs, staring out the window at the creek. At last she says, "There's so much at stake."

"Ma'am—Beth?"

"Our country's going to shit. You know that, right?"

"It's a challenging time. Politically and socially." I'm mimicking my boss—her husband—but can't think what else to say.

"Brad's a good man. He could get things done. Big things, I mean, national things, if he's given the chance."

"I agree." And I do. Whatever you might say about his liberal interpretation of marriage vows—and I could say plenty—Pendleton has been a visionary governor who's helped improve the lives of millions of Ohioans.

"It's crucial he get this nomination. Crucial that nothing screws it up."

"I agree—"

"You say you agree, but then you turn a blind eye to what's going on. You let it happen. Do you understand it's not just about him? It's about me too. I've got a role in this. I'm also going places. I've sacrificed—given up everything to support him, to get him—to get us—to a position where we could really make a difference. And you don't seem to get that. So I'll ask you again, why do you hate me?"

"I don't hate you—"

"Oh really? Then what?" She glares at me, eyes bright, lips parted.

"I—"

"Jesus Christ. You hate me, and you're so fucking dense," she says, leaning over and grabbing my face and pulling me close and kissing me so hard I gasp as I struggle to catch my breath. I resist for as long as I can, but it's a losing effort—it's been a long decade. Five minutes pass before we pull away, staring at each other like wild animals interrupted in a struggle for their lives.

"I love you," I say.

"Take me home," she replies.

* * *

Turning off Broad onto Parkview and heading toward the residence the next morning, I find myself still thinking about our encounter, but for just a moment in a different context. In light of Lincoln's second visit to the Statehouse, in February 1861, during which he received official word of the electoral college vote. I thought about Beth's lecture. *He could get things done. Big things, I mean, national things, if he's given the chance.* A chance like Lincoln was given? The greatest president in the country's history?

To my surprise, Pendleton is standing by the small cottage housing the troopers who man the residence 24/7 when I pull up a few minutes later. He's chatting with the groundskeeper, an elderly, bent man who's maintained the grounds all the way back to the era of Jim Rhodes, the governor who called out the troops on the Kent State students. It's unusual for my boss to meet me outside. He shakes the groundskeeper's hand, offers his usual warm smile of departure, and climbs into the Tahoe.

"Good morning," I say. He nods. I glance at the daily calendar I'd printed out that morning from home. "Upper Arlington?" I say in even tones, the way I always do when *WFD** is on the schedule.

To my surprise he shakes his head. "I had to cancel that. Head to the Riffe. I'll be there most of the morning. But I need you to do something for me." He lowers his voice. I feel my heart skip a beat.

"Of course."

"Ben"—the groundskeeper—"says he saw someone lurking around this morning. Someone that didn't seem like he fit in the neighborhood."

"Did he tell the cottage?"

"Of course. And normally I'd let them deal with it. But with everything going on, I'd rather you check it out as well."

"If you really think—"

"We can't take any chances right now. It's probably nothing. Don't tell Ben we talked—he'll take it personally. You know how he is. Just check out the perimeter. You can brief me later. I've got the green-energy bill signing at three o'clock—you can drive me back here after that."

"Yes sir."

Forty-five minutes later, Pendleton safely ensconced in the Riffe, I'm back at the residence. I'm standing by a pair of paw-paw trees as I talk to a young trooper outside the cottage when I hear my name called. I turn and see Beth. She's standing on the patio that looks out into the garden of native Ohio plants and flowers. She's wearing a sleeveless green tank top and yoga pants. She calls again, tone formal. Mistress to servant. I apologize to the trooper and walk slowly up to the stone house.

"I'm sick of all this," she says, shaking my hand.

"Sick of what?"

"Everything," she says. I trail her inside. We walk through the library and the dining room and into the kitchen. None of the usual residence staff are there, I notice. She moves past the industrial-grade refrigerator and stove and leads me into the pantry off to the side. I don't need her to tell me to use my right foot to swing the door shut behind us.

"You don't know how hard it is," she says, throwing her arms around me.

"I'm sorry," I say, staring into her eyes.

"You should be."

The next day, a reception for visiting provincial lawmakers from a sister prefecture in Japan. The governor and First

Lady are standing in the middle of the giant inlaid marble county-by-county map of Ohio in the crypt—what they call the first floor of the Statehouse—just outside the gift shop and around the corner from the visitors' center. Pendleton's hearty "*Ohayou gozaimasu!*" for the delegation's sake—"Good morning!"—with the usual joke about the homonymic similarity to "Ohio." The usual polite laughter follows—I've heard this quip five times in ten years. Afterward, I escort my boss to his office in the Riffe. Ten minutes later I'm back in the crypt, accepting the handoff of the First Lady from her chief of staff. We walk downstairs and I open the Tahoe's passenger door for her. We don't speak as I start the car and drive through the garage and up and out into the October sunshine. I don't turn right, toward the residence. I head left. We're at my pastel-blue split-level in Hilliard twenty minutes later, and upstairs in my bedroom not a minute after that.

"We've got a little problem," she says afterward, tracing a line down my chest and onto my abdomen. I've worked hard to keep fit over the years. Not as easy as you'd think given Pendleton's schedule. I'm glad I've done so—I'm at least a semi-match for Beth's yoga-conditioned body.

"Tell me about it."

"I will."

She rolls over and across the bed, reaching for her purse. I eye her firm behind, already feeling myself stiffen again. I hear a rustle of paper. She rolls back and hands me a stapled report.

"What's this?"

"Our little problem."

I glance into her eyes, seeing nothing. I look at the top document and my own eyes widen. "Holy shit," I say after a few seconds.

"Yeah."

It's single-spaced biography, oppo-research style. Subject: Amanda Purnell. Who is not Amanda Purnell at all, it turns out, but someone named Ashley Purvis, whose background may or may not include digital marketing but whose other past experience includes dancing at Sirens Call men's club on the aptly named Godown Road on the northwest side. The report includes a darkly lit photo of Purvis curled around a pole on a small stage. The lighting is bad and someone's finger is blocking part of the view, but there's no question it's her.

"For Chrissake—it's a setup," I say, unable to stop myself.

"Apparently."

"How did you—"

"I hired someone. Just in case. I always do."

I stare at her, dumbfounded.

She frowns at my discomfort, sympathy in her eyes. "I'm sorry," she says, patting my thigh. "I know the timing's bad."

"Does the governor—"

"We're going places. You know that, right? Whatever happens with the nomination, it's not over. It's not stopping here. He's a good man, doing good things. People are better off because of him. I don't mean conceptually. I mean literally—he's saved lives through his policies. That's not going to end. Do you understand what I'm saying?"

My mind reels, as if I'm back in high school after sneaking inside early on a Sunday morning, stinking of booze, arms and legs akimbo as my bed spins round and round.

"I didn't—"

"I relied on you. You may not realize it but I did. I understand Brad. I understand how men like he operate. Good men. Men who save lives. That's why I put my faith in you."

"I—"

"And now this needs to be fixed. Do you understand? Not just for him, or me, or you. For all of us. For the people of Ohio. For the country."

"Fixed," I say.

"Fixed," Beth says, rolling up and on top of me, her breath hot in my ear as she whispers my name and reaches for me.

The smile on Ashley Purvis's face was so authentic when she opened the door that night that I couldn't tell if she was genuinely glad to see me or if it was part of the put-on. She knows my face, of course—the man with the stony expression who stands beside her lover at atrium receptions, who scans rotunda alcoves for shooters, who drives the Tahoe that delivers Pendleton into her arms. The man guarding Lincoln. Either way, the smile and her hesitation were enough to get me inside the door and onto the golden-honey bamboo flooring of the condo foyer without a fuss. Years of training kicked in after that.

A few minutes later, as she lay on her side on the high-pile oval throw rug with concentric circle design in the living room, trussed with zip ties, gagged with an extralarge red bandanna, I placed an index card and pen in front of her hands and explained in a quiet voice that I needed all her passwords—to her phone, to her computer, to her Flickr account. All of them. "Cooperate, and it'll be all right," I told her. She hesitated and after a moment nodded, eyes bright as chips of Ohio River shale after rain. While she wrote—printing tiny and crabbed as her bound hands labored with the pen—I retrieved her laptop from the marble-topped kitchen island and plopped down on the couch above her. It took me two hours, going through search histories, checking her sent e-mail, exploring the hard drive. I had to prod her a couple times for new passwords when I found new storage websites. Finally, I was satisfied that I'd located all the pictures and videos she'd secretly recorded of her and my boss, and equally satisfied she hadn't passed them on to her client yet, which was probably a mistake on her part. Perhaps she'd succumbed to the legendary Pendleton charm even in the throes of her deceit—not that it mattered now. Finished, I shut down the laptop and pocketed the index card of passwords. And then I got off the couch, feeling a twinge in my left knee as I lowered myself to the floor, slipped on a pair of blue latex gloves, and broke my promise that everything was going to be all right.

The announcement comes three days later. It's the news they hoped for. That *we* hoped for. Pendleton's been given the nod for veep. He's going places. An official event is scheduled for Friday afternoon, in the rotunda, with Pendleton to stand before the Lincoln Vicksburg Monument with the candidate. I'm to liaise with the Secret Service for security protocols. I'm expecting criticism of the Statehouse, with its warren of back rooms and passageways that don't always add up, but I'm pleasantly surprised by their affability.

"Shit," says the lead agent in a drawl that brings to mind barbecue and sweet tea. "This ain't nothing compared to that mess over in Indianapolis."

Still, I'm nervous, and rightfully so. This is my house. It's my boss. I screwed up once with Ashley Purvis and only thanks to Beth did that mistake not cost us everything. I can't let my guard down again. That's why, at her quiet, hushed insistence as we lay together once again, the morning after the announcement, I'm prowling the cool marble corridors late Thursday evening—down in the crypt, over in the atrium, up in the rotunda. I just need to be sure. Beth needs me to be sure.

I'm staring at the monument, thinking of Pendleton, and of the three times Lincoln stopped at the Ohio Statehouse. The first time, addressing a crowd during that 1859 campaign. The second time, speaking before the House and receiving word of the electoral college vote in 1861. The third—but I'm interrupted by my phone buzzing with a text.

The Wright Brothers. How safe?

Beth. I know right away what she's thinking because I've told her my own concerns. West side rotunda alcove, upper walkway. The doors accessing the passage and its low wooden railing locked and "private," but what does that mean today? Perfect place for a shooter. I walk up the first flight of stone steps, use my Statehouse master key to let myself in on the lower level, and take the stairs two at a time to the top. I unlock the interior door from the inside—I'm in a darkened Senate caucus room—and step out. I eye the hard-looking steps far below that lead to the Broad Street entrance and the McKinley Memorial. Too far down to survive a John Wilkes Booth *"Sic semper tyrannis!"* moment, but does that matter in an age when shooters don't care about escape? Satisfied that all's clear, I'm turning to head back downstairs when I hear the door behind me open.

I stare. "Beth?"

"I'm sorry," she says. "I had to be sure."

I glance through the door closing behind her. I can't tell if she's somehow eluded her normal security and has come alone, or if I spied a watchful figure in the shadow of the room beyond. She's wearing her black yoga tights—odd for the evening—along with a slimming black sweatshirt, hood pulled fetchingly over her head. I look at the ring of keys in her right hand, her access to these private passages. I realize I've seen them before. The day I gave them to my boss—

"What are you doing here?" I say. "Be sure of what?"

She steps closer, looking around. "That we're still going places."

"I thought we decided that. I thought we . . . fixed things."

"You did," she says. "And I'll always be grateful for that. Because thanks to you Brad's going places. I'm going places." She leans closer, standing on her toes, bringing her face up to mine. "You're going places."

I lean in, breathe in her perfume, unable to help myself, but it's too late. I should have guessed she had the strength in her, from all that yoga, and from our time beneath the sheets. Yes, I should have. She braces her legs, bends her knees, and shoves me, hard. Startled, I lose my balance and flip over the rail and then I'm falling, falling, falling . . .

The man guarding Lincoln, without a guard himself.

It comes to me in the split second before I meet the stairs. Honest Abe's third visit to the Ohio Statehouse.

April 1865, lying in repose in the rotunda on his long, final journey west—

HONOR GUARD

by Tom Barlow
Clintonville

Tommy is on his usual rant as I drive him to O'Reilly's Pub to celebrate Veteran's Day with a couple of their monster cheeseburgers. He's wearing the ball cap I bought for him online, with the insignia of the USS *Yorktown*. He's showered with the soap-on-a-rope I made the mistake of buying him for his birthday, so he reeks of Old Spice.

"Well, shit," my father says as we turn onto High Street from Weisheimer Road, in the heart of the Clintonville neighborhood where he's lived for fifty years. He points to the empty lot catty-corner from Panera Bread. "They're putting up another apartment building where Novak Funeral Home used to be. I seen a lot of my buddies laid out there. They already tore down that other funeral home, I forget its name, for more fucking restaurants. By the time I pass there won't be a place left for me."

"I thought you wanted to be cremated," I say. His sister Alice and I have commiserated about this new propensity of his to curse. He was always so decorous back when he was entirely in his right mind.

"I still want a service. And I want you to get ahold of the Navy, arrange some sort of honor guard. I didn't spend four years on that boat for nothing."

Tommy refused to even discuss his time in Vietnam when I was a boy, denying me the chance to take pride in his service.

But since Mom passed he's not only opened up about it, he's become quite the bore.

All the way through our three-mile drive, he keeps up his tirade against the gentrification of Clintonville, which is driving property values up so fast he's struggling to pay his taxes. When we pass Dough Mama he blames the millennials for that and all the other locavore restaurants that are rapidly replacing the modestly priced places like White Castle and the A&W drive-in that once populated the neighborhood.

"Who the fuck eats at these places, anyway?" he says. "All those queers? They must have a lot of fucking money is all I can say." He isn't happy with Clintonville's new reputation as a particularly gay-friendly neighborhood either, although his cousin Bob Harper has been out of the closet for decades and he never held that against him.

Rag-O-Rama, a swanky used-clothes place, draws disparaging comparison to the Volunteers of America on Indianola, where Tommy buys his shirts secondhand on half-price Tuesdays. When we pass Cup o' Joe, he launches into a harangue about people who would spend five bucks on a fucking cup of coffee, when they could get one for a buck fifty at Nancy's Home Cooking just up the street.

I used to argue with him, back before I understood it was senility speaking. Back when he was still "Dad" and not "Tommy." He improved slightly when they put in four stents a year back, but it didn't last. Now, I just bite my lip and hope no one can overhear us. Although I'm out of the real estate game after having failed to sell even one house in a year when the market was red hot, I still remember the agency manager pleading with me to try to make a habit of cultivating goodwill with strangers.

When we finally reach the pub, most of the parking spaces

out front are filled, although it's only one p.m. on a weekday. Tommy leads as we climb the two steps into the bar and darkness. It takes a moment for my eyes to adjust before I discover most of the booths are full and there are only two empty stools side by side at the bar.

"Where you want to sit?"

"Come on," Tommy says, pulling at the sleeve of my jacket. He leads me to the left through the dining area and out the side door onto the smoking porch, where we grab the only table available.

"What are you doing?" I say. He knows I've just quit cigarettes after twenty years of enslavement and he hasn't smoked since his Navy days. However, as soon as we take a seat at the only open table, he pulls a pack of Marlboros from his jacket pocket, sticks one in his mouth, and, with hands shaking, fires up an old Zippo lighter that carries a Navy insignia. I've never seen it before.

"Since when do you smoke?"

"Don't tell my sister," Tommy says, winking at me. I add this to the symptoms of his growing dementia. Alice has been on his ass to go to a doctor, get diagnosed, get help, but he's so deep in denial there's not a chance he'll ever agree.

I glance around the porch. Half a dozen tables are set on the asphalt in an area walled in by wooden lattice, allowing the late-fall wind to blow the smoke out the back. The crowd is all men.

A moment later a barmaid steps out of the building carrying four bottles of Budweiser and a plate of chicken wings, which she deals to the table of men around Tommy's age seated behind us. One of the men is wearing a USS *Yorktown* ball cap identical to Tommy's. I can predict a maudlin scene if Tommy spots him, so I hold my peace.

The barmaid turns to us. "What can I get for you?" She is cursed with a baby face—fat cheeks and Kewpie lips—but exudes an air of contentment that I find appealing. I have an ex-wife of sour disposition who taught me a lesson about choosing looks over attitude.

I suggest we celebrate the day with a couple of ales from Lineage Brewery, just across the street, but when the barmaid tells Tommy they run seven bucks a glass he glares at her before ordering a Busch. She waits for his food order, and I have to remind him how much he likes their cheeseburgers.

The guys at the next table are talking Ohio State football. We're only a couple of miles from the stadium, and most of the city is convinced another national title is in the offing this year. I quit paying attention to football when I left the Realtor gig, no longer needing to pretend to share my potential clients' passion just to get into their wallets.

Interrupting my eavesdropping, Tommy says, "So, you planning to go back to the post office?"

I'm surprised he even remembers my situation. I'd carried mail for twenty years before convincing myself I could earn a better living sitting on my ass selling houses, which proved to be false confidence. Now my unemployment is going to run out in a week and alimony is due on the first of the month. "They wouldn't rehire me now," I say. "Not the way I left. Besides, I couldn't do all that walking anyway, not with my back."

"I told you to take that plumbing apprenticeship out of high school, but no, you were too good to do what your old man did. I was never out of work, not once. Good economy, bad economy, people gotta shit." He lays the cigarette pack on the table as though to tempt me.

"I thought you hated being a plumber."

"Who says work is supposed to be fun? Maybe that's your problem."

Eventually the barmaid returns with the beers, and the cheeseburgers, thick and juicy. She places Tommy's in front of him and says, pointing to the adjacent table, "These gentlemen are picking up the tab for your meal. Happy Veteran's Day." She hands me my plate and returns to the bar.

Tommy turns in his chair to face the men. All four are looking his way as he grabs his can of beer and holds it up. "Thanks, guys. Much appreciated."

"No problem," says the one in the *Yorktown* hat, a guy I'd guess is about Tommy's age. "Thanks for serving."

I can see the moment the man's hat registers with Tommy. His eyes get big and his lips compress. "You were on the *Yorktown*?" he says. His tone carries a nuance of doubt.

"'67 through '69," the man says. "You?"

"'65 to '69." Tommy stands up and takes a step to the side so that he can extend a hand.

The guy also stands, holding onto the back of his chair with one hand. I note that he cants to the left, like someone with a new hip. They shake awkwardly.

"Ed English," the man says after Tommy introduces himself.

"What did you do?" Tommy says. "I don't remember you, but I don't remember a lot of shit these days."

"I was on the arresting gear crew. You?"

Tommy's forehead creases. "Catapult. You said '67 to '69? In 'Nam?"

"Of course in 'Nam. Everybody was in 'Nam."

"Well, you see, that's funny," Tommy says, taking a step closer to the man, "since the *Yorktown* left Southeast Asia in June of '67 and returned to Long Beach for a refit. We never went back. I guess any asshole can buy the hat, though." He reaches out and flicks the bill of the man's cap with his middle finger.

"You calling me a liar?" the man says. His cheeks are now bright red and he's let go of the chair.

"You wear that hat just to get free beer?" Tommy says, as I grab the back of his coat and try to pull him away. "Nothing's lower than some shithead that lies about serving."

"Let it go, Ed," one of the other men at the table says. "He's drunk."

"Me drunk?" Tommy says, raising his voice so that everyone in the smoking porch is now paying attention. I don't know what to do. I've never seen my father quite this belligerent.

"I don't care if he's shitfaced," Ed says. "You owe me an apology, sailor."

"I never saw you around the flight deck, and I knew those crews like my own family," Tommy says, shoving Ed English in the chest.

Ed reaches out and returns the shove, and before I can stand and enclose my father in a bear hug, Tommy cocks his right hand and throws a jab, the one he polished boxing Golden Gloves as a young man, as hard as he can at Ed's chin. To my horror, the punch lands right on the button and Ed's head snaps back. He catches his foot on a table leg and falls backward, smacking his face on the chair seat on his way down. Blood gushes out of the cut on his forehead, and Ed isn't moving.

Everyone on the porch is on their feet, craning to see the body. Tommy steps back, rubbing his knuckles, as one of the men at Ed's table kneels next to his friend. Another has his cell out calling 911, while the third grabs Tommy by the arm and says, "You're not going anywhere."

Tommy shakes off his hand and sits down. He turns his chair a little so he can see Ed, and then, to my disbelief, starts to eat his sandwich. I remain standing, helpless.

Nobody leaves before the fire department ambulance arrives from up the street. The EMTs search for a pulse, can't find any, so they try to shock Ed back to life. No success. Nonetheless, they toss him onto a gurney and hustle him out to the ambulance. As they leave, a police unit pulls up.

Every person on the porch is eager to tell the two patrolmen what they saw, and every one of them thinks Tommy is guilty of murder. Except me. I try to explain that Ed did some pushing too, that it was a fair fight, although Tommy—"My dad," I say—got in the first blow. He sits, seemingly oblivious, smoking.

To quell the chaos, the cops walk my father out to the cruiser and place him in the backseat. I ask to accompany him and they agree. We sit there uncomfortably for a couple of hours while the crime scene people take their photos and some cops in plainclothes show up to interview all the witnesses.

On the way to the station downtown Tommy is fixated on convincing the cops that Ed was a poseur as a Navy man, implying that this makes his actions completely justifiable. I try to shut him up, but he is having none of it until the cop riding shotgun tells him to put a sock in it.

At the downtown jail they treat Tommy like a criminal, which fires him up even further. I am sent to cool my heels in the waiting room while he's booked, but I can hear him protest at the top of his lungs that he is "being treated like a fucking coon!" Half the faces in the lobby are black, and I presume he is going to encounter more in the holding cell. He raised me to treat people of other races without prejudice, and this ugly change makes me sick to my stomach. Nonetheless, if I had any religion I would pray for his safety. Instead, I call my cousin Emily, who is an attorney with Zeller and Beachy, a large firm in town.

She shows up an hour later, appearing more perturbed than sympathetic, perhaps because she has heard about Tommy's increasingly antagonistic attitude toward Aunt Alice, her mom.

Emily talks to the officer staffing the desk and is led inside. It is only ten minutes before she returns.

"I had to explain to him who I was." She shakes her head. "He'll be here until tomorrow at the earliest. There will be an arraignment in the morning if the prosecutors decide to file charges. If they do, a judge will set bail. Can Tommy afford it? It'll be substantial, probably six figures, for which he'll have to pay a tenth in cash to a bail bondsman."

"Yeah, he can afford it," I tell her, not willing to divulge the depth of Tommy's economic problems. The dumbass, working for himself, hadn't given a thought to retirement until he was in his fifties, and the only thing of real value, if you don't count the life insurance policy he's always bragging about, is his house. He has a line of credit on it that he set up to pay his mom's medical bills from the Alzheimer's unit. That debt is almost paid off, but this will set him back big time.

Emily promises to accompany him to the arraignment the next day and sends me on my way. I'm short on cash for a cab so I take the High Street bus back to the bar to retrieve my car.

The next morning Tommy is taken to the Franklin County Municipal Court around the corner on South High where the city prosecutor charges him with manslaughter. He pleads not guilty at Emily's suggestion and posts bail, drawing on his line of credit to pay the bondsman, and is home by early that evening. I offer to come over and play some pinochle, which we do every once in a while, to take his mind off his troubles. He says he wants to be alone.

A few days later, I'm in line at the bank to cash the check I received when I sold off my ex-wife's ruby pendant, the one she thought she'd lost, when my phone rings. The caller introduces herself as Celeste Brown, the daughter of Ed English, the guy Tommy punched. I recognize the name from his obituary. She claims to have something urgent to discuss with me, but not over the phone. She insists we meet face-to-face. I reluctantly agree, and suggest the Crimson Cup coffeehouse on High near Tommy's house. I did a lot of networking there when I was a real estate agent, so it is familiar turf.

I arrive early and grab a couple of chairs and my usual Americano with an extra shot. A few minutes later a lady about my age enters, scanning the room. I raise my hand.

Her hair is long, dark, thick, and curls when it reaches her shoulders. Her sunglasses are perched on her head like pussy-cap ears. Her lips are slightly lopsided, one of those flaws that makes a woman more attractive. She's dressed in a silky mauve tunic and yoga pants stretching fetchingly over a lithe frame. In another context I'd be attracted to her, but in another context she wouldn't give me the time of day.

She walks up to me and says, "Mark Rucker?"

I stand, nod, and stick out my hand. Hers is soft as chamois. I ask her if I can get her anything. She says pumpkin spice latte, a little pricey but she's hard to say no to.

Once I deliver it, she says, "I asked you here because your father refuses to talk to me." She raises her eyebrows as though we are in sympathy with Tommy's difficulties.

I have to remind myself we are adversaries. "About what?"

She purses those lips. "I talked to one of the witnesses who told me all about the murder. Now, I could go to an attorney and sue your father in civil court for every penny he's got."

"But the city could still decide to drop the case."

"That doesn't stop the civil suit," she says. "Remember O.J.? Anyway, I went to school with one of the prosecutors, and she checked out the case for me. She said they'll push it unless I say otherwise."

"Okay, I'll bite. What do you want?"

"Two hundred grand. If I go the lawyer route, I could get five times that." She is leaning forward and her hair hangs like curtains framing her face.

The only way Tommy could come up with that kind of money is to sell the house, and then where would he live? With me in my tiny one-bedroom walk-up in Olentangy Village? That isn't even an option; my love for him demands some distance.

"And an apology," she says. "In the *Columbus Dispatch*." She pulls out a sheet of paper and hands it to me. It appears to be a screenshot from the Internet, a list of the crew of the *Yorktown* from 1969. Ed English's name is highlighted. I go down the list and find Tommy's name too. So Tommy was wrong. Figures.

"So the money and the ad, that will make up for your loss?" I can't help but sound a little acerbic.

"You don't know anything about me. But you should know I'm serious, and I need that money fast; Dad was helping support my husband, who's dying of Lou Gehrig's disease, and he has bills. Tell your father he has until Friday if he wants to avoid losing everything. And if he tries to bring an attorney into it, I'll have to do the same, and the deal will be off the table." She stands, and, leaving the balance of her latte on the side table, does a dramatic exit, head held high, not looking back. I can't help but notice she has a great ass.

That evening I'm drinking with a bowling buddy of mine who dropped out of law school, and naturally I tell him about the situation. His considered opinion is that she has a good case, both civil and criminal. He advises me to settle.

I stop by to talk to Tommy the next afternoon. I find him standing atop an extension ladder trying to snake a hose into the downspout of the gutter on the northwest corner of his house, the one that a towering silver maple has been filling with whirligigs for twenty years. He's dressed in a threadbare T-shirt, although the temperature is in the forties.

I try to get him to let me take over, but as usual he doesn't trust me to do it right. He does let me turn the spigot on for him, and a geyser of water comes flying out of the top of the plugged-up downspout, soaking him. He teeters on the ladder for a long moment while I hold my breath, before his balance returns. He descends pretty briskly for a seventy-year-old.

He leaves the ladder in place and we enter the house through the screened-in porch. Once inside, he drops his sodden trousers on the kitchen floor, then kicks them into the corner. Standing in his underwear, he pours us both cups of coffee from the ancient electric percolator that he inherited from his mother, which makes coffee the consistency of molasses.

I broach the subject of Celeste and her demands after he settles onto a kitchen chair across from me. "She's got a case," I warn him. "She could cause you a world of hurt."

He gives me a raspberry, and I feel a mist of spittle reach my hand. "The guy had his fucking chance. It's not my fault he didn't defend himself. If that took place on the flight deck of the *Yorktown*, you'd have had officers stopping the fight until they could make book."

"You sucker-punched him," I say. "Any jury would see that."

"He got what he deserved. You really think I'm going to give up my house to pay that bitch just because her old man was a fraud?"

Telling him about the evidence Ed's daughter had shown me of his service on the *Yorktown*—proving Tommy screwed up—would just rile him up more, so I don't mention it. "I think you need to come to some sort of agreement with her if you want to stay out of jail. She seemed desperate to me, so she might just take less money. I'm thinking we offer her fifty grand cash if she agrees to drop her civil case and convince her friend in the prosecutor's office to kill the charges."

"You're pretty quick to give away my money. And who put you in charge, anyway? This is *my* business." He pulls a pack of butts out of the Porky Pig cookie jar on the table and fires one up. I lean forward to catch some of the smoke.

"Remember," he says, "when that kid bullied you in fourth grade?"

"Yeah." I'm shocked he remembers. "You did nothing." Paul Peters had kicked the crap out of me every day for a couple of weeks, and Tommy pretended like nothing had happened when I came home with a black eye or a ripped shirt. I heard him and Mom arguing about it the first night it happened. She never won such battles with Tommy, though; he'd simply prolong the dispute until she grew exhausted and gave in.

"I thought eventually you'd get the idea," he says, "that you can't expect other people to stand up for you. To this day, you still let people walk all over you."

"And that's what you were doing when you killed that

man? Standing up for yourself?" I slide his pack of Marlboros my way and tap one out. I'm not going to smoke it, but my hands need something to do.

He's rapping the table with his thumb. "You don't get a fucking honor guard for turning the other cheek," he says. "Where's this bitch live?"

"I don't know. Why?"

"Maybe I'll pay her a visit."

"For God's sake, don't make this worse."

Eventually, he dismisses me so he can take his daily stab at the crossword in the *Dispatch*. I've been looking at them after he's done and he's taken to filling them in with gibberish.

I head home, but after considering the situation, turn before I arrive back at my apartment, and instead drive to Aunt Alice's house on West North Broadway, a typical Clintonville Dutch Colonial overlooking the river.

She's cleaning house as usual, although her place is always antiseptic. I'm invited in for tea, which means cookies, which she still bakes weekly although she usually ends up throwing them away for lack of company. Her friends are dying off so fast she has several mourning outfits in case one is at the cleaners when needed.

We take a seat in the alcove where the early-winter sun has raised the temperature enough that both her cats are sprawled on the rug. She knows about the fight, but when I tell her about Celeste and Tommy's threat to visit her, she shares my concern.

She stirs her tea with a tiny spoon until it reaches room temperature. "A week ago he tried to kick Dulcie when she ran between his legs. He can't control his emotions anymore. This must be so hard for you."

"You know how I love him. But I'm afraid if he faces a judge he'll go ballistic. He could lose everything."

"He's reached the point where you have to wonder about his competency. Maybe it's time he moved to one of those facilities like where we put Mom."

"I can't imagine having that conversation with Tommy." I pick up a cookie, then put it back.

"You're his only child," she says, pointing at me. "He had to do that for his mother. Now it's your turn. And after all, it's in his best interest."

"Even if I could convince him, he couldn't afford one of those places." A chill comes over me. Maybe a breeze is leaking through her old aluminum windows.

"You'd be surprised. There's government money, and his house is worth a lot, even after paying off that lady. And I have some of your uncle's life insurance money that I could contribute."

"You'd do that? He treats you like crap."

"I promised Mom to look out for him," she says.

"She's been gone for, what, ten years?"

She shakes her head so slightly it might be a tremor. "A promise is a promise."

"So how much life insurance money do you have?"

We reach an agreement: she'll lend me the fifty grand to buy off the woman, to be repaid from Tommy's life insurance after he passes. She's that sure she'll outlive him.

Although I now have the cash in hand, I find reasons to postpone calling the victim's daughter. First, I have an interview at Beechwold Hardware. They're in need of someone to fill in during the Christmas season, but as I talk with the owner it's quickly apparent to both of us that I don't know enough about home maintenance to provide the advice that Clintonville homeowners have come to depend upon. I wouldn't know a spud wrench from a spud casserole.

Second, I'm still reluctant to cross the old man. I try to convince myself that paying off Celeste is in his best interest, but that role reversal comes at a cost. If he becomes the one who must be looked after, who will I turn to when I'm feeling overwhelmed?

Then Emily calls to tell me the prosecutor's office is taking the case to the grand jury. She's had the opportunity to look over their case and is worried that it's a slam dunk. I ask her about a plea of mental incompetence, but she is doubtful the court will buy it without a previous history of diagnosis and treatment.

This and Alice's persistent inquiries finally prod me into action. I call Celeste, suggest we meet again. I figure I can negotiate better face-to-face.

This time we meet at the Global Gallery, a vintage gas station a few blocks north of Aunt Alice's house that has been converted into a gift shop and coffeehouse. Celeste is waiting for me as far from the cold wind leaking through the porous overhead doors as possible.

I grab a coffee and join her.

"It's your meeting," she says as I settle. Her expression is steely, telling me she's ready to end this.

I wonder what Tommy would think of me now. He taught me to hate liars, but she's forcing my hand. "You should know that Dad doesn't have much. His mom was in a nursing home for two years before she passed, and he had to take out a second mortgage to pay for it."

"Not my problem." She has makeup on today, or perhaps she's just blessed with the skin of an infant.

"But it is, like it or not. His equity is about shot. You take him to court, maybe you could garnish his Social Security, but he always underreported his earnings so that isn't much either."

"Then why call the meeting?" she says.

"I have a 401(k) with about $50,000 in it. It's yours, on a couple of conditions." I show her the check I've made out in her name, hoping to provoke her greed.

"Go on."

"You agree to not sue him, and you call your friend and get her to forget about the grand jury."

I can hear her heel tapping against the floor as she thinks. "That's the best you can do?"

"Cross my heart," I say.

She takes the check from my hand. "What about the ad?"

I promise her I'll place it that afternoon. She's not happy for the delay, but what can she do?

She has already prepared a written agreement which she pulls out of her purse. She crosses out the 200k and writes in the amount of the check, then we both sign it. She promises to mail me a copy.

I, Tommy Rucker, hereby apologize to the family of Ed English for suggesting he did not serve on the USS Yorktown from 1967 to 1969. I was wrong; he did indeed serve with honor on the arresting gear crew.

I have the paper run the four-inch ad the next day, in the food section, hoping Tommy will overlook it. Unfortunately, he still has a few buddies with wives who cook, and one of them wakes him at seven a.m. that morning to point it out to him. When I stop by at ten a.m. to take him on his weekly grocery trip, he's waiting for me.

"What the fuck is this?" he demands, shaking the paper at me. He's perched on the lip of the couch.

"It's what's going to keep you out of jail," I say, too nervous to take a seat. "I met with the guy's daughter; she demanded that. It wasn't my idea."

He snorts. "You think? Then why did Emily call this morning to let me know my case is going to the grand jury?"

He's seated next to an old photo of the three of us. In it he's probably about my age, and I'm about ten. Mom has her arm around him and he's grinning like a fool, as though he'd been into the Jim Beam since breakfast. I have nothing but fondness for the man in the picture, and struggle to remind myself the same guy is ranting at me now.

"The daughter was supposed to tell her friend to drop the charges," I say.

"The bitch that kept calling me? She won't be happy until I'm in jail."

I excuse myself and walk into the kitchen to call Emily on Dad's landline. She confirms Tommy's statement: there's no chance the charges get dropped. I tell her about my deal with Celeste.

She says, "I don't understand. I met with the daughter yesterday. She is planning to sue, and she didn't indicate she knows anyone in the prosecutor's office."

A pall comes over me. "A tall, good-looking brunette?"

"Short, blond. Missing her left arm at the elbow."

I smack the wall with the old phone handpiece so hard the Bakelite cracks around the speaker. I've been played. Demanding the ad, while risky, had been the master stroke. Because of that, I never questioned the woman was who she said she was.

"What made you think the bitch would drop the charges

anyway?" Tommy says when I return to the living room.

I tell him about the fifty grand, too embarrassed to admit I'd been conned. I thought he was mad when I arrived, but now he turns it up a notch. "You threw away my sister's money? What? You sweet on that woman? I warned you about thinking with your dick."

"I did it for you," I say. "You'd have done the same for me if I was facing a prison sentence."

He throws the newspaper at me, but it comes apart in midair and sections land all over the carpet. "Let me tell you something, you dumbass. We didn't want you. We were saving up to buy a storefront to start a flower shop. Then you happened, and your mom had to quit working, and there went our fucking plans."

"That's not you talking," I say. "You never treated me like you didn't want me."

"What the fuck was I supposed to do? A man doesn't take out his anger on a child."

"I'm still your child," I say, and am immediately embarrassed for doing so.

He stands, crosses the room to me, and slaps me across my cheek. "What do I have to do to get you to grow up?"

I let him smack me again. He's my father, I owe him that. I barely notice the sting this time.

He smacks me a third time, but now there is less power behind it, and he's breathing hard. "You think I don't know what's going on? I saw my mother lose her mind until she couldn't even remember how to breathe. I can't go through that. You claim you still love me, be a man and prove it." He strikes me again, but this time it has no more sting than a love slap.

"What do you mean?"

"Kill me," Tommy says, hands dropping to his side. "Before I lose my mind. You owe me that much."

"You don't mean that." I grab him by the shoulders. He shrugs me away.

"You know what happens to a man in prison," he says. "And by the time I get out, I'll be a drooling vegetable like my mom."

Out of nowhere comes a memory, Tommy handing me my first ball glove, playing catch with me at ten feet's distance, a big smile every time I snag one of his tosses. Baseball was the one thing I was good at in high school, and he never missed a game. That was the last time I could remember feeling competent.

When I fail to reply, he says, "Just help me clean out the fucking garage so I can get the car in there. I'll take care of the rest."

But in the end, I have to help him with the hose, and I pack some rags under the garage door to seal up the gap once the car is inside. He looks a bit bewildered, sitting there behind the steering wheel. I can tell his grasp on the situation is slipping, and I suppose I could talk him back into the house at that moment.

But I don't, because I love the man. After all, who am I, who has failed at most everything he's attempted, to dishonor his father's decision?

I even momentarily consider riding shotgun, but I'm not as brave as the old sailor. He tells me to go home. I like to think he is concerned that I might be found guilty of abetting. Instead, I return to his kitchen to fire up a cigarette.

There, rolled up in the cookie jar next to his smokes, is his life insurance policy. I'm already furious at myself, but that is magnified when I find myself picking it up to check for a suicide exclusion.

Checking in vain.
Some kind of honor guard I have proven to be.

AN AGREEABLE WIFE FOR A SUITABLE HUSBAND

BY MERCEDES KING

South End

Gerald shifted on his barstool at the Scioto Downs clubhouse, mildly aroused by the cocktail waitress who'd kept the drinks coming and had spent part of the night in his lap. Her smile widened each time he slid her another dollar on the opposite side of his Pabst Blue Ribbon. She rubbed up against him like a cat, and didn't seem to mind when he looked down her blouse and grabbed her rear. At closing time, she agreed to a little fun in the backseat of his Oldsmobile. He thought her name was Crystal but wouldn't swear to it.

After they buttoned up, he gave her some money, told her to buy herself something nice, like more of that perfume she was wearing. She readily accepted but said she could use more, her rent being due and all. Gerald obliged. Times were troublesome with another energy crisis on the horizon, thanks to that idiot Carter taking over in the White House. Gerald had a soft spot for struggling, hardworking gals like her. Said he wouldn't mind seeing her again—maybe take her to the Ponderosa.

"You know where to find me, handsome."

With that she scooched out of the car, straightened her skirt, and gave a little wave over her shoulder as she walked across the empty lot to her car.

If only his wife could be that agreeable, that much fun in the sack. But what could he expect? Annette grew up on a farm in Kentucky, slaughtering hogs. While she could stir up sausage gravy and Bisquick biscuits like nobody's business, she wasn't much more than a rag doll in the sheets. Sure, she didn't nag him like Andy Capp's wife in the comics, but she never teased him or wore any of those silky or see-through nighties with fur on the edges he was always buying her. Gerald got behind the wheel and felt a sudden rush of disgruntlement hit him, washing away that feel-good vibe from Crystal.

The track's clubhouse wasn't his regular spot. He had no luck gambling on horses, and the drinks were too pricey. But gals like Crystal made it worthwhile on occasion. The stench of horse manure reminded him too much of his own bluegrass upbringing, where summers were spent baling hay and hanging tobacco. His family hoped he'd take over the farm, but working sunrise to sunset didn't appeal to him. Instead he traded a life of permanent dirt under his fingernails for factory-greased hands.

He'd be staring down forty before long. The six years— or was it eight—he'd been with Annette weren't what he'd expected. She was married before. The husband—Harlan— dropped dead from a heart attack or something. It happened. Two boys resulted from the marriage. Gerald didn't mind them much. They kept out of his way mostly, since they were afraid of him. He liked her because she had a bit of money, an all-right figure, and a hankering to leave Kentucky. They put the Old Country, as they called it, behind them and the money went toward the down payment on their house. The gray smokestacks of Columbus and its growing industry became home.

Then life became a dull routine. Carrying the basket of

dirty laundry downstairs, yardwork, keeping the cars spotless and tuned up, carrying the basket of clean laundry upstairs. Ordinary. All Gerald wanted was a good time, an escape now and then from the talk at Buckeye Steel about layoffs, from the boys wrestling and breaking things as they pretended to be the Bionic Man. That's what nights like this were about for him. With girls like . . . Crystal? Smoothing the edges and helping him tolerate the boredom.

It was a good thing Scioto Downs was a short drive up Route 23 to his home in Jefferson Meadows. What was it tonight, five beers and three shots of Black Velvet? That's all he could remember. As the road swam before him in the dark, he wished he was headed anywhere but home to Annette.

Annette flinched when she heard Gerald's car bang into the aluminum trash cans as he pulled into the garage. She glanced at the clock: almost three in the morning. She was still at the kitchen table, studying for her real estate class. The clamor prompted her to peek out the window, more concerned that the neighbors had been bothered than about Gerald's condition. No lights appeared from either Bob and Alice or Bill and Carol, giving her a fleeting sensation of relief. She watched Gerald stagger-stumble toward the door and thought: *Here we go.*

"What's this?" Gerald leaned against the doorframe after he made it in, pointing to her books.

"You know it's for my real estate class."

"Real estate class? What's that for?"

"I've told you. So I can get my license and sell houses. And keep your voice down." At least her boys knew by now to stay in their room, no matter what they heard.

"You already got a job, and that ain't paying much bills."

Annette couldn't argue. Waitressing at the Western Pan-cake House, across from the Great Southern Shopping Center off South High, she felt like she brought more home in leftovers than tips. But working evenings, weekends, and a double shift here and there proved easier than asking Gerald for money when the boys needed new sneakers or a banana seat for their bike.

"You think you can do better than me at providing?" Gerald said, managing *providing* despite a belch that seemed to sneak up on him.

"Now that's nonsense, Gerald," she said, carefully. "No such thing as a better man than you." She forced herself to kiss his cheek—and that's when she smelled it, the flowery scent of another woman. Now that she was closer to him, she noticed the traces of lipstick on his mouth. Annette realized her face must have betrayed and exposed her sudden anger, as she caught Gerald looking at her. His brow furrowed, and she knew he wanted to turn things into a fight, because that was all he was really good at, all he really knew how to do well.

She defused it instead: "We'd better get you to bed." Annette slid her arm around him. "Get you undressed and tucked in." She patted his chest. "Wouldn't want you to be late to work, would we?"

He seemed confused, as though he'd forgotten what he was mad about. His forehead thumped into hers.

"Maybe I could get lucky with my woman."

"Well, let's see if you can manage." She gave him an en-couraging smile.

It took time getting him up the stairs, especially with him trying to play frisky, but once his back flopped onto the bed, he was out.

Annette stood at the end of the bed and looked at him

as the intensity of his snoring increased. She thought back to the first time he hit her. A laundry basket in his way. It was his own fault since he left it there, claiming he couldn't be bothered with *women's work* anymore, lugging that thing up and down the stairs. Not that Gerald would ever admit his own folly. He aimed his wrath only at her, which Annette was grateful for. The boys learned quickly to avoid him, but truth was she didn't want them around an abusive man. Not again. Not after what she went through with Harlan.

The worst was the night Gerald grabbed her by the face and clicked open his switchblade right by her nose. She thought he was going to kill her—and her boys would find her body. He'd gone on about some guy starting a fight with him at Pit Stop, said he wanted to cut that guy's throat right there in the parking lot, but maybe she'd have to do instead.

That was the night she decided. The night she was done putting up with a broken marriage, done playing the charade of a happy family. She was done risking her boys' future.

The night she decided Gerald had to go.

Gerald did his part on Saturday and felt proud of himself. Dropped the boys off at the Scioto Trail pool, trimmed hedges, mowed the lawn after a couple beers, because that's the kind of man he was. He let his neighbor Bill borrow his bag of charcoal, because they were barbecuing with family later, then checked the used Cub Cadet that neighbor Bob picked up, because it sounded awful. Needed a new belt, and Gerald happened to have an extra in the garage. That's the kind of man—and neighbor—he was.

Jefferson Meadows was a modest collection of ranches and split-levels, accessible from Rathmell and Lockbourne roads, and within walking distance of the local schools. Built in the

MERCEDES KING // 143

late 1950s, when Rickenbacker Air National Guard Base was at its zenith, most homes still reflected pride of ownership. Gerald's house, along with his neighbors' houses, included a backyard and a steep embankment that, at the bottom, bordered a ball field for Little Leaguers. Franklin County offered the homeowners the extra land at no expense, not wanting to bother with maintenance—which turned out to be the exact reason Annette didn't want the land, saying it was worthless. But Gerald made the final decision, and the county paid for chain-linked fencing to surround and divide the properties.

Mowing the damn hill became a bane for Gerald with the summer heat beating down and the land's steep angle.

At the bottom of the embankment, he kept a spot for burning trash, something only the homeowners with the extra tract could do in this neighborhood. Useful for burning yard debris, the boys' dead hamster the one time, anything he wanted rid of, really. Today, when Bob and Bill weren't around, he tossed Annette's real estate books into the pile, along with a lit match. Sweat-soaked from the day, he smoked a cigarette and guzzled another beer while the fire crackled and the pages were consumed. Parents and players gawked as they drove by slowly. Gerald lifted his beer their way as he offered a toast.

Ain't having no woman think she's better or smarter than me.

Carla, not Crystal. The cocktail waitress from Scioto Downs. He saw her several more times, picking her up from work on occasion and treating her right by taking her to the E-Z Sleep Motel on South High, just over the bridge on the other side of 104. They had a time, until she helped herself to his wallet one night and found a faded picture of Gerald with Annette and the two boys. She tore into Gerald, even pounded him on the chest, but he grabbed her wrists and squeezed her until she yelped; it was the only way to get her to listen. He admitted being married. It hadn't come up before since Gerald quit wearing his ring years ago. He told Carla that Annette didn't mean anything to him anymore, that he hated every bit about being trapped and tied down. That calmed her.

They shared a beer and he got her back into the mood for another round, but it wasn't the same. He thought he could make up for it by giving her more cash and promising to take her someplace fancy next time, maybe the LK Restaurant and Motel off Alum Creek. She didn't light up, not like she did when he took her to see *Smokey and the Bandit* or when he gave her that nightie. When they parted ways, Carla said nothing about getting together again.

Gerald blamed Annette. Like always, she ruined everything for him.

He stomped the gas pedal in the Olds as he left the motel and made his way to Pit Stop, his favorite bar. Located off Williams Road, Pit Stop sat beside Columbus Motor Speedway, a paved, figure-eight-style track that hosted demolition derbies, school bus races, and other events. Fans and drivers were always coming and going, bringing the smell of motor oil and burned rubber with them. Gerald preferred a barstool over the grandstand but enjoyed the stories people shared.

He'd stayed away because the barmaid he'd been friendly with, Doris, had a husband who caused trouble awhile back. Gerald and the guy ended up in the parking lot, fists at the ready. Knowing the man could take him out with a few swings, Gerald whipped out his switchblade, an eight-inch knife with a pearl handle he kept on him when he stopped in for drinks. Gerald threatened him before God and every tipsy patron who stumbled outside to watch. The guy spat his own threats but both walked away with neither of them throwing a sloppy punch.

Gerald belonged at Pit Stop. He didn't care if Doris—or

her husband—was there or not. His switchblade was in the glove box, where he usually kept it, out of sight from the boys. Hadn't used it on anyone but he knew there were plenty of mean drunks out there. Paid to be smart.

Sitting in the Olds, parked at Pit Stop now, Gerald gripped the steering wheel. After getting scorned by Carla, all he wanted was a bottle of Jack and to complain. He opened the glove box, pocketed the knife, and steeled his nerves before heading inside. He'd duck out if he sensed trouble. When he swung the door open, George Jones greeted him from the jukebox with "Why Baby Why." Familiar faces smiled, waved him in. Yeah, he was home.

Annette looked at the movie screen, trying to figure out why women swooned over Burt Reynolds. She never cared for his films—he was no Charles Bronson. Watching Burt speed around and make a fool of Jackie Gleason felt like another petty torment. Lately, life was full of such torments.

Life with Gerald Reed had been nothing like Annette had expected. She had fallen for his charms, just like Doris, the Pit Stop barmaid. And now the latest mistress. But in the beginning he'd been hard to resist. Gerald had taken to her, even though she was widowed and had two young boys. They had shared a desperation to leave eastern Kentucky, and eloped after a few weeks of courtship, if late-night talks on the porch swing were considered courting. They wasted no time packing up and heading to Ohio, where they moved around a couple years before making the South Side of Columbus home.

That's when it started. After they settled in, Gerald's discontent and drinking ramped up. Every evening demanded a six-pack, until drinking at home lost its luster. Then he found Pit Stop—and the company he craved.

And now Annette was sitting two car lengths back from Gerald's car at the drive-in, where he'd taken whichever girl this was for the evening. *Smokey and the Bandit.* Hmph. The last time he'd taken her and the boys out, to Long John Silver's, Gerald complained, like he always did. Mad the boys didn't finish their hush puppies. So long ago she couldn't remember.

Annette watched as the Olds shimmied and the windows fogged. She didn't know why being a good wife wasn't enough, why Gerald went chasing after other women. For the last seven years she'd taken care of him, their home, and gave in most every time he turned to her in bed and flashed that smarmy grin he thought was his best charm. She bore his lousy grunting and drizzling sweat and told him he was fine when it was over. And she never made a fuss, a peep, or a production over *her* needs. What more could a man want?

A shiver streaked through her, recalling how her first husband had been the same way.

Were all men self-absorbed and unaware? Did that explain why Gerald paid no attention to being followed? Because when it came to tomcatting, Gerald proved careless. He left receipts in his pockets. Maybe that would teach him to do laundry—*women's work*—now and then. He must have thought Annette wouldn't realize he'd rummaged through her panty drawer and taken one of those skimpy lingerie pieces from the back—one trimmed with leopard fur.

It was a good thing he made mistakes. Because in her mind, it was only a matter of time before Gerald was done with her. He'd already held that switchblade to her face, threatened her. She was bound to end up dead by Gerald's hand, unless she acted first.

Annette didn't like what she'd have to do—the task needed

to get rid of Gerald. But bathed in the glow of the movie, looking at her bare arms and caressing the scars on her skin from her hog-butchering days, she set her mind to it. *You gotta be quick . . . certain.* Just like Daddy taught her. *No hesitatin'!*

Yes, when the moment was right, Annette would be ready. Her life depended on it.

The knock came one balmy evening in August two weeks later. Gerald glanced at Annette questioningly. Their friends and neighbors knew they never bothered with the front door and only used the back sliding door. They'd finished supper and the boys had gone off to play in a neighbor kid's tree fort down the street.

Gerald opened the door to a man wearing slacks and an elbow-patched blazer over a dress shirt.

"Evening, sir. I'm Detective Holbrook. Columbus Police, homicide division." He showed a badge. "I'm looking for a Gerald Reed."

"That's me."

"Sorry if I'm interrupting your dinner, but I'd like to talk to you about a case I'm working. Your name has come up quite a bit."

"Did you say homicide, as in murder?" Gerald noticed Annette didn't join him at the door, just stayed in the kitchen, listening with interest. That irked him.

Holbrook nodded. "Yes."

Gerald nodded along.

"Would you mind if I come in, Mr. Reed? Might be better to have this conversation inside."

Of course Gerald minded. Cops meant nothing but trouble to him, and he knew better than to trust them. But if it helped get rid of him faster . . . Gerald held the door open wide, welcomed the man in with a stern glare and arched eyebrow. He watched *Starsky & Hutch*, knew his rights. Holbrook took in the living room. Gerald hated how the man was already making judgments. Holbrook exchanged hellos with Annette, turned down her offer of coffee.

"You folks may have heard," Holbrook said, "if you catch the news, that a young lady was killed recently. I'm lead on the investigation, and, Mr. Reed, it seems she's connected to you. What can you tell me about Carla Wilson?"

Gerald hesitated. His face scrunched. "Can't say the name's familiar."

"You sure about that?" Holbrook's gaze narrowed. "She's a waitress at the Scioto Downs clubhouse. Well, she was. Her body was found nearly a week ago in Big Walnut Creek. I believe that runs behind your house, on the other side of that ball field."

Gerald said nothing. Hell, he didn't know the name of that creek anyway.

"I've talked to her sister," Holbrook went on, "a few of her friends and coworkers. They've told me she was seeing you."

Gerald shifted and looked at Annette, then returned his attention to the detective. "I—I don't know who you're talking about." Best not to admit anything, he figured. No need to fall into any traps. Let the detective show his proof first.

"You drive a blue Oldsmobile, Mr. Reed?"

"What's that got to do—"

"Several people claim they've seen Carla getting into a blue Oldsmobile—and that a man fitting your description picked her up from work on occasion."

"Can't be me." A smugness tainted his voice.

"How about the name *Gerald Reed* that we found on receipts from the E-Z Sleep Motel? The clerk also described you, mentioned the car."

"Well, the car, that—what did you say her name was?" Gerald scratched his neck, ignored the perspiration surfacing on his body.

"Carla." The detective gave it emphasis, as if that might trigger Gerald's memory. "Her sister Judy has been particularly helpful. Told us you and Carla carried on an affair for a couple months, until Carla found out you were married and called it off."

Gerald heard Annette gasp. He turned and saw she had a hand over her mouth, her eyes wide.

Detective Holbrook looked past Gerald to Annette. "I'm sorry, ma'am, if this is news to you."

Gerald watched as Annette bent her head, closed her eyes, as if she were praying. He didn't understand her reaction, didn't care either.

"Judy also said you wouldn't leave Carla alone," Holbrook continued, "that you kept showing up at the racetrack after she ended the relationship. In fact, Judy claimed Carla yelled at you—and that you made quite a scene."

Gerald thought his head would explode, taking in the detective's words. Sure, he'd gone back to Scioto Downs a couple of times to see if Carla missed him, hoping to woo her back. He'd always had a way with women, could turn on the charm whenever he wanted. She gave him excuses, though, said she was tired, then said she had a cat to feed, that sort of thing.

He missed the action with Carla. Truth was, he'd planned on telling her he'd leave Annette, if that's what it took to get more tail. Went down there, week ago or so, for that very purpose. But things didn't go right that night. Carla was slutting around with some other guy while she worked. Touching him, making sure he could see down her shirt, same way she'd acted with Gerald in the beginning. Gerald took a table in the back, watched the two of them while he put away several beers. Crushing the cans as he finished did little to ease his growing anger.

After the man left, Gerald went up to her, confronted her about what she was doing, called her names. Carla told him to get out, called him a creep, told him never to come around again or she'd call the police. Gerald couldn't swear to it, the memory fuzzy from all those beers, but he thought he knocked the tray from her hands, maybe threw a glass he grabbed from a table as he rushed out.

Now she was dead?

"Mind if we have a look in your garage, Mr. Reed?" Holbrook asked.

"For what?"

"The car, Mr. Reed. Mind if we take a look inside it?"

"There's nothing in it . . ."

"Fine. How about we make sure?"

"Don't you need a warrant for something like that?" Gerald didn't like the detective's tone or feeling pushed around.

"I can get a warrant and a few officers, and we can come back, put you and your wife in handcuffs, have you wait outside while we search the car and the whole house. If you feel that's necessary . . . and have something to hide."

Gerald gaped at Annette. He didn't know what to do, but the storm in her eyes told him she'd do him no favors. That burned him up on the inside, knowing she was going to stand there and pout while the police accused him of something he didn't do. Maybe he didn't expect sympathy from her but concern would've been nice.

"Let's get this over with," Gerald mumbled.

He got his keys and, with Annette following at his heels,

led the detective out back by the detached garage. He hadn't put away too many beers, not for it being a Sunday, but still his head throbbed, and now he was more irritated with Annette than usual. Once they were alone—after he proved there was nothing in the Olds and the detective told him how sorry he was for the bother—Gerald would smack that look off Annette's face once and for all.

He fumbled with the keys and wondered why in the hell he stayed with Annette. Far as he was concerned, there was no need being miserable, not when there were women like Crystal—*Carla*—and Doris out there who knew how to make a man happy. That was it, he decided. He'd leave her and the boys tonight, right after he popped the trunk of the Olds. Let her figure out what to do, how to get by. Gerald didn't care anymore. He'd go to Doris or find another gal like Carla. Agreeable.

He inserted the round key in the trunk and opened it. He stared. A reddish-brown stain covered the trunk lining. All three pairs of eyes went wide, though none wider than Gerald's. Detective Holbrook whipped a crisp white handkerchief out of his pocket and dabbed the area. The stain was dried and crusty.

"What the hell is that?" Gerald pointed to the blemished carpet in disbelief.

"Looks like blood, Mr. Reed."

Annette gasped, covered her mouth with her hands again, and turned away.

Gerald felt the detective's strong grip on his arm. "Mr. Reed, I need you come with me."

Annette took a seat in the interview room across from Holbrook but passed on his offer of a cigarette. She wanted one, badly, but he didn't smoke Salems, and she needed to keep her focus sharp, not get too comfortable or casual around Holbrook. Two months had passed since Gerald's arrest.

"Thanks for coming down again," he said, after lighting up and puffing away. "I know it's a bit inconvenient with the boys and all."

"Carol has been great about watching them."

"Before the trial begins, I wanted to go over a few things."

Annette waited. She didn't know if it was normal, being interviewed three times, but she was used to it by now.

Once again, they covered the same laundry list of questions; she replied with the same steadfast answers.

"We've got a lot of evidence against your husband, Mrs. Reed," the detective said, rifling through papers. "Blood in the trunk of his car, a switchblade from his glove compartment with blood smears—both matching Carla Wilson's blood type. Then there's a piece of a work glove we found in the ash pile at the bottom of your embankment, that also has Carla's blood type on it."

"It's so hard to believe," she murmured.

"And there's testimonies. Carla's sister gave us plenty of details about the affair and the last time Carla and your husband were seen together at the clubhouse. We've also talked to your neighbors, and Doris over at Pit Stop." He paused. "You know what they've told us?"

"I'm sure they've had a lot to say about Gerald."

Holbrook nodded. "Especially about his temper, about how he treated women, and how he treated you. Carol and Alice both mentioned seeing you with bruises. So did your coworkers."

Annette stared down at the tabletop and pressed her lips together. She nodded.

"They told me how Gerald never came straight home after work," Holbrook said, "that he always went to Pit Stop or the clubhouse or some other bar. I've seen this plenty. Man mistreats his wife, and there isn't much we can do about it unless we walk in on the guy while he's hitting her. That kind of life, well, I can understand how that might wear on a person after a while and might eventually cause her to snap."

"Snap?" Annette said.

Holbrook leaned back in the steel-framed chair. "Revenge is one of the oldest motives for murder."

"I don't understand, detective—"

"It wouldn't be unheard of, you know, an abused wife wanting to escape her circumstances. I could see it. Because if you ask me," he came forward, rested his forearms on the table, "all that evidence against your husband almost seems too convenient. It's like we found enough to hang him at every turn."

"What are you saying?"

"Don't get me wrong, Mrs. Reed. Your husband's as low as they come. He probably deserves being punished for what he's put you through. But two things keep me from sleeping. First off, Gerald hasn't shut up about being innocent. My guys are running out of Anacin and Rolaids from all the chirping he does from his cell. He even suggested you set him up."

"He *what?*" Annette's surprise was genuine.

"Then there's the evening we found the bloodstain in the trunk," Holbrook continued. "Pains me to say it, but Gerald was taken aback, as if he really had no idea it was there."

"I don't know what you want from me, detective." She couldn't hide a tremor in her voice and the slip of her Kentucky accent, which happened anytime she was nervous or around her family.

"I'm just after the truth."

Holbrook's head tilted slightly, empathy pooled in his stare, daring—no, encouraging—her to trust him, to bare her soul and secret sins.

"Would you feel better, detective, staring at my body in the morgue or at my home after my husband beat me to death after—finally—one too many beers? Because, like you said, there's nothing you could do, unless you caught him hitting me." Annette kept her voice metered. Made a production at blinking back tears. "Is it really so hard to believe that instead of me, his fury released on someone else? Or would you sleep better if two young boys didn't have their mother?"

Holbrook stayed silent.

"There's nothing I can tell you, detective, that I haven't already."

After Gerald's trial concluded—guilty on all counts, straight to the Ohio State Reformatory in Mansfield for life—Annette sat on the edge of her bed, watching Fritz the Nite Owl on the color Zenith she'd treated herself to. The boys were asleep but hopeful that tomorrow would be blanketed with the predicted snow. They were excited about sledding down the embankment, the only thing it was good for, Annette thought.

Beside her was the day's copy of the *Columbus Dispatch*, featuring an article and black-and-white photo of Gerald. In the photo, he was being restrained after apparently lashing out at the judge, declaring his innocence. The title simply read, "South Side Man Gets Life for Brutal Murder."

She thought again about the night she'd gone to Scioto Downs. Sat in the rear of the bar, her hair pulled back into a tight ponytail, which she'd never worn around Gerald. Phony glasses from one of the boy's school plays were cheap but passable for a disguise at a dimly lit bar. It was the night Gerald made that explosive scene over Carla flirting with another man. The night she knew it was time to make her move.

For all his faults, Gerald hadn't been half as bad as her first husband, Harlan, the boys' father. Harlan had beaten her daily, drunk or sober, and enjoyed being cruel. Her family told her that was marriage, that a man could do as he pleased; her job was to make the best of it.

So she did, mashing up those lilies one day and adding the juice to his moonshine flask.

Annette figured she was fortunate Detective Holbrook never found out about Harlan—or the half million–dollar life insurance policy she cashed in after his death. That money, and Gerald, had been the assurance of a new start. So had Columbus. It was the clean slate she and Gerald had wanted. Far enough away from family but not too far. Opportunities abounded, as did the chance to build a life away from pecking chickens and outhouses. And hogs.

Not telling Gerald about the money had been for the best, Annette figured, although he seemed like a good man at first. When he wasn't drunk, he was hardworking, helped around the house, appreciated her cooking. He'd been suitable. But drinking got the best of him.

Now that he was gone, Annette had decided that when school was out for summer she'd leave Jefferson Meadows. Find a better community in another part of town, like Whitehall or Reynoldsburg. She'd finish her real estate classes—already had her new books—and earn her license. In the meantime, she'd get by on the insurance money, still having most of it tucked away in a safe-deposit box. Plus, it was time to move on—or escape—from the well-meaning but suffocating sympathy, and endless tuna casseroles, that Carol and Alice provided.

But there were some things she'd never escape. Like the way her accent slipped back that day with Holbrook. Or like knowing how to slaughter a hog. Daddy instilled two things in her: *You gotta be quick when you grab 'em and certain when you slice 'em. They get squirrelly in a heartbeat, so you gotta knock it in the head, stun it, then slit that throat in a swift motion. No hesitatin'.*

Turned out, Annette discovered, the same proved true for unsuspecting women in poorly lit parking lots.

It was possible she'd never escape the nightmares either. The ghosts of Harlan and Gerald still crept nightly under her sheets, invaded her slumber. She'd jolt awake from Harlan's wrath, him yelling in her face as he strangled her, or from Gerald, as he gripped her throat and stabbed her in the eyes with that switchblade. If poor sleep was the price she had to pay, so be it. More coffee would compensate.

Her deepest regret was Carla. That night at the house, when Holbrook said that Carla had ended the affair when she found out Gerald was married, Annette's shock had been real. But she shoved aside the guilt and sorrow that threatened, reminding herself that sacrifices had to be made. *No hesitatin'.*

She'd figure out how to raise her boys and how to build a life without depending on a man. It wasn't that she was a man-hater; she'd gone into both marriages hopeful, in love. What happened to Harlan and Gerald gave her no satisfaction, but self-preservation and survival did. From here on out, she decided, being on her own, focusing on her boys, was best. Because if nothing else, experience had taught her there was no such thing as a truly suitable husband.

TAKE THE WHEEL

BY DANIEL BEST

Short North

I just want to be behind the wheel. Is that too much to ask? Instead, I'm sitting in the backseat of a Tesla. The arrogant driver is reckless as he brags about his baby's features. He smiles as he turns the wheel of my life in and out of oncoming traffic, always just fast enough to swing the car back to safety. Soon he'll drive us both into the Olentangy River. Then brown water will rush in through my nostrils until my lungs become dirty sponges. And what will I have to show for my life?

The steam wand on the espresso machine hisses at me, the scalding moisture bites at my cheeks. *His* voice drives the thoughts from my head.

"Could you make that *breve?*" Terry asks me. It really isn't a request. Nothing he says ever is, really. He disguises his demands as questions, even nice enough to put in some rising inflection as if someone's squeezing his balls. We're supposed to be partners in the coffee shop, Terry's idea of *I'm sorry for letting you take the fall ten years ago*. Not all partnerships are created equal. His retaining 70 percent ownership is proof of just how sorry he *actually* is.

I flip on a few switches, as commanded, grinding beans on one end and distilling dark drips of espresso into shot glass–sized measuring cups on the other. I look up from the machine to see Terry leaning over the splintering wooden counter to talk to a girl whose cleavage is Grand Canyon–deep. His smile, which highlights the dimple deep in his chin, isn't fake. He's flirting with the customers, again. The line is backing up nearly to the outdoor sandwich board with *Grindz Coffee* drawn in blue chalk, but it's all the same to Terry. He's a lost cause. The titanium ring on his finger doesn't dampen Deep Boobs's enthusiasm. She's drawn to his lush black hair, prismatic green eyes, and surprisingly deep tan for a white guy. Guess Terry wants to be dark like me. Poseur.

But still, few could resist a face like that. Unfortunately, not even Terry's wife. I quell the anger rising at my helplessness of her loving him when he barely gives a damn about her. Right before he tells the girl about his Tesla's features, I turn to him.

"Terry," I say louder than the whirring espresso machine. He comes to, visibly annoyed, and notices the line as if for the first time. Deep Boobs pats him on the shoulder. I skip the foam art that I usually make out of steamed milk and shove her the drink.

The door swings open and a man steps inside—homeless, judging by his appearance. Neglected dreadlocks are coated with dirt and grime. They look like logs rolled through riverbank mud. The patrons waiting to order do their best not to stare.

Some even smile.

That is the beauty, and sometimes the beast, of co-owning a coffee shop located in the Short North. Progressive, artistic, and filled with stores that sell nine-dollar craft beers and six-dollar scoops of ice cream—a place where the new locals and patrons make it their business to scrub away the crime and grime from the pothole-filled streets and concrete benches where the homeless make their home. But the homeless that remain aren't pushed out, just socially pressured to leave.

I wave the man to the front of the line. Terry glances at me, probably wondering if he and I know each other. And not because we're both black, but because just two years ago this man, for all Terry knows, could have shared real estate with me under the CSX Upper Scioto River Bridge like teens having some slumber party on Neil Avenue. Could have listened with me to trains chug along while getting sucked off by mosquitoes and the elite Columbus residents watch from sleek million-dollar condos. Maybe they'll donate a hundred bucks to some charity to feel like they're making a difference.

But I didn't live with him. The man I shared a mattress with OD'd a few months before Terry offered me a job. But I know everyone loves a warm drink, so that's what I'll give this resident of the streets. I pull two espresso shots and pour them into a paper cup and extend it to him.

He nods and says, "Thanks." The stench of rotten chicken mixed with the bitter scent of stale cigarettes fills my nostrils. I nod back. He turns and leaves.

"Not sure that'll help or hurt my Yelp reviews," Terry says.

We work through the orders, making lattes, mochas, and, our specialty, double-dark honey cream. Finally, the last customer gone, Terry grabs the sandwich board from outside, locks the door, and pulls the sterling silver chain—draining the *Open* sign of its neon-blue blood. It's just us now.

Terry smiles like a kid on Christmas Day and gestures for me to follow him to the back of the shop. He knocks out a wood panel from near the desktop computer on the other side of the leaky faucet and reaches in, biting his tongue and giving me a hopeful expression as if he's feeling for a prize. Since I'm the one who gets him stuff, the dramatics are extra.

He tosses me a vial the size of a cologne sampler. I catch it with one hand. The fine white powder inside entices. He takes his own, and we each lift them under our noses and inhale, our nostrils vacuuming up the crystals. The cocaine finds the happy receptors in my brain and all of a sudden I'm floating. Terry too, judging by the euphoric expression on his face. For as often as we do this, I'm surprised we feel it *this* quickly.

Something ain't right.

"Terry," I say, "this is stronger than the stuff I got you."

"I know!" Terry's eyes bulge. "I wanted a harder hit, so I made my own connections and tried something new."

I stare at him blankly. Not all street drugs, like coffee-house partnerships, are created equal. Bumps don't come with FDA-approved labels. Who knows what this coke is cut with?

"You should try the brown sugar," Terry says. "Chase the Dragon is what they call it. *That* will knock your dick off. I tried it once and nearly died. Would've if the wife hadn't been there."

"Brown sugar? Heroin? That stuff is dangerous, Terry."

He guffaws. "Thanks, Nancy Reagan. Don't worry, I'm done with it. Stuff's too strong. I'm selling the rest of it."

"Sell it? That puts us both at risk. Puts our shop at risk."

Terry shrugs. "My shop, mostly."

He's still looking around when we hear someone outside. The lock prevents whoever's trying to rip the door open from getting their caffeine high. I gesture to the would-be-patron that we're closed for the night. But Terry doesn't shoo them off and over my protests opens the door. A man dressed in a skirt and long red wig struts in.

"What are you doing *here*?" Terry asks.

"Oh that tone," the skirt says. Her voice reverberates

through the air with a deep layer of sexiness to it. "No way to treat one of your new favorite . . . *friends.*" The skirt sighs once she sees Terry's not in the mood, and gets to the point: "Listen, hon, your kid's pedaling the stash I sold you, at a premium. I want the windfall."

I glance toward Terry. He's grinding his teeth hard enough to crush coffee beans. His kid—his stepkid—has been an issue since Terry married the mom a few years back. Lilith. I shut my eyes, allowing one quick stroll up and around her curves.

"How'd you find me?" Terry asks.

The skirt laughs. "Terry, I know *all* about the people I mix for." A dark look crosses her face. "Including where they live."

Silence . . .

"Hang on," Terry says. He goes to the back and returns with a stack of bills. He counts a few out and hands them to the skirt. She swishes hard enough to break a hip as she comes forward. A lavender scent wafts around her. She flips out her hand in a flourish.

Terry counts out four fifty-dollar bills into her right hand. "That should cover it."

The skirt keeps her hand there, batting inch-long eyelashes. "You can afford that Tesla and this *fancy* coffee shop. I know rent in the Short North ain't cheap." She throws a kiss at him. "So pay up."

Terry glares, but gives her one more.

She pockets the money, grips his hand, and yanks him in. "A word of advice. I know you, Terry. I know what you can take. You can handle the amount of spice in that batch I made you."

"What are you saying?" Terry replies.

"Others ain't so strong. There've been some ODs recently. A few lucky folk got Narcan in time. But not everyone. People are pissed. Someone's gotta pay. And honey, it won't be me. So get your house in order before someone burns it down."

Terry's stopped breathing. He's not used to threats. Had he and I swapped places ten years back, maybe his reaction would have been different. Maybe.

The skirt blows Terry another kiss and swishes out the door. Terry's eyes are darting around as if he's following some invisible game of Ping-Pong. I remember the look. Guilt. He had the same one when the cops stopped us.

That day a decade ago, I knew what was in Terry's backpack before the cop made it within ten feet of us. If he found what was inside, Terry's life would've been over. He was going to Ohio State University. Me? I had no plans for life or the future. He'd probably drop me once he made some real friends in his dorm anyway.

So I took the bag from Terry and told him to scram. When the cop saw Terry running, I opened the backpack and dropped its contents on the ground. I stopped the cop, told him the backpack was mine. That included the seven hundred grams of cocaine inside.

The judge could have given me two years, the mandatory minimum. But since I stayed quiet to protect Terry, I got the max he could give, eight.

Terry's phone rings. He pulls it out of his pocket, checks the name, and ignores the call. After a few seconds the buzz in his pocket stops. Then mine rings. I pull it out. Terry's wife's name appears on the screen.

I answer: "Hey, Lilith."

"Hey," she says. The single syllable sends shivers spiraling. My coke-infused brain recreates Lilith in my mind. Her form is nearly perfect—her lips, her breasts, her hips make me think dirty. No one sees her like I do. No one ever can. They don't deserve her. Not Terry, not her kid, no one.

"Is Terry there?" she asks. "I called him. He didn't answer."

I glance toward Terry, who shakes his head roughly. He's a scared pup. He better not piss on the floor.

"He's in the back," I say. "What's up?" I bet she's wearing a soft pink robe.

"Some guys came here looking for my son. Someone overdosed. They say he dealt them some bad stuff . . ." She goes quiet.

I absorb the information and remain silent. I picture her at home, her supple breasts nearly spilling out of her robe as sadness slouches her shoulders. This angel's tears are Terry's fault.

I glare at Terry, who stares at me with wide eyes. Seven hundred grams. Eight years. Not all partnerships are equal. An idea strikes me.

"I'll find him," I say into the phone.

"Thank you," she says softly. It must be the coke, but I can feel her warm breath on my cheek as she whispers into her phone: "Please. Bring my boy home."

I close my eyes, allowing all the times I dreamed of being inside her play again. Blond hair flows over her face. Full lips with a tint of crimson. Heavy mascara cakes to her slender face, though there's not enough to cover the bruises Terry leaves on her when he's high. Despite the bruises . . . she's beautiful.

I open my eyes. "Let me get to work."

"What'd she want?" Terry asks after I cut the call.

"Her kid home."

"Why'd she ask you?"

I make sure to smile. "She wanted it done." Terry's mouth draws into a slim line. "Know where he is? Sounds like he hasn't been home for a while."

"No clue."

"Where's he been staying the past few weeks?"

"No idea."

"What *do* you know?"

"That you talked to *my* wife."

"Because you ignored her."

"I'm stressed."

"Prison teaches the best stress management. Too bad you missed out."

Terry puffs out his flat chest. Gym rat he is not. "I'll find the kid."

"What do you know, Terry? Seriously?"

"Enough."

"And where you gonna look first? Call your accountant? Your lawyer? Hop in your Tesla and drive till you find him?" I shake my head. "No, man. Let me find him. I know some people that have probably seen him."

Terry screws up his face. "Why are you so interested? Why do you care?"

An image of Lilith running her hands up my thighs plays in my mind. "Because you ain't seen your kid in a while. He could be on the streets. Ain't no place for the kid."

"And what do you want for your good deed?"

I shrug. "Fifty-fifty partnership."

"No way. He ain't even my kid!"

"Is that what you're gonna say to Lilith when he turns up at the coroner's with your heroin on him?"

Terry considers. "I'll give you 10 more percent."

"Give me 50 or I'll take 100 . . ." I let the statement hang.

Then I add, "Judging by how you treat his mom, the kid will turn you in for the drugs. Probably say that you gave it to him to sell. You won't worry about what percent of Grindz you own behind bars."

Terry rolls his tongue along his bottom lip. "Fine. But you bring him here, not to his mom so she can coddle him. I need him to understand what happens when he screws me over."

I don't respond as I leave the shop.

A Columbus Division of Fire ambulance parked outside the grilled-cheese joint across the street bathes the Short North red and white with its lights, coloring people walking up and down the streets. Passersby watch wide-eyed. Someone drank too much or ate too much.

It's a brisk spring night out, but a light jacket from a discount department store is plenty. White-chalky powder stains the road, remnants of salt to melt ice. I gotta keep walking until I find one of my contacts—they'll know something if the kid's peddling.

I don't get as many looks as I used to, even though the stench of the streets isn't quite off me yet despite two years of Grindz and Terry's "charity." I glance at an organic ice cream shop window and see the homeless man I'd been reflected back. His jeans are spotted with stains and his ashy knees are visible through holes. His shirt is plaid and three shades darker thanks to dirt and grime. His beard is tangled and the edges of his 'fro beads like oil drops on water.

The diners inside have no idea. Patrons wearing designer jackets and scarves and orthodontist-perfected smiles eating ice cream that sells by the half-scoop. They're all like Terry. I imagine how they'd react if they saw the old me staring at them. Probably ignore the man I was, as if I were a ghost.

Becoming translucent is part of being homeless, like some-one taking a light dimmer and turning the dial counterclock-wise. I survived on these same streets once upon a time, but they were different then. Columbus of days past wasn't always so nice, so sterile. The Short North used to bleed with wounded gangbangers whose faces were covered by white sheets. It's come a long way, but with each thousand dollars the average income went up, another layer of scum was scraped away.

I wouldn't stand a chance now, not because of the night crawlers, but because of petitions, enforcement, and social pressure from well-intentioned people thinking that pushing a problem to the edges solves it.

"I know you."

I turn toward the voice. She's set up next to a bench by an ATM.

"Hey, Becca."

"Hey back at ya." Becca's my age, I think. Though I don't know how, she manages to keep her face and dark-brown hair somewhat clean. The only indication of her being homeless is her soggy cardboard sign with *Make up the Wage Gap* written on it with a thick black marker.

"Looking good," she says. "Job going well? Barista at Grindz, right?"

I'm impressed she knows this. "Co-owner."

"Oh, nice," Becca says. There's no bite in her tone. "How'd that happen?"

"The owner tried to repay a debt."

"Must have been a crazy debt."

"About eight years' worth."

"Good for you. Was it hard to go back to *normal*?"

And that's how it feels too. It changes you . . . the streets. Each person who ignores you changes you. Each person who doesn't ignore but glares like you're shit stuck to her heel changes you. Each time you wake up with someone running their hands along your fly . . . changes you.

"Mostly," I say. "Shop helps."

"Terry's your partner, right? He's got a sharp Tesla in the *Owner* spot."

"Yeah. Know him?"

She nods. "I know his kid too."

I perk up. "You know his kid?"

"He's pushing the hot new brown sugar on the street. Not sure where he got it. Some guys on Goodale OD'd on the stuff a few nights ago. They snorted it since they didn't have needles."

"Chase the Dragon."

"You ever see anyone OD?"

I nod at a memory. "Yeah. A guy I used to share a mattress with."

"Dang. Your roommate? Sorry to hear."

I'm not sorry at all. Meant more room on the mattress for me. "Thanks."

"So, yeah," Becca says. "Friends are pissed. And the coroner is gonna get suspicious."

"Hey, know where the kid is?"

"I know he ain't home."

"Care to share?"

"He's with a daddy. Guy named Clint."

"A daddy? I didn't know the kid was gay."

Becca shrugs. "He'll be whatever's needed to live on the street."

"Know where they might be?"

"Tilt, if I had to guess. It's the club near Hubbard."

"I know the place."

"I'll be headed there later," Becca says. "Drunk guys give out the best cash."

I offer a small smile. "I'm gonna find the kid before he gets himself killed. You should drop by the shop. I'll have some coffee and a meal ready for you—deal?"

She gives me a wide smile. "Thanks."

I head off.

"Hang on, hang on," Becca draws out. "Mr. Fancy Coffee Shop Owner." She shakes her can.

I drop a few bucks in, gesture at the *Folgers* label. "Don't tell me you drink that crap."

Becca scoffs. "I've got standards."

I turn the corner by a creole shop known for its spicy shrimp gumbo and flaky, crust-like garlic bread. A steady thump of music draws me like a moth to flame. The beat's got an attitude. It punches at the confines of the building as if ready to break out of its soundproofing cage. It reverberates throughout the Short North, reaching as high as the cranes hanging above the steel skeletons of yet another luxury apartment complex or a building filled with thin-walled condos.

A cop stands guard near Tilt's entrance. His tanned skin and short gray hair ping my memory like icicles hitting my brain. But he doesn't react—well, almost. I chuckle when he shifts nervously. I don't need to read his badge to know it says *Officer Snow*—which I always thought was ironic.

Similar to the skirt with her customers, I recognize mine anywhere.

Officer Snow glances around, jaw clenched. I'm not sure why he's nervous. We have an unspoken deal, back to the time he first caught me with a few grams when I was carrying a delivery for Terry. I was happy he only took a third of my supply, but he wasn't being altruistic. He was buying my silence. Since then he does a scripted stop near Goodale Park every Tuesday to confiscate his fix from me.

It ain't Tuesday and Officer Snow must be wondering why he sees me. I hope he doesn't think I'm here to cause trouble. It'd be mutual destruction with both of us arrested. Though we both know who'd fare better in prison.

I nod, and he tells the Tilt employee checking IDs he'll be right back.

"Never seen you here before," Officer Snow says. His voice sounds like his dad punched his nose so hard it caved in and they never got it fixed.

"I need your help. There's a kid inside that's in some trouble." His hand floats toward his gun. I shake my head. "Not that kind of trouble." *Not yet, anyway.* "I just need to find him and get him home."

"Get him home?"

"Yeah, he's fifteen." I gesture to the door. "Got any of those in tonight?"

"Official answer is no."

"We're beyond official, officer."

"What's the kid look like?"

"White, brown hair . . ."

Officer Snow blinks at me, dumbfounded. He glances around. A dozen guys smoking outside match the description.

Point taken. "Let me in."

He waves me forward. "Okay. See you Tuesday?"

"Wouldn't miss it."

Inside, the jumping and shouting reminds me of riots back in prison. The ultraviolet light makes everything glow. Bartenders with metal spikes through cartilage and contacts that make them look like nocturnal animals pour glasses filled with vodka and only a splash of coke. Their teeth aren't normal-looking—the UV light makes them demonically white. The bass shakes my stomach so hard I think I have another heartbeat.

I look to the column next to me and see two men, eyes glassy as the coke goes home. I notice one has his fly open, letting the other's hands disappear inside. I make eye contact, but he either ignores me or doesn't register. I've seen that expression before on Terry after doing a line.

I keep my head on a swivel as I head toward the dance floor, where the largest number of people pool. Red, blue, and green lights scan the gyrating flesh of hundreds of dancing bodies like products being checked out at Kroger. It's an ethnic salad bowl inside. My eyes dart around as many people as possible, looking for the kid.

Hands rub all over me as I walk across the floor. It takes all my will not to attack when someone cups my manhood. *You're not on the street anymore. You're okay. You're here for a reason.* I force smiles and take a deep breath.

A woman with beauty-model looks tilts her head back as another woman with hair shorter than mine rolls her tongue along her neck. She places something in her mouth and then turns to me. Her own glassy eyes sparkle as lasers pass over them. She sticks her tongue out at me, revealing a small white pill, and smiles.

I don't pay attention to her long because the kid is right next to her.

I push through the crowd, sliding past slick bodies, my shoes pock-pocking from something sticky on the floor, ignoring the splashes from light beer and mixed drinks from animated dancers who forgot to suck them down.

I see the crown of the kid's brown hair, laser lights showing enough sweat to make it look like he's dunked his head in the Scioto. I grab his shoulder, warm and wet, and turn him around.

He's all smiles when he faces me. It's a sharp contrast to the sad kid who seemed to be drawn to life only with several shades of gray each time he was with Terry. Lilith bends over backward to keep Terry, her sugar daddy, happy. Too bad that includes letting Terry put hands on her son.

The kid swivels his head to the side as he squints. Recognition registers. Other than looking a few pounds lighter, he seems to be in good health, though the way he's swaying implies he's had several drinks too many.

His eyes open wide, pleasant. "What are you doing here?"

"Here for you, kid," I say, eyeing the drink in his hand. "Time to go."

"Can we help you?" A guy with an exposed barrel of a chest is suddenly in front of me. The man doesn't seem to miss a day at the gym. Must be Clint.

"Kid's gotta go now."

"Like hell he does. He's with me." Clint flexes, nipples aimed like cannons.

"I don't want any trouble."

"Good," Clint says, pulling the kid toward him. "Beat it."

"You're gonna let him go."

Clint turns to me. "Or what?" He pushes my chest with two fingers.

Pulsing music or not, the other dancers take notice, though they don't care enough to intervene. They only step away, enlarging the circle around us.

"Or . . ." I lower my voice, "I'll take him."

Clint gives me a once-over, greasy smile popping on his lips. He nods to himself as if contemplating. I've seen this posturing before, always from the new guy serving time. Clint thinks I don't notice him shifting his weight backward and balling his fist. It's a dumb technique. He probably went to some kickboxing cardio class—one that told this man he could fight. He should ask for a refund.

Before he brings his arm up to hit me, I snap my elbow, launching my fist into his nose. I feel the bones shatter around my knuckles. Blood explodes skyward in tune with people next to us flinging up drinks from too-full glasses. I catch Clint as he stumbles back from my blow. I pull him close. His sweaty skin smells musty.

"Listen up!" I shout in his ear. Blood from his nose trickles onto my shoulder. "The kid's coming with me. You might like them young, but he's only fifteen. I know the cop outside. Make my life hard and I'll have you in cuffs before you wake up from me knocking you out." I push him away and stare into his now-wide eyes. "I know how much guys like you bleed."

The words sink in. His flight skills have him bumping guests and running past dancers before the song ends.

The kid glares at me. "Dude! You just blew my cover!"

I cut to the chase, grabbing his head and pulling him close so he can hear the words I shout into his ear over the music: "People are OD'ing on the heroin you stole from Terry!"

He's suddenly sober. He doesn't protest as we leave.

I'm walking the kid back toward the shop. It's in the same direction as his mom and Terry's place, the Jackson, a luxury condo complex shoehorned into the Short North.

"Now what?" the kid asks after minutes of silence.

"I'll do what I can, but some guys already went to your mom. Apparently one of your customers stopped breathing. He didn't start again."

"People are . . . dead?"

"Yeah."

"Shit, dude. It was Terry's. I thought it was safe."

"Why'd you take it?"

The kid shrugs. "I hate Terry. Especially how he treats Mom. I figured I'd sell it and make enough so she didn't need him anymore."

I already know something's wrong when we pass a pitch-black Grindz. We always leave security lights on. Terry's Tesla is still in the *Owner* spot.

A sliver of light in the back room draws my attention. Someone appears, disappears. It's so quick I wonder if I imagined it. Is someone in there with Terry? Lilith said there were guys looking for the kid. If they didn't find him at the Jackson, the shop is the next logical place. My shop. Prison taught me how to protect what's mine. My body inches toward the street.

"Why are the lights off?" the kid asks.

Just for a second I'd forgotten about him. If they see him, he won't be any better off than Terry is right now. I need to get him home.

We ride the elevator to the Jackson's top floor after Lilith buzzes us in. Inside, I take in granite countertops, shiny walnut-colored cabinets, and stainless steel appliances. A world apart from the one-bedroom apartment I rent above Bodega down the street.

Lilith wears a dark-gray robe open a bit at the neck and legs. She smells good, like she just got out of the shower.

The kid and Lilith rock side to side as they hug. She whispers promises of how different things will be, whispers of how Terry will keep his hands off him. But the heavy mascara caking

Lilith's face tells the truth of how much she can really do to stop him.

"Go get showered," Lilith tells the kid. "Then we'll get some food. Goody Boy sound okay?"

He smiles and then walks up to me. "See you at the shop?"

I give him a small nod. "Kid?" I say as he retreats around the corner. "Give it back." He stares at me for a beat, and then looks at his mother. "She already knows."

The kid empties his pockets of a half-dozen packets of heroin and leaves them on the counter. He takes off his shoes, revealing and then removing more packets. He strips off tattered jeans, producing a couple more bags taped to his calves. He also gives me eight hundred in cash before continuing up to the bathroom.

Lilith and I stare at the packets of brown sugar on the counter. Tears stream from her eyes, though she doesn't move. She's a beautiful crying statue. Each stream reveals more of her bruises. I approach and run a hand along her blue-tinted cheek.

"They don't hurt so much anymore," she says. She glances up the stairs. "I'm worried about him. Terry's so tough on him. So . . . cruel." My brain scrambles with how to help her. It shuts off when she places hands on my hips. "Thank you for bringing him home." She pulls herself to me, leaving not even a sliver of light between us. Heat spreads through my body and I stiffen. She presses against me, her strength matching my hardness. She pulls me down and bites my lower lip. I massage her through her robe—her tongue snakes into my mouth. She moans as if she hasn't been kissed in ages.

I start to open the robe when she pulls back.

"Sorry," she says breathlessly. "I shouldn't. Terry." Before I protest she rubs her cheek. Then I realize she's not in the driver's seat of her life either. Terry is. His name makes me a noodle again. He doesn't deserve her. I know what I need to do. I grab a plastic Kroger bag and throw the kid's brown sugar inside.

"Keep him here for a while," I say. "I need time to smooth things over."

Lilith watches me as I leave, lips parted . . . in desire? Or fear?

The shop's lights are still off and the door's unlocked. Our barstools are kicked over, our espresso machine leaks water on the floor by the bathroom door. Our paintings purchased from shops up and down the street during Gallery Hop are torn to shreds.

I take steps slow enough to remain silent as I move toward the back room. I see his feet first. They're splayed like the feet of a cartoon character crushed under a boulder, twitching in comic relief. But this ain't funny at all. His jeans are soaked. Water? I take a whiff. No. Terry pissed himself. His shirt's un-tucked and blood plasters his hair to his face. His lips and nostrils look like he strolled through a mist of baby powder. He must have done some lines to escape the pain.

He smiles at me. Missing tooth makes perfect Terry less so. Good.

"You should see the other guys." He laughs but then grips his rib cage.

"What happened?" I ask, clutching the bag filled with the brown sugar.

"Some guys from German Village were pissed their buddy died. The batch is laced with a little fentanyl. That's why it's so strong. I can handle a small amount, kinda. The skirt pointed them my way like I'm the dealer. I told them caveat emptor.

They ain't like that much." He reads something in my eyes. "I kept the kid out of it, took the blame." His face darkens red. "I'm gonna kill him, though." He squints a swollen eye at me. "You find him?"

"Yeah, he's safe."

"For now." He winces. "I need a bump. Mind helping? Then you can drive me home." He chuckles. "I know you always wanted to drive my Tesla."

I nod at the instruction. I grab a small vial of cocaine from his stash, and then take one of the packets the kid was dealing. I dump the vial's powder and replace the contents with the brown sugar. I hold it under Terry's nose. He smiles at me. Flashes of Lilith's bruises and what Terry's done to terrorize the kid play in my mind. Flashes of her robe too, and what lay beneath. I lift the vial higher into Terry's nose. He doesn't realize it's full. He empties it in one strong sniff.

Chase the Dragon, friend.

"Thanks," he says. "I owe you one."

I don't respond. Drugs are best the second they hit the brain. The nasal passages are broadband compared to the dial-up speed the blood provides. This will hit Terry quick.

It does. Within a second his eyes widen as his cerebellum's G-spot lights up.

He lies back, letting the morphine erase his pain. His eyes widen again. I wonder then if he knows. If he does, his tongue is too thick and heavy to accuse me.

Instead, his eyes just close. Just like that.

I saw this happen once when I was homeless, the roommate I told Becca about. We alternated sleep space, switching who got to use the mattress and who had to sleep on the quilt. I hated sharing, hated not being in control. So when my homeless comrade decided to do some heroin, I watched out for him, yeah. But instead of slapping him around to keep him awake, I let him fall asleep on the mattress. I waited until his pulse slowed, and then stopped, as his body forgot to breathe.

I take Terry's wrist in my hand. I feel for a pulse. I feel a faint thump every ten seconds or so. I look at the man who saved me from the streets, his eyes closed, his head rolled to the side. After a minute I don't feel a beat anymore. I place a finger under his nostrils to see if I can feel the hot air of life. There's none.

Now Lilith won't have a thing to worry about. I picture her sliding off her robe and pressing herself against me—all smiles. I smile too. I'm coming. I make an espresso shot and grab Terry's keys. I turn to the corpse before heading to the Tesla, playing back his final words.

"No, Terry," I say. "We're even."

THE DEAD AND THE QUIET

BY LAURA BICKLE

Union Cemetery

There was no going home again.

Not after this.

Sarah tugged the sleeves of her hoodie down over her knuckles and wrapped her arms around her chest. *I will not cry*, she thought. *I will not cry.*

The young woman sank down on the concrete steps of the bus stop and stared at the empty road before her. To her right, a train rumbled over a railway bridge. Behind her, the hospital shone softly in fluorescent light and blue glass. Even in darkness, this place still hummed with seething activity . . . not that it helped her in any way.

She blinked back tears and bit the inside of her cheek to focus. How had she gotten here? Pete dropped her off at the Riverside ER five hours ago. He told her not to come home without a bottle of Oxys or something better. The ER was clean, to the point that Sarah could see her reflection in the floor, and she felt nervous. Maybe this was a place for rich folks, and this could work for or against her. Rich people got everything they wanted, right? And if rich people were here, maybe someone would give her what she wanted so she'd leave quickly.

Sarah told the people in brightly colored scrubs that her back hurt. That she'd been in a bad car accident, hit and skip. No, she hadn't reported it to the police because she had no insurance. Yes, it hurt. It hurt from her tailbone all the way up to her skull, a sharp throb whenever she moved. She was in pain, and she needed help.

That last bit wasn't a lie. Not really. Sarah had run out of Oxys yesterday morning. Her body had begun to ache without them, as if the very marrow was roiling inside her bones in search of something to numb it.

The nurses and the ER doc looked at her skeptically. Sarah had played this riff at several other area ERs, with mixed success. Some just wanted her out of the hospital and wrote her a scrip. Others kicked her out immediately, as if they read some secret file on her that caused them to know what she was after. The folks here were thorough, though . . . they sent her for X-rays and a CAT scan. She protested, because she knew she had no hope in hell of paying for any of it. But she went anyway to the sparkling machines, hoping the images would show that her body needed something, pretty much anything. She'd even take some Percs, not as good as Oxys, but she was desperate at this point. Maybe they'd give her that. But the doctor came back and told her that she was fine . . . as if that was good news! No injuries. She was a reasonably healthy woman in her twenties who should get some rest and see the dentist. She should take some ibuprofen when she got home and go see her regular doctor next week.

Sarah gritted her teeth. *What* regular doctor? A nurse gave her a sheaf of paperwork containing a list of doctors accepting new patients and a pamphlet called *Resources for Opioid Dependence*. Sarah threw it and the rest of the papers in the trash on the way out. Even the trash can was clean and empty.

She rose to her feet at the bus stop now, rocking from her heels to toes, afraid of what came next. She couldn't go home to Pete. The last time she dared return without scoring some drugs, Pete forced her to have sex with his friends. Pete got five Vikes for that, and Sarah was hit so hard she lost two teeth. She hung onto those teeth for a long time, as if some generous tooth fairy might slide her a couple of bucks for them. They rattled around in the bottom of her jacket pocket now, feeling light and brittle. Those two teeth had been the price of crossing Pete once. There was no going home. Pete said he would kill her, and she believed him.

She knew the number 1 bus would come to this stop . . . eventually. She dug through her pockets for change. Only five coins, not enough for bus fare. Even if she had enough, she didn't have any friends she could couch-surf with, anyway.

She walked down the steps and out onto the sidewalk. Olentangy River Road was lit up in the distance. She thought she remembered a Golden Arches maybe a mile and a half down the road. Ohio State University sprawled farther south, buildings crammed cheek to jowl along the muddy Olentangy River. Maybe she could find some lost change and hop the bus for a little while, be someplace warm to think.

She started walking. March nights were cold here. Winter hadn't let go of the city yet, and she regretted not wearing anything warmer than her jeans, T-shirt, and hoodie. It was likely going to get down to freezing tonight; she was going to be screwed. But it was still better than heading home to Pete. Right?

She crossed North Broadway, ducked under the freeway overpass, and went south along Olentangy, walking on the cracked sidewalk. She walked past closed restaurants, an auto repair shop, and a new hotel. There was a cemetery here too, spreading on the east and west sides of the road, the largest she'd ever seen. Rows of headstones set in brittle grass stretched into the darkness, reflecting bits of passing light from car headlights. Leafless trees reached out of the plots into the sky like dark hands. There had to be thousands of people here.

Sarah shuddered and kept moving, not letting her gaze slip into the graveyard. She wasn't particularly superstitious, but she knew enough about bad luck not to want to court any more than she already had.

"Where you headed, young lady?"

Sarah nearly jumped out of her sneakers. She stepped back to stare at a man in a long coat leaning against the cemetery fence, his fingers resting on the bars. Though it was dark, she had the impression of an old man, wearing all of his clothes at once, the way homeless guys did. Right now, that was looking really smart to her. In a thick voice, but kind, he repeated the question.

"Um. To Micky D's."

"Will you buy something for me?" The man reached a wrinkled ten-dollar bill through the fence.

Sarah stared at it.

"You get something for yourself too. Just bring me back three cheeseburgers and a bottled water."

"Why . . . why not go yourself?" She peered into the dark for evidence of an injury, for a cane or a crutch. Maybe the old man couldn't walk that far.

He coughed into the elbow of his coat. "They kicked me out for loitering some time ago." He made a face. "I asked the wrong guy for money. But anyway. They won't mind you. You're young and clean. Would you please? I'll wait right here."

She paused. What was the catch? The guy sounded honest enough, and there were bars between them.

"Sure," she said at last, taking the rumpled money from his hand. She pocketed it, gave him an uncertain smile, and walked the rest of the way, past a shuttered strip mall with faded parking stripes.

The night crew gave her no hassle. She ordered five cheeseburgers and two waters. She wasn't sure the next time she would eat, but her stomach was growling. She scarfed down two of the cheeseburgers and drained a bottle of water. She carried the bag back to the spot in the fence where she saw the old man.

He was there, waiting for her. She passed the bag through the gap in the fence.

"Your change is in the bag," she said. There wasn't much there, but it was his. "Thank you."

"Thank you, young lady." The old man didn't even glance in the bag. He eyed her as she stood on the other side of the fence, shivering. "Do you have a place to stay?"

She looked down, biting her lip. She didn't know what to say. She knew better than to trust a stranger, and she didn't trust her own voice, for fear she'd burst into tears. But a stranger couldn't be worse than the people she knew. Right?

"I have a fire just down there, by the freeway." He gestured back toward the hospital. "Why don't you warm yourself for a little bit, collect your thoughts, and then you can be on your way?"

She nodded slowly. The old man could be a criminal, a rapist, or worse . . . but worse was waiting for her at home.

She walked north on one side of the fence, in the light of the road, while the old man walked on the other, in the graveyard. She jammed her hands in her pockets and shuffled her feet. They walked at the same pace, the iron divide between them.

"My name's Mose," the old man said.

"I'm Sarah."

"It's nice to meet you, Sarah. This is Cricket." He opened his coat, and Sarah took a step back, figuring she'd encountered a flasher and ready to run. But Mose pulled out a cat, black with a white spot on his chest. The cat meowed softly.

Sarah reached forward, through the bars, to touch the cat. Cricket blinked green eyes and purred as she tickled his chin. "How do you take care of a cat . . . out here?"

"You mean as a homeless guy?" Mose chuckled. "I do the best I can. The cat always gets fed first, and when that happens, everything else pretty much falls into place."

"Where did you get him?"

"I found him as a kitten in a railyard in Atlanta. Kitten didn't have anybody, and I didn't either. He made the tiniest meows, like a cricket. So I took him with me."

The fence ended abruptly at the edge of a hotel property. Sarah realized the cemetery wasn't fenced in at all, there was just a length of fence with gates along the roadside, designed to keep car traffic out. Mose came up beside her, holding the cat.

"You know, most people take my money and run," he said in a gravelly voice thick with mucus.

She blinked at him. "What?"

"The money I sent you to get burgers with. Most people just take it and don't come back."

"People are shitty," she said. But she knew she was one of those people too. Shitty people went to the hospital to scam pills.

"So why'd you come back?" Mose asked her.

She shrugged. "I may be shitty, but I'm not an asshole." Only an asshole would steal from a homeless guy.

Mose had a little encampment hidden away on a slope below the freeway. There was a dense thicket of wild honeysuckle and scrub pine trees that hid the clearing from pedestrian eyes, maybe seventy-five feet back from the road. Plastic tarps were strung up on ropes to collect rainwater, rattling a bit in the wind. Plastic bottles littered the area. A mattress of flattened cardboard was pressed to the ground. He'd been here for some time. . . the ground was worn free of winter's dried-out grass. A rusty trash can sat in the center of the little clearing, holding still-warm embers.

Mose poked at the contents of the can with a stick. He took a piece of wood out from under a torn trash bag and placed it in the can. Soon, fire was flickering through the rust holes. Sarah kneeled before it and put out her hands. They shook. Her head was pounding, and she felt sweat prickling on her brow.

Mose watched her carefully. He took apart his sandwiches and fed most of the meat to Cricket, who picked up the pieces delicately. When Cricket was finished, he ate the remains of the sandwiches he held in his gnarled fingers.

"What brings a nice young lady like you here?" he asked, as if he were striking up conversation in a diner over a piece of pie.

Sarah thought about that for a moment. She thought about not just tonight, about looking for pills, and all the times before that, but about what *really* brought her to this place, to a homeless man's encampment in March with nothing more than the clothes on her back.

"I think . . . I think it was high school love gone wrong," she confessed. What was the point in lying to a homeless guy? "I met a guy. Pete. My parents hated him, said he was no good. But I was wanting to prove that I knew myself, and that I knew him better. I dropped out of school to follow him here. It was only after we got here that I realized maybe my parents were right. Realized he had problems."

"Problems," Mose echoed. Cricket slid out from under his

fingers and pressed himself against Sarah's side. She stroked the coarse fur of his back. It didn't feel like the fur of a domestic cat; it felt like the thick coat of a feral cat in her parents' barn when she was a kid.

"Yeah. He always liked to smoke some weed and drink back in high school. No big, then. But once we got here, to the big city, he found out there was a lot more interesting stuff to try. He did meth for a bit, but he likes Oxys, benzos, a little heroin once in a while. And . . . and I followed along." There was no sugarcoating it; she'd been a passive follower, and it had come to bite her in the ass.

"That ain't good." Mose lit a cigarette. He offered her one, and she accepted.

"Yeah. I can't go home to him. I've got nothing to take."

"Take?"

She explained to him about the hospital and the drugs, her cheeks burning in shame. It seemed so much worse to say it out loud, but necessary, somehow.

"Can you go home to your parents? You're still young. Parents forgive a lot of youthful indiscretions." His eyes were dark and kind on her.

She shook her head and her lip trembled on the cigarette. "Can't go there either. Mom and Dad are gone. I didn't even know about it until last year, that they died. They were in a car accident with a semi. The semi won . . ." Her voice trailed off in a whisper, and a tear splashed on Cricket's back.

The old man patted her shoulder. "I guess you're right. There ain't no going home, girl. Take it from an old man. That much I know." He pursed his lips and turned his head away to cough, a wet, rickety sound like gravel in a storm drain.

Sarah struggled to pull herself together. "You don't want to go home?"

He chuckled. "You think I'm on the run?"

Sarah peered down at the cat. "I'm sorry."

"You're not wrong. I'll be honest with you, since you've been honest with me. Forty years ago, I killed a man back in Texas."

Sarah froze, heart pounding. A murderer. He could kill her too . . .

"I was young and I was dumb." He stared up at the sky. There were only a handful of stars to be seen, this close to all the light and sound of the city. "You see, my mama married a man who wasn't my daddy after Daddy went to prison. The man she married was cruel to me and my brother the instant he darkened our doorstep. One day he was beating my little brother, and I thought he might kill him. I really did." Mose took a drag off his cigarette. "I went into their bedroom, got the shotgun out from under the bed, and I shot him."

Sarah's hand flew up to cover her mouth. "Oh my God," she muttered through her fingers.

"I called the police. I called and told them what I did, what happened to my little brother, and how I shot the bastard dead." The old man's mouth was a hard line. "I told my brother to go to the neighbors', to tell them everything. And then I ran."

"I'm so sorry," she said.

Mose's shoulders fell. "I am too. I mean . . . I shoulda taken my brother and run. We could've started over, someplace new. I coulda taken care of him. But I made a twelve-year-old boy witness a murder. There's no forgiveness for that. Not from the law, and not from anybody else."

"It wasn't your fault," she said. And she meant it.

Mose gave a sad smile. "It's kind of you to say that, Sarah. But no matter how far we run, some things you just can't shake."

Sarah nodded. "But you did what you had to."

Mose's wrinkled fingers tapped his lower lip. "Maybe."

"Maybe?"

"Thing is, when I stood there with the gun, he stopped what he was doing to my brother. He backed off. Said he was sorry. Changed his tune right quick."

"But?"

"But I shot him anyway. Because I just couldn't be sure." He paused. "That's what I'm running from."

"What do you mean?"

"Shooting him anyway."

The old man draped a blanket over her shoulders and walked away to the cardboard on the far side of the fire. Sarah lay down with Cricket purring in the curve of her arm, and she slept a thick, dreamless sleep.

"This is no good for you, girl. No good."

Sarah awoke to violent tremors racking her body. Cricket skittered away, and Mose's hand was on her shoulder, pulling her to a sitting position. Cold sweat stuck her hair to her scalp, and her teeth rattled in her head. She immediately threw up the cheeseburgers she'd eaten last night, a stream of foul-smelling vomit. She slunk away from the camp to shit in some leaves, feebly wiping her ass with leaves and cheeseburger wrappers, humiliated.

Mose was unfazed. He helped her back to the clearing, gave her water, a sip at a time. "That poison—those drugs. It's no good for you. Your body wants to reject it."

"I have to . . . I have to get some. Just a bit."

He shook his head, crouching before her. "No. It's time for you to be done with that. All of it. Are you ready to do that?"

Sarah paused, her tongue stuck to the top of her mouth.

It had been a long time since someone asked her what she wanted. And it was not this.

She nodded.

"Okay. You can get through this. Up with you." Mose pulled her to her feet. Her vision swam. Cricket wound around her legs. "We're going for a walk."

She shook her head. "I can't . . ."

"You can. We're going to walk it all away, down with the dead and the quiet."

Leaning heavily on Mose, she walked to the graveyard. Cricket trotted ahead of them. They went to the old part that she'd passed last night. It was vaster than she'd expected, acres on acres, a necropolis of ornamented stones turning black with age. A person could get lost here.

"People don't usually come to this section," Mose said. "They go to the new part, across the street, and put flowers on people they remember. The recent dead are there. It's pretty . . . nice flowers and mausoleums. I only saw that because the railroad tracks are beyond it . . . as you can tell, I like to avoid most people. The old part is a nice, quiet place between the freeway and the university. Still. A little bit forgotten."

She nodded, her stomach lurching. She paused at the edge of the graveyard, feeling she was going to be sick again. Sick, or shit herself. Mose stopped and took a coin out of his pocket.

"What are you doing?" she whispered.

"I wound up in New Orleans with a lady who told me that you never enter a graveyard without making an offering." He kissed the nickel and placed it beside the grave. "If you do that, Oya will keep you safe among the dead."

"Who's Oya?"

"The goddess of the graveyard gate."

Sarah turned and vomited again. Cricket purred sympathetically around her ankles.

Mose helped her to her feet after she hit the dry heaves. He produced a bottle, gave her a sip of water to rinse the taste of bile from her throat. And they walked.

They walked for miles in that graveyard, with excruciating slowness. Mose would pick a minty-flavored ground weed for her, creeping Charlie he called it, and bade her to eat it when she could. Over the next few days, they walked together and separately. She saw ghosts, hallucinations poured from her toxic brain like vomit and shit. She knew that's what they were when she saw them, pale shapes moving between the tombstones, denizens of the kingdom of the dead. She found sleeping ghosts lying with their heads on the pillows of gravestones, holding trees that had sprouted from their hollow chests. Those acorns and walnuts they'd been buried with split open coffins and heaved the ground, the trees beginning to bud out from that death. In an area with a dozen dead children, with small white grave markers shaped like lambs and doves, she heard children laughing. One of the lambs, the size of a toaster, had fallen from its base onto the ground. Its edges were blackened with age, and it seemed that tears had stained its eyes. Carefully, she put it back in place, and it seemed to her that a little girl sighed happily when she did so.

She fell to her knees before a stone that was inscribed with the word *DADDY*, missing her parents so much that she fell asleep before that stone, her hands clinging to the top. Cricket found her and led Mose to her, and Mose drew her back to the camp, where she slept in the flickering light of the fire.

They talked in this time, in between hours of companionable silence. Sarah told him about her life in rural West

Virginia, how all the people she grew up with had parents who worked at the local chemical plant until it shut down. She told him about growing tomatoes with her grandmother and summers spent playing in the sprinkler as a child. Mose told her of riding the rails, of jumping trains and moving north and east, always getting at the railyards when he could see light after a night of riding. He told her all about cities she'd never seen: Nashville, Huntsville, Baltimore, Pittsburgh, Detroit.

Each time they entered the graveyard, Mose offered a coin. Sometimes it was no more than a penny, but he always produced it, tucking it into the frozen dirt. When she went alone, she did the same, uttering a prayer for peace to the goddess of the graveyard gate, or whoever might be listening.

One afternoon, she stood at the edge of the cemetery. She'd left Mose at the campsite. He wasn't feeling well; his coughing had rattled throughout the night. She had wiped his face with cold rainwater, and he'd waved her on to the grave-yard. She left Cricket with him for comfort while she entered the burial grounds to walk her now-familiar circuit.

There were no coins in her pocket, she realized. Just the teeth she'd forgotten about, loosened by Pete's friend, now coated in lint. She cleaned them up and gently pressed them into the dirt. The graveyard had granted her a great wish—it had brought her to sobriety. Though she still felt weak and un-certain, her head was clear. She'd come out on the other side of her hurt, walking with the dead and washing in rainwater and sleeping on the earth. There was no pain now, and she vowed never to return to it. For the first time in a while she thought about the future. Considered going back home, to the town she grew up in. Maybe see if her great-aunt still lived in the area. Maybe . . . She walked as she had for all this time before, threading among the stones, pausing to read. There were no ghosts here anymore, just silence.

She sat among the stones, her hands in her lap, as the sun went down. She closed her eyes, still feeling the warmth of the sun on her face and breathing in the smell of freshly sprouted grass. Car exhaust filtered down from the freeway, and the sounds of traffic echoed in the distance. She chewed a piece of creeping Charlie, feeling the sharpness of it against her empty tooth sockets. She cleared her head and thought of nothing, just feeling the earth and the gathering dark support-ing her. She fell asleep, resting on the stone of the youngest child there.

"You owe me. You owe me everything."

Pain flashed though her skull, and Sarah sprawled on the ground, breathless.

She brought her hand up to shield her face, hearing the familiar voice hiss down at her.

Pete. Pete was here. *No!* How had he found her? She scrambled up to her hands and knees, intending to run, run back to camp. But his swinging boot crushed her ribs, and the wind was knocked from her. His hands were winding into her hoodie collar as he slammed her against the ground.

She didn't understand. He wanted her to leave . . . he said not to come home, and she'd obeyed him . . .

"How could you leave me? I gave you everything," he snarled. His voice was teary and wrathful at the same time, as it had been in so many of their fights. He *wanted*—wanted her, wanted the drugs, wanted something she could not give him. He didn't know what that was. But it was not anything that she could summon for him.

"You destroyed my life," she sobbed. Saying it aloud, it

had the ring of truth. She squirmed, kicking, and fought to get to her feet. Breaking free, she lurched away from him.

"You're dead, damn it. Dead," he howled behind her. And she knew he meant it.

She screamed for help, but there was no one to hear her in this city of the dead. She ran, weaving through this necropolis that she now knew by heart, leaping over stones and sweeping through rows in the falling darkness. Breath slid cleanly from her lips as she plunged into the children's section of lambs and doves. If she could outrun him, then . . .

Behind her, she heard a thunk. She paused, turning. Pete had tripped, right over the *DADDY* tombstone, landing face-down in the grass. He swore, struggling, a dark slash of blood over his eye.

Sarah sucked in her breath. He would pursue her, she knew. She could not outrun him. There was no outrunning some things. Like Mose and his stepfather.

She reached down to find the headstone with the broken lamb. She picked up the lamb with both hands. It felt solid and cold in her grip, the jagged edges digging into her palms.

She walked over to where Pete lay on the ground, dazed and gasping like a fish. She stood over him, feeling power singing through her for the first time in her life. She could leave him now. She could run far, far away. She was free . . .

Pete groaned. Barely conscious. She looked down at him struggling unsuccessfully to rise. He wasn't going anywhere anytime soon.

But Mose's voice rang in her skull: *I shot him anyway. Because I just couldn't be sure.*

Sarah needed to be sure. She lifted the lamb high, swinging it over her head, and slammed it down on Pete's head with all her strength.

Not once. Twice. Three times. By then, Pete stopped twitching and the lamb slipped from her hands. In the darkness, she saw the sharp glitter of broken teeth and the shine of something black and viscous splashed on the surface of a gravestone. Pete's skull was open and oozing, like a cantaloupe someone had dropped on pavement, exposing gleaming seeds of teeth and bone and bloody gore inside. The lamb sculpture lay beside him, stained black with Pete's blood.

Her hands shook, and she gulped in air.

She turned on her heel and ran back to camp.

"Mose?"

The old man was wrapped up in his sleeping bag, his head propped up on a disintegrating cardboard box.

She reached toward him, and the sleeping bag moved. Cricket poked his head out of the top, blinking, and wormed out of the bag.

"Mose," she said again. "Mose, I've done . . . something." She couldn't bring herself to say *a terrible thing*. Just that she'd done something. A thing that was neither good nor evil, but a thing that had to be done.

Mose didn't move. She reached out to touch his neck, and recoiled, feeling cold flesh. She reached out again, found no pulse. She shook him. Sobbing, she pressed her ear to his chest. There was no movement, no cough, no nothing. Cricket leaned against Mose's shoulder.

"His cough," she said to Cricket as she wiped a string of snot from her nose. "It was his cough, wasn't it?"

Cricket mewed softly and stared forlornly at Mose.

"Don't worry," she said to the cat. "I'll take care of you."

She laid Mose down carefully on his cardboard mattress and lovingly arranged his hands over his chest. She found two coins left in his pocket that she pressed into his hands. She didn't know if the graveyard goddess wandered this far, but she wanted her to receive Mose as gently as she could.

She quickly took inventory of Mose's belongings, packing up what she could carry in his army duffel bag. She donned his coat that smelled like cigarette smoke and cheeseburger wrappers. She picked up Cricket and tucked him into her hoodie. He curled up next to her chest as if she were wearing a baby carrier.

She kneeled and kissed Mose on the forehead. "Thank you."

And she kicked the fire out. She struck out to the new cemetery across the street and the railroad tracks beyond it. It would only be a matter of time until a train paused and she would be on her way. Not home, though. She hoped the train would go south, far away from here.

She had paid her fare, and she was free.

PART III

BUCKEYE BETRAYALS

THE LUCKIEST MAN ALIVE

BY LEE MARTIN

San Margherita

I t's late when I step out of Johnnie's Tavern, and traffic is
light along Trabue Road, just a car or two from time to
time, tires hissing over the wet asphalt. Fog is starting to
settle in, and I can barely make out the stoplight on McKinley Avenue to the east, and the lights of the Quarry apartment complex where I bunk while my wife and I try to decide
whether it's time to cut bait. I've been there a summer, and
now that we've made the turn to autumn, it's starting to feel
not quite like home, but instead like a necessary adjustment.
I live in a pocket of Columbus just west of the Scioto River,
almost in San Margherita, almost in Marble Cliff, almost in
Grandview, almost in Upper Arlington, but not quite. A place
without definition where someone like me can hide.

"Hey there, pie face." A voice comes out of the fog, a
woman's voice, and I spot the cherry of her cigarette. "Come
on over here, puss pie."

For the record, I like to keep things above board. I make
it a point to stay away from the Private Dancer gentlemen's
club up the street. I never take my money to the backroom
poker game at the San Margherita Market. When I drive up
Fifth Avenue, cross the Scioto, and cruise through Grandview
by its large clapboard two-story houses, and its smaller Cape
Cods set back from tree-lined streets, and its trendy strips of
restaurants and shops and breweries and pubs, I watch my

speed, keep my eye out for cops, try to steer clear of trouble. Trust me, I'm carrying enough of that.

I hesitate, but then the woman starts to cry. It's one of those whimpering cries you'd barely notice if you had enough noise to cover it, but on this night there's only the hiss of the tires and the fog, and though I still can't see the woman, I can sure as hell hear her, and it tears me up inside.

"Don't cry," I say.

This woman whimpers a time or two more, and then she's quiet. I'm just about to take a step when she says, "Why don't you come over here and make me?"

I know I should find my truck and head on to my apartment. Call it a night and hope for tomorrow, but now I'm curious about this woman who seems all boo-hoo one minute and so hard-assed the next.

"Well," she says, "you coming or what?"

I find her at the edge of the gravel parking lot, standing in the tall grass. Her hand comes out of the fog and catches me by a belt loop. "It's about time," she says. "I want you to take me somewhere."

The woman—a girl, really—is a slip of a thing. She's wearing a short black skirt with black fishnet hose and a pair of stilettos. Her dark hair has a blue tint to it, and her lipstick is blue to match. She has a silver stud in the corner of her nose. She has sunken cheeks flamed with rouge, and the kind of eyes I know the girls call smoky—plenty of liner and shadow and mascara. She throws her cigarette on the gravel and tries to grind it out with the toe of her shoe, but all that really happens is the butt sinks down into the gravel and continues to smolder.

"Where do you need to go?" I ask her.

"Saint Margaret of Cortona," she says.

"The Catholic church on Hague Avenue?"

"You need a map, puss pie?"

"I know where it is."

She steps up close to me. She grabs my shirt right at the collar button, and pulls so hard I feel the collar cut into my neck.

"Good," she says in a whisper. "Then take me."

I drive out Hague, and she doesn't say a word. She cries a little more. She tries to light another cigarette, but her fingers shake so badly, she can't manage it. The match burns her fingers, and she tosses it and her cigarette out the window of my truck. She looks so small, curled up against the door, her chin wobbling when I hit a pothole.

When I get to the church, she tells me to pull right up to the front door and to shine my lights on the statue of Saint Margaret. The fog swirls all around the saint in the beams of my headlights, and though I've never been the religious sort, something about the fog and the girl and her hushed voice catches me by the throat and won't let go.

The girl makes the sign of the cross. Then she tells me the saint's story—the patron saint, she says, of the falsely accused, of the homeless and the insane, of the orphaned and the mentally ill.

"And," she says, "probably a few more that I'm forgetting."

Then she gets out of the truck and goes to the statue and puts her arms around it and starts to cry again. She says, "Please, please, please." Then she whispers something that I can't quite make out, but later, when I'm trying to sleep back at my apartment, I swear that what I heard her say was, "I didn't mean to kill her." I tell myself I'm crazy, and I tell myself to forget it. Then on my way to work the next day, I snag a copy of the *Columbus Dispatch*, and I see the story about a girl's body pulled from the abandoned rock quarry just west of McKinley, and I have a sick feeling I can't shake, no matter how hard I try.

My daughter was a girl named Star. Starlene, really, but her mother and I called her Star because she was the light of our lives. A little blond-haired girl with dimples and the sort of blue eyes that could make you believe there really was something called God—that we were all part of a grand design instead of floating, alone and lost, the way I feel I am now.

"I used to believe in heaven," my wife said to me just before I moved out. "Now I'm not so sure."

Once upon a time, I swore I was living in paradise every day of my life. "Me too," I told her, and for just an instant I wanted to grab onto her and never let her go.

Then she said, "Now it's all I can do to look at you."

Here's the story. One day back in the winter, when the snow was on, I pulled Star down the street on her sled, but she quickly got bored with that. She was ten by that time, and she was eager to test her limits.

"Faster," she said. "Go faster."

We lived in Grandview, in the house my father built in 1957. A white clapboard with green shutters at the windows, and a porte cochere at the side where my father usually kept his Mercury Comet parked, and a front porch that faced west. The house was on a rise, and when I sat in the porch glider, I could see the Scioto River, and the old rock quarry, long closed and filled now with water. I could see kids sneak in under the chain-link fence to go swimming even though they were constantly being warned that it was a dangerous thing to do. I could also see the vineyards behind the houses along

Trabue Road, the long rows of grapevines the Italian immigrant quarry workers put in the ground in the early 1900s. Many of the workers came from the commune of Pettorano sul Gizio in the Province of L'Aquila in the Abruzzo region of Italy. They brought with them the patron Saint Margaret of Cortona, the woman who'd established a hospital for the sick, the homeless, the impoverished. In order to get nurses, she started yet another order known as *le poverelle*, the little poor ones.

I know all this because what I didn't tell the girl who called me pie face and puss pie and wanted me to take her to the church was that I'd been there many times, always at night, just like her, always because I had something I couldn't stop confessing.

"Star," I said that winter day, "let's take this up a notch or two."

I grabbed a log chain out of the back of my pickup and wrapped it around the axle, using a slipknot just like my father taught me. Then I did the same thing with the other end and the frame of Star's sled.

"This doesn't seem safe to me," my wife said. She stood just inside the garage, looking out to where Star was lying on the sled on her stomach.

My wife had on black jeans and a black turtleneck with a red cardigan sweater over her shoulders, the sleeves knotted loosely around her neck. She'd always been a timid sort, someone I found easy to nudge this way or that. It shames me now, and will haunt me forever, to recall how la-di-da I was when I said, "Ah, Gayle, don't be a wet hen."

"Ed," she said, "I don't know. . ."

But there was the sled, all hooked up and ready to go, and Star was in her snowsuit and her boots and her mittens with the little fuzzy balls at the ends of their strings and her sock hat and her Ohio State Buckeye scarf wrapped around her face.

She pulled it down a bit and said, "Mom," drawing out that one syllable in a way that said, *Please?*

Gayle looked at me. She raised an eyebrow. That was as close as she could come to asking me to not get behind the wheel of my truck. Now I can't stop living in that moment, that stretch of time when I had the chance to stop what was going to happen.

I got in the truck. I stuck my head out the open window and shouted to Star. "Hold on!" I said, and away we went.

Everything was fine for a while. There was no traffic on our little street, and I was taking it nice and slow, glancing in my mirror from time to time to make sure Star was holding on. Then at the end of the street, I made a left turn and caught a patch of ice, and started to slide. I steered into the skid the way I knew how—a reflex from years of driving on snow—and that's what whipped the chain and sent Star's sled off to the left where it struck a curb and shot her off into a yard. I watched her catch air, and everything seemed to slow down, and I swore she'd be fine. I believed it all the way up until she landed. She hit her head on a landscape stone and came to rest finally in the soft white snow.

Everyone told me afterward—after the days at the OSU med center, and the hematoma, and the life support, and the decision, finally, to let Star go—that it wasn't my fault. It was just an accident. No rhyme or reason, but I knew better, and so did Gayle.

We talk a little now and again, but it's like talking to a stranger.

That's the story I could have told the girl at Saint Margaret of Cortona, but I didn't. Instead, I took her where she wanted to go—one of those brick duplexes along Glenn Avenue in Grandview.

She started to get out of my truck, but I grabbed her by the wrist and said, "Wait, what's your name?"

"No." She tugged her arm free and jumped out of the truck. Right before she closed the door she said, "You don't get to know that."

Then she ran up the walkway and went into one of the duplexes. I sat there awhile, waiting for a light to come on, but it never did, so I went on to the Quarry and I sat in the dark in my apartment and looked out at the lights in other people's apartments reflecting off the lake, until finally I lay down to sleep, awaking later with a start, hearing the girl's voice clear as day, confessing to killing someone.

The girl they pulled from the rock quarry is a Jane Doe—no identifying marks, no wallet or purse with a driver's license, no scars, no match with the national dental record database. I look at the police sketch in the *Dispatch*. A face like mine—round and fleshy—with bangs hanging into her dark eyes. Suddenly, it comes to me. Pie face—a face as round as a pie.

She was wearing a red OSU hoodie, Levi's, and a pair of black Vans. Around five feet four inches and 165 pounds. A stout girl, who somehow ended up floating facedown in that quarry, her lungs filling up with water.

The boys are yakking about it the next day at work. The general consensus is suicide. A desperate girl takes a dive and drowns. End of story.

Me? I'm not so sure.

"Who's to say it's not murder?" I say to my buddy A.J.

We work for Decker Construction, filling potholes, paving

streets—that sort of thing. Today, we're working near my old neighborhood, just a few blocks to the north on the fringe of Upper Arlington. I keep imagining that at any minute Gayle might come driving by, and I'll wave at her, and maybe she'll wave at me, and there'll be that moment when we remember that once upon a time we had everything right where we wanted it. We were a family—Gayle and me and Star.

A.J. is shoveling Flash Fill into a pothole. Flash Fill is made from coal fly ash. It's got a lot of calcium in it, and that's what causes it to set up fast. We call it a flash set, the hardening that comes when mixed with water. We use it to fill what we call void areas. We use it, in other words, to fill holes.

"Paper give any reason to think someone killed that girl?" A.J.'s a scrawny dude, on the other side of sixty. A bachelor all his life. His blue jeans bunch up around his knees and sag off his hips. He pulls a blue bandanna out of his hip pocket and uses it to wipe sweat from his face. He leans on his shovel handle. He chews at the corner of his long mustache. "Any gunshot wounds? Any stab wounds? Anything like that at all?"

"Not that the article mentioned," I say.

"Then why would you think . . ." He cuts himself off and narrows his eyes, squinting at me there in the sunshine. "Oh," he finally says.

The maple trees along the street are brilliant with their crimson leaves. They drift down and land on the lawns, on the low stone walls, on the windshields of parked cars. Crows call somewhere nearby, their caws sharp in the crisp air. I hear the scrape of a rake in a lawn. I lift my head and see a young mother raking leaves into a pile for her kids to romp through, and I have to squeeze my eyes shut to get that image out of my mind. I have to forget Star and that last autumn we had together, time running short outside our knowing.

A.J. is the only one I've ever talked to about Star and what I caused to happen to her. He's sat with me in my apartment long into the night, letting me speak my misery and regret, unable to do anything to help me, outside of being there as witness. He knows now that I want the girl's death to be suspicious because I want to hold everyone to account. I'll be even more direct—I want as much proof as I can get that we're responsible for the people we love and then lose, that effect follows cause, that there's no God to save us. There's only our own stupidity and the ruin we make. I don't want to be alone.

"There was this girl," I say.

"I know, I know," says A.J., and I'm not sure if he thinks I'm talking about Star or the girl from the paper, so I set him straight.

"Not the drowned girl. Another girl. Last night. She was outside Johnnie's. She said, *I want you to take me somewhere.*"

"No, man." A.J. starts back to work with his shovel. "I don't want to hear about you and some girl."

"It wasn't like that," I say. I tell him about taking the girl to Saint Margaret of Cortona and how she cried. "She got out of my truck and went to the statue. I think she was making a confession. I swear she said, *I didn't mean to kill her.*"

A.J. stops shoveling. He studies me. Again, he squints. "Did you hear her say that? Are you sure?"

"I think I did."

"But you aren't positive?"

"She was crying real hard. It was tough to make out all the words."

That's when his face crumples, like all hope has left him, like he's finally lost patience with me and he's about to tell me what's what. I want to say to him, *Aren't we all the saintly and the damned? Aren't we all the little poor ones?*

"Man, you got to stop this shit," he whispers. "You got to stop blaming yourself for Star. Straight up, man. You got to stop getting off on everyone else's trouble. Own up to what you did. Then let it go."

But I can't. I keep thinking of that girl from last night and the way she depended on me. I made sure she got to where she needed to go, and then I took her to that duplex on Glenn Avenue. After work, I drive over there, and I knock on the door.

I'm not sure what I'll say if she answers. Maybe I'll just get right to the point. Maybe I'll say, *Are you in trouble?*

A dog inside starts barking. I can tell it's one of those yippy dogs, a real ankle-biter. Then I hear footsteps, and a man's voice shouting, "Brutus! Shut the hell up!"

The man has the dog, a Pomeranian, cradled in his left arm when he opens the door, a bit of reddish-yellow fluff with shining brown eyes and a Buckeyes bandanna around its neck, folded into a triangle that hangs down its chest. The man's short and husky, with a nest of gray hairs poking out of the vee of his buttoned-up cabana shirt. The shirt's white with a wide black stripe down the middle where the buttons are. He smells like something fried—that and just a hint of peppermint. He's too old to be the girl's lover, at least in any kind of decent world, and I wonder whether he's her father. If so, I wonder what he knows or doesn't know.

"Is she here?" I ask.

"Which one?" he says.

Just like that we're in the middle of a conversation that assumes I know things I really don't.

"The skinny one," I say. "The one with the blue tint in her hair and the smoky eyes."

"Tina?"

"That's right." Now I have what she didn't want me to have, her name. "Tina," I say. I snap my fingers several times like I'm trying to come up with her last name. "Tina whosit . . . ?"

"Tina Monticello."

"That's the ticket. She's the one I'm looking for."

"Can't help you, bub." He starts to shut the door, but I stick my foot over the threshold and bar my forearm across the door. "Hey, what gives?" he says. "Who the hell are you, anyway?"

"I gave her a ride last night. I wanted to make sure she's okay."

"She gets like that. She's a hothead. Meggie knows how to push her buttons."

Meggie, I think. The pie-faced Jane Doe they pulled from the rock quarry. "Yeah, Meggie," I say. "What can you do?"

"Tell me about it." The guy relaxes his pressure against the door. He even gives me a grin. "Why I put up with 'em, I don't know. Last night's fight was a doozy. *You don't like my hair?* Tina said. *Well, maybe I don't like your fat face.* Meggie didn't take kindly to that. *And I don't care much for those smoky eyes either, if you want to know the truth. You look like a whore.* That's when I left and came back here. What happened next, I don't know. They always make up. Wasn't Meggie with Tina when you gave her a ride?"

"She was outside Johnnie's over on Trabue in San Margherita."

The guy nods. "Sounds about right. The shit hit the fan at the Private Dancer. It wouldn't surprise me if they both got tossed out."

"The strip club?"

"Tina knows a girl who dances there. Sometimes we have a few drinks."

"So where's Meggie now?"

"Beats me. I haven't seen either one of them all day. They come and go, you know? It's not like I'm their father."

"Who are you, then?"

They guy narrows his eyes and studies me. The Pom starts to bark, and he closes his hand around its muzzle and holds tight. Then he gives me a wink. "Me?" He chuckles. "I'm the luckiest man alive."

That's what does it, that wise guy remark—*the luckiest man.* When I leave the duplex, I'm already thinking, *What kind of man?* I have to drive around a long time, trying to ignore the rage rising up in me. What kind of man lives with two young girls and doesn't care about their welfare? He shoved me out the door and slammed it and locked it. I heard him inside talking baby talk to his Pom.

"Who's Daddy's girl?" he said.

The Pom yipped and whined, and I heard her nails scrabbling about on the floor.

"Such a happy dog," the man said. "You're such a happy dog."

Like there wasn't a misery in the world.

I drive up King Avenue to Northwest Boulevard and shoot over to Upper Arlington. The day's turned cloudy, and now the light's going, a reminder that we're speeding ahead toward winter. I drive the side streets in UA: Waltham and Cambridge and Tewksbury and Doone, those winding streets where I can get lost and not care. I'm content to drive past the brick Tudors, chimneys reaching to the sky, and the old stone homes with the manicured hedges and the low stone walls. I like to see the lights on in those houses and the people inside: a woman in a cardigan sweater reading a book in lamplight, a man reaching for an apple from a bowl on a dining table, a girl playing a grand piano. These are the lives of the blessed, and the funny thing is, I don't envy them, not a bit. In fact, I'm happy for them and what appears to be their flawless lives, and I let myself believe, just for a while, that I'm one of them.

Eventually, though, I find Lane Avenue and go out past the Scioto Country Club where a foursome is heading to the clubhouse in the dusk. I imagine they're eager to get home, to be once again with their wives and children, and I get that fluttery feeling in my stomach I have each time I imagine I'll never again know what home is. I'll live alone the rest of my life, and I can't bear the thought of going to my apartment in the Quarry and listening to the sounds of my neighbors: the muted voices from upstairs, the noise of a radio next door, the faint laughter all around me among people who are thankful for their companions.

Headlights are on all along Riverside Drive, and I make the turn onto Fifth Avenue and head east. It's the supper hour and since it's Wednesday, it's four-dollar burger night at the Brazenhead pub.

That's where I am when I hear a voice say to the bartender, "Gin and tonic, puss pie."

It's her all right, the girl with the smoky eyes. She's sitting at the bar, one leg crossed over the other, her skirt riding up her thigh. She's got on a black felt hat with a long red feather coming out of the satin band.

I leave my table and sit down next to her at the bar. "Hey, Tina," I say. "What's shakin'?"

She plays it cool. She takes a quick glance in my direction. Then she stares straight ahead at the mirror behind the bar. I do the same. What would someone think, I wondered, if they happened to take note of us? They'd have no way of knowing, of course, about my sweet Star and the burden that grief and guilt ask me to carry. They wouldn't know, either, the feeling that wells up in my heart when I think about Tina and Meggie and all the girls out there tonight trying to make their way through a world filled with stupid, thoughtless men. How can I ever take care of all of them? How can I ever keep them alive?

"How do you know my name?" Tina says.

The bartender delivers her gin and tonic, and she moves the swizzle stick around in lazy circles.

"Are you in trouble, Tina?" I let the question hang there between us awhile. Then I ask the other question: "Where's Meggie?"

Tina stops stirring her drink. For the first time, she turns her head and stares at me. "Someone's been busy," she finally says.

Then she sips at her drink through the swizzle stick, like she's got all the time in the world.

I press ahead: "You read the paper this morning?" She doesn't answer, but I swear I see the corner of one smoky eye twitch. "I heard what you said last night when we were out at the church." I remember how she cried and how desperate she was for me to help her. I do what I wish I'd done last night. I take her hand. "I heard your confession," I say. "I know you killed her."

It's a crazy thing I'm doing. I should be talking to the police, but something about the way Star trusted me that snowy day when I said I'd pull her sled behind my truck has gotten all mixed up with the pain Tina's carrying, and I don't know what I want from her. All I know is I don't want to let her go.

"Let me help you," I say. "Please."

She lets me cover her hand with my big mitt, and I know I'll be forever grateful to her for that kindness.

When she finally speaks, it's in a shaky whisper, the sound of someone giving up. "There's no helping me," she says. Then she starts to slide her hand out from under mine. I try to hold on. She bows her head a moment. Then she looks at me and her cheeks are wet with tears, and she says, "I'm no killer. Please. Just let me go."

Then she's gone. It takes me awhile to notice something's fallen from her jacket pocket. I see the glint of something shiny on the floor, and I pick it up.

It's a key. *Do Not Duplicate*, it says on the back. A house key, I figure. I close my fingers around it and hurry out into the night. I look up and down the street, but Tina's nowhere to be found.

I slip the key into the pocket of my jeans, and feel it there when I go back into Brazenhead and sit down at my table. I take a few bites of my burger, nibble on some fries, but I'm not hungry anymore, so I pay my bill and go out to face the rest of the night.

A light rain is falling. The streets are shiny with it. I watch the drops come down in the glare from headlights moving along Fifth Avenue.

Whenever it rained, Star used to get so sad because she couldn't go outside and play. That's when Gayle would tell her the story her Slavic grandmother always told her, the story of Dodola, the goddess of rain, who was milking her heavenly cows, blessing the earth with life.

"It's not a sad time," Gayle would say. "It's a time of thanksgiving. A time to be happy."

Then she'd do the dance her grandmother taught her—the waving of arms and swaying of hips—and soon Star would be laughing with delight, and I'd close my eyes and listen to the sound of it, never once thinking that someday I'd have to do my best to recall it.

I get in my truck and drive west toward the river and my apartment on the other side of it. I tell myself that's where I'm going, but already I know I'll make the turns that will take me to where I used to live. I park along the street and look at the lights in my old house where my wife now lives alone.

A motorcycle leans on its kickstand beneath the porte co-chere. I don't recognize it, but I take it for what it is, a sign of life moving on for Gayle. Before too long, a man comes out the front door, slips off his boots, and leaves them on the mat before going back inside. I see his shadow move across the drawn curtains in the front window, and then the lights go out.

I sit there a good while, waiting for them to come on again, and when they don't, I pull away from the curb, an ache in my throat as if someone has punched me.

That's how I end up back at the duplex on Glenn Avenue. I don't know where else to be. I don't want to be alone in my apartment. I know A.J. will tell me to get a grip if I swing by his place. Crazy as this is, I stand in the rain at the front door, and I hear the Pom yipping and people laughing, and music playing, and I do it before I can stop myself. I put the key in the lock, turn it, and open the door.

The people inside—Tina, and the guy who called himself the luckiest man alive, and a blond round-faced girl—stop the dance they've been doing and turn to me, their eyes alight with wonder.

The man is holding the Pom who's stopped barking. Tina has the round-faced girl by the waist. The round-faced girl holds a bottle of Wild Goose beer in her hand. The music is zydeco, and hearing it, I don't know how anyone couldn't be happy to stumble upon these people and the looks of rapture on their faces.

Tina glows with the radiance of someone who believes in second chances. "Look," she says to me. Then she nods at the round-faced girl. "Meggie. We had a fight, but she came back."

The rain is falling on me, soaking my shirt, running down my face. I know I should be happy that what I suspected has turned out to be something I imagined, but I can't quite manage the appropriate measure of relief. I think about the girl they pulled from the rock quarry, the Jane Doe, the body of someone's daughter, someone who waits and waits for her to come home.

I take the key from the lock and hold it out to Tina on my palm. My fingers tremble. *Look what I found,* I want to say. *Look what I've brought you.*

What else can I do? How else can I say the hurt that's brought me here?

"Oh, pie face," she says to me, "did you really think I could—"

I find my voice and I stop her. I don't want to hear it said aloud. I don't want to hear these people laugh at me, or to have to explain why I decided Tina was begging for forgiveness last night at the statue of Saint Margaret of Cortona. I don't want to admit I've manufactured a life for myself that depends upon the foul deeds and sorrows of others. I don't want them to know I've had to do this in order to survive.

For the first time since Star died, I admit I no longer know how to love people. I only know how to look for the wounded and the maimed, so I can wrap them up in my arms and try to love myself.

"Oh, puss pie," Tina says to me with such a sad voice. I

know she understands, without having to hear my story. I'm one of them. She lets Meggie go. Then she comes to me and plucks the key from my palm. She brings it to her lips and kisses it. Such a tender kiss. I bow my head, and she presses the key to my forehead. It feels cool there. In a whisper, she says to me, "It's all right. Whoever you are, and whatever you've done, it's okay."

She takes my hand and gently pulls me inside, into the glow of the lamplight, and the swell of the accordion and the fiddle, and the company of Meggie, risen from the dead, and the man with the Pom who puts his arm around my shoulders and says, "That which was lost has been found. How's that for luck, buddy?"

I tell him it's something. It's really something. Tonight, it's almost enough.

THE VALLEY

BY YOLONDA TONETTE SANDERS

Whitehall

"One one thousand, two one thousand, three one thousand . . ."

Nine-year-old Kellie counted out the numbers, resting her head on her forearm as she leaned against the tree while her friends and brother found their hiding spots. Though her eyes were supposed to be closed, she squinted, peeking just enough to get a general idea of the direction some had gone in John Bishop Park. Kellie couldn't see everyone without turning her head. She resisted the urge to do so to avoid being accused of cheating like last time. Kellie did manage to see where a few people had gone. Andy, a boy who lived down the street, ran behind the tree on her left. Skyla, their neighbor, was crouching at the base of the slide. Jeffrey, her little brother and youngest kid in their playgroup, was running around in circles complaining he couldn't find anywhere to hide like he always did.

At six, Jeffrey was only selected to be "it" as a last resort or when he started crying, threatening to tell his and Kellie's parents that Kellie wasn't playing fair. No one, including Kellie, liked to hide with him because he couldn't keep quiet and he always whined if he got caught before he wanted to. Truth be told, he was a brat, and the only reason Kellie brought him to the park with her was that their parents made her. Reluctantly putting her resentment aside, Kellie closed her eyes and kept counting. Almost immediately she stopped, interrupted by the blast of heavy metal music.

She peeked again, glimpsing two teenagers in a blue van before resuming the game.

"Eighteen one thousand, nineteen one thousand, twenty one thousand. Ready or not, here I come!"

Kellie opened her eyes and at the same moment, she heard a scream. She looked around but saw no one outside of their hiding place. Had she imagined the sound? Stepping away from the tree, she saw the blue van heading for the exit. Kellie made eye contact with the driver for a quick second. He smiled, and she smiled back. Then, to her shock, he laughed and gave her the finger as he peeled out of the parking lot and disappeared down the street.

Confused by the driver's actions and slightly perturbed at the intrusion, Kellie stared after the van for a long moment. Boys could be so stupid. They were also unnecessarily annoying if she included her little brother in her assessment of males. Kellie was pleasantly surprised to see that Jeffrey had apparently found a hiding spot. She smiled. Perhaps her baby brother wasn't as stupid as he was annoying. With the park finally quiet again, Kellie repeated her charge.

"Ready or not, here I come!"

Kellie first ran in Andy's direction. He peeked around the tree and saw her coming. He took off toward the base, which was the tree from which Kellie had been counting. She was never going to catch him. Other kids ran toward the base as well, but Kellie was fast enough to tag Skyla as she came from behind the slide. "You're it!"

"Aw, man!" Skyla moaned. Together, Kellie and Skyla walked back to base where everyone took a moment to catch their breath and talk about their hiding spots. Finally, Skyla asked, "Y'all ready to go again?"

The kids were off in a flash as Skyla began counting.

As Kellie jogged away, she looked around for her brother. "Hey, has anyone seen Jeffrey?" No one paid any attention. They were all too busy running for safety. Kellie searched to no avail.

There was no sign of him. She was so perplexed she didn't hear when Skyla had finished counting. "Tag! You're it!" Skyla shouted a few moments later, slapping her on the shoulder.

Laughter erupted as other kids ran to the base, teasing Kellie for having been caught so quickly.

"Guys, I can't find my brother," she explained.

"He's probably still hiding somewhere," one of the boys said. "Last time I saw him, he was by the parking lot. I bet he's behind one of the cars."

Kellie ran in that direction. Other kids followed. He wasn't there.

"Let's check the shelter across the street," suggested Andy. He and a few others crossed Etna Road while Kellie stood paralyzed in the parking lot. Pretty soon all the kids were scattered around the park in search of Jeffrey. Everyone was shouting his name. Their efforts were in vain. A pit forming in her stomach, Kellie ran the three blocks home to face the wrath of her parents who had warned her to keep an eye on him.

Upon delivering the news that she couldn't find Jeffrey, her dad hopped in the car and sped out while her mom quickly called the Whitehall police. Soon, several of the neighbors—adults and kids alike—scanned the streets looking for her brother. Owners of cars that were left at the park for whatever reason were contacted and questioned. Hours of searching turned into days, and after a week, hope was fading. Officers interviewed each kid who was at the park that day, wanting to know every detail they could recall. Kellie told them about the van with the teenage boys, wondering if they were responsible for her brother's disappearance. She left out the part about the scream, afraid it might bring further resentment from her parents about her irresponsibility. Besides, she wasn't sure if she had really heard anything. She kept the detail to herself, even after her brother's body was found in the wooded area of the Whitehall

Community Park, a mile or so from John Bishop Park. He'd been raped and strangled.

One one thousand, two one thousand, three one thousand—

Kellie abruptly awoke. She looked at the clock. 3:13 a.m. Sighing heavily, she reached to the nightstand for the two bottles she kept there. She opened the short plastic one, removed two pills, and popped them into her mouth. She opened the tall bottle and took a long gulp of the brown liquid, washing down the pills in an attempt to escape the nightmare from twenty years ago.

The moonlight glow coming through the open blinds of her bedroom window shed enough light that she could read Psalm 23:4 inscribed on her wall. *Yea, though I walk through the valley of the shadow of death, I will fear no evil.* When Kellie was younger, her dad stenciled this verse for her after she'd had a series of bad dreams. "Remember, God will always protect you," he would say. "Whenever you wake up from a nightmare, I want this verse to be the first thing you see. Allow His word to comfort you."

Well, that advice worked when she was a child, before Jeffrey's murder, but now she was sure it was the two bottles— the benzodiazepines and the liquor—that really calmed her. For all her parents' religious talk, they failed to internalize it after Jeffrey died. By the following year, her dad had lost his job and caved to alcoholism. Thankfully, he had a small inheritance from his family that kept the mortgage paid and the utilities on. If there was a bright side to things, Kellie would say that she always had a roof over her head and food on the table, even if she had to prepare it herself.

Kellie's mother had passed long ago, losing her struggle with depression by succumbing to suicide nearly three years to the anniversary date of Jeffrey's death. Kellie would never forget the day she headed to the bathroom to brush her teeth, hoping against hope they'd actually purchased toothpaste. She was so tired of using pure baking soda as a substitute. As Kellie pushed the bathroom door open to enter, she could hear a steady drip. It wasn't water as she'd assumed, but blood. Her mother lay in the bathtub, her arm dangling over the side with blood dripping from her wrist onto the ceramic floor. She'd used a kitchen knife to do the damage. In the tub with her was a picture of her favorite child.

No one needed to verbalize that Jeffrey was the favorite of both parents. It was always implied. As the oldest sibling by three years, Kellie was the one scolded for any- and everything that went wrong, even if it was Jeffrey who had done it. "You should have been keeping a closer eye on him," one of her parents would say. Or her mother's favorite line, "If he did do something to you, I'm sure it was in retaliation to whatever you did to him." Jeffrey could do no wrong in their parents' eyes. After his death, instead of appreciating the fact that they still had one child left, both parents mourned as if Jeffrey had been their only offspring. The beatings Kellie suffered and the verbal attacks after he died were clear indications that they blamed her. After her mom's death, Kellie was pretty much left to fend for herself as her dad was often too drunk to care about her needs. His were all that mattered.

"Kel, come here," he'd called her from his room one night.

"Yes, sir," she'd timidly answered before entering. She'd witnessed him load up on drinks less than a half hour earlier. Nothing good ever happened when he drank. She knew that. She braced herself for verbal abuse, which was often followed by a beating.

"Come *here*." He patted the bed next to him and smiled.

Kellie found herself letting down her guard. His voice was soft, not hard as she'd grown accustomed to since Jeffrey died. She eagerly approached the bed and sat down next to her father, who put his arm around her.

"Things are going to be different now that your mom's gone. It's just the two of us now, you know that, right?"

Ignoring the stench of liquor on his breath, she nodded. "Yes, Daddy."

Gently, explaining his physical needs and how she was to fulfill them, he slid his hands underneath her shirt to unhook her training bra and instructed her on how to touch his genitals. Paralyzed by shock, fear, and unimaginable emotional pain, Kellie complied with all her father's wishes that night and countless others as the abuse lasted well into her twenties, until he'd gotten too sick to function.

Kellie shook her head, trying to erase memories of her sexual experiences with her father, the only man to ever know her in a biblical sense. Though Kellie now lived alone in this three-bedroom house, she could not remember the last time she'd set foot in her parents' or her brother's room. She was never allowed in Jeffrey's room after he died, and she'd spent enough time unwillingly in her parents' bed being raped by her father that there was no desire to ever walk across that threshold again.

Her father eventually drank himself into cirrhosis before passing away about four years ago, leaving Kellie as the sole recipient of the house and the money that was left from the malpractice settlement he received from the doctor who had failed to inform him of his diagnosis for an entire year thanks to a communication lapse in the doctor's office. If there was one thing Kellie's father knew how to do, it was live well off other people's money. Kellie, too, now lived off those means.

As a high school dropout, there weren't many opportunities for her anyhow. She was both uneducated and a loner since all her childhood friendships had dissolved in the years after Jeffrey's death. No friends, no family, no lifelong goals, she spent most of her days watching the Investigation Discovery channel, *Forensic Files*, or the local news simply to ensure that she didn't completely lose touch with the outside world. Kellie found comfort in alcohol though she wasn't addicted like her father. She told herself she only drank to take the edge off. She was in control—unlike her father.

Kellie read the inscription on her wall once more. *Yea, though I walk through the valley of the shadow of death, I will fear no evil.* She never painted over it because it was a re-minder of a time in her life when she was loved by her father in a genuine, untainted way. Recalling his words about protec-tion, Kellie couldn't help but ask, *God, why didn't You protect me from his sexual advances? Why didn't You protect Jeffrey from dying?*

The next day, Kellie stared at the TV in numb disbelief.

"*I'm on site at John Bishop Park in Whitehall on the city's East Side where a five-year-old boy has gone missing,*" reported a newswoman. "*Alyssa Jackson told police that she and her children were the only ones at the park earlier today when she left young Mark playing on the swings to take his younger sister to the restroom. The mother is certain that she wasn't gone longer than a few minutes. When she returned, her son was nowhere to be found.*" A picture of the boy flashed across the screen. "*In-vestigators are asking that if you have seen this boy or have any indication of his whereabouts, please contact the Whitehall Police Department immediately. We'll keep you up to date about this case as details emerge. Allen and Janel, back to you.*"

Kellie's stomach knotted, waiting for the shoe to drop. It didn't take long.

"*We've been informed that John Bishop Park is the same location where a six-year-old boy disappeared twenty years ago,*" Allen said, shaking his head with dutiful sadness. "*Jeffrey Sullivan was playing hide-and-seek in the park with his sister and a group of neighborhood kids when he went missing. Unfortunately, his body was found in a shelter at another park. Police aren't sure if the two cases are connected. Sill, as Leah stated moments ago, please contact the Whitehall Police Department if you have any information.*"

"*That is so sad,*" remarked Janel, mimicking her coanchor's concern. "*We certainly hope there's a better ending for the Jackson family.*" Then her face brightened. "*Next up, we'll explain how a new law passed by Congress will affect local gas prices.*"

Kellie muted the TV and sought comfort in her bottles. Could this really have happened again? The same park—a boy about Jeffrey's age? She used her cell phone to search for news articles about Mark Jackson. She stumbled across a clip of the boy's parents, pleading for their son's safe return. Putting the phone down, she remembered something.

Rising with difficulty, Kellie stumbled into the dining room, making her way to the table buried beneath papers, books, and unwashed dishes. It took her several minutes but finally she found the file. The typed white label at the top simply read: *Jeffrey.* She carried it back to the couch, sat down heavily, reached again for her bottles, and then opened the file.

At some point in the fog between the end of her father's abuse and his death, Kellie had hired a private detective to investigate Jeffrey's murder. Tim Barnes, a retired Whitehall police officer, had spent a tremendous amount of time looking into Jeffrey's disappearance. Kellie had hoped if she could find answers—find the killers—maybe it would appease her father somehow. Maybe he wouldn't hate her so much. Fat chance. Barnes tried, but kept hitting dead ends. There simply weren't enough clues out there that the police hadn't combed through three times over.

Kellie had briefly gone through the file a time or two before, but today when she pulled it out, she took her time reading all the articles and notes. There were never any suspects in the case. Kellie—like the police and Mr. Barnes—didn't think the killers were residents of Whitehall. The community was too small. Someone would have reported a connection with teenagers and a blue van if one existed in the area. Had it been a van she'd seen at all? What if it had been a truck, or perhaps a green van instead of a blue one? As an adult, her subsequent run-ins with the cops over their lack of investigative progress made Kellie question everything she thought she remembered about Jeffrey's case. The only clue she had for sure was the digital sketch of the driver whom apparently no one else saw but her. The other kids were too busy hiding, she supposed, and Kellie did not get a good look at the passenger.

She came to the last two items in the file—a computer-enhanced image of the driver as he might look now that Mr. Barnes had produced at the end of his fruitless investigation, and a single scrap of paper with the name *Paul Ackerman* written on it.

It didn't take long. Within a week Mark Jackson's body was found. He had been raped and strangled like Jeffrey, then dumped behind a local thrift store. Shortly after the news of Mark's murder was aired, Kellie sifted through the file again. Before she knew it, she was picking up her phone.

"Tim Barnes here, how can I help you?"

"Well, h-hel-*lo*, Mr. Barnes. This is Kellie Sullivan. How are you doing?"

"Doing as well as an old man can, I guess." A long pause. "What about you?"

"I'm fine with a capital F, I suppose."

"You sound like you've been drinking."

"Oh, just a little bit," Kellie pinched her fingers together as though Mr. Barnes were in front of her and could see how little she claimed to have drank.

His sigh was an indication that he didn't believe her. "What can I do for you, Kellie?"

"Oh, Mr. Barnes. You sound irritated. Don't . . . don't be like that. I thought you were my friend. You are my friend, aren't you?"

"Listen, sweetheart, I'm busy right now. I'll give you a call later."

"I wanna tell you something important!" Kellie said, trying not to slur her words. "It's real important. Another boy got murdered. And . . ." she lowered her voice, "he disappeared from the same park as Jeffrey." She waited for Mr. Barnes to respond. "Hello? *Hel-lo*." A look at her phone screen revealed that he had ended the call. *Jerk*, Kellie thought right before taking another drink.

The sound of her phone's ring awoke Kellie from her stupor. She'd passed out, drooling on top of notes from Jeffrey's case file. She'd known that something had gone wrong, but she wasn't sure what. As she found her phone and a missed called from Mr. Barnes, she started putting together the pieces. Shame and sorrow filled her as she timidly called Mr. Barnes back.

"Tim Barnes . . ." he answered.

"Mr. Barnes, this is Kellie. I'm so sorry about what happened earlier."

"You really should seek help, Kellie. You—"

"I'm sorry, Mr. Barnes, okay? I don't want to talk about whether you think I have a drinking problem or not. I called you about something else. Have you heard about the recent kidnapping and murder of a young boy? He was taken from John Bishop Park like Jeffrey."

"Yes, I've been keeping up with the news."

"Do you think the cases are connected? This boy was found somewhere different from my brother."

"It's a possibility. I'm sure the police will do a thorough investigation."

Heat flushed her cheeks. Prior to hiring Mr. Barnes, Kellie had several drunken encounters with neighbors and others, ending in her arrest for one reason or another. She'd accused several community members of being her brother's kidnapper and killer over the years and had consequently developed a reputation for crying wolf. She hired Mr. Barnes knowing if he brought a suspect to the police's attention, they would find him credible.

"Would you mind calling any friends you have on the force and asking about any possible links they've found? Me and the Whitehall PD haven't really been able to establish a healthy working relationship."

"I shared with you everything I know. I have other cases and can't get involved at this point," he said softly.

"Fine, whatever!" she spat, finding it hard to hide her disappointment. "I have one more question. I saw on the back of one of the papers that you'd written down the name Paul Ackerman. Who is that?"

He repeated the name and then paused in thought. "He's a longtime Whitehall resident. I found his name on an old message slip with no other information. I don't know who wrote it or why. I went to see him, but he was suffering from Alzheimer's and his wife didn't know any reason why his name would have been connected with the case."

"Do they have any children?"

"A son, as I recall, but Mrs. Ackerman said he was in his sixties and has lived in Missouri since graduating from college. The Ackermans themselves were in their eighties. Neither the father nor son would have been close to the age of the teenager you saw." Barnes sighed. "I wish I would have gotten a chance to speak with Paul Ackerman when he was still in his right mind. Now, whatever information he may have had is forever locked up in his head."

"That's unfortunate," Kellie replied.

"I suppose. But who knows if it has any bearing on the case. Listen, I have to run. Please take care of yourself. I'm concerned about you, Kellie. You can't keep drinking like this, or—" Mr. Barnes stopped short of finishing his sentence, but Kellie knew what he would say. Contrary to what he thought, Kellie was nothing like her father.

"Thanks for taking the time to speak with me, Mr. Barnes."

"No problem, sweetheart."

She hung up and decided she would do some more investigating on her own. But first, she needed another drink.

Kellie drove up and down Yearling Road past the police station several times, wondering if she should stop. Nope. The cops would likely dismiss her as they'd done many times previously. Instead, she turned off Yearling and pulled up in front of the address she'd found for Paul Ackerman. The house sat on a corner about a block or so down the street from Etna Road Elementary School. She rehearsed what she'd say. Yesterday, between drinks, she spent countless hours looking for unsolved child murders in Missouri. One came up from thirteen years ago when a nine-year-old boy was found along the interstate in Springfield. He had been raped and strangled. There were no suspects. No witnesses. No leads. While it could have been a coincidence, Kellie wanted to be sure. Since Mr. Barnes wouldn't help her, she'd decided to take matters into her own hands and see if she could get Mrs. Ackerman to give her additional information about her son. Once Kellie got what she needed, she'd contact Mr. Barnes. If she did so now, she'd be lectured about not getting involved and how she needed to get help for her "drinking problem."

After taking several deep breaths, Kellie found herself drinking more courage from the little flask that she kept in her purse. She *didn't* have a problem. The liquor burned her throat on the way down. After the sting settled, she blew out one long sigh, exited the car, and headed up the Ackermans' driveway.

The screen door was open and a young girl—ten or so—was standing in the living room playing some kind of dancing video on her game system. Kellie knocked lightly, not wanting to scare the girl.

"Yeah?" she said, looking up but not moving from her spot.

"Hi. I'm looking for Paul Ackerman."

"Dad!" the girl yelled. "Some lady is here asking about Great-Grandpa." When no one responded, the girl took off around a corner without saying anything. Moments later, she returned with a man Kellie assumed was her father.

"Can I help you?"

Kellie swallowed, looking at the man. Recalling the age-enhanced photo in the file she'd received from Mr. Barnes. Besides the pinched nose and dark hair, he didn't look much like the sketch or the photo. She wondered if she was on the verge of accusing an innocent man as she'd done many times in the past, but the steady flow of alcohol that day caused boldness to shoot through her veins. She was already here. Why not let this confrontation run its course?

"Lady," the man said, "something I can do for you?"

His curt tone deflated her confidence a bit. "Um . . ." *Man, did she need that flask right about now.* "I'm looking for Paul, um, Paul Ackerman."

He gave her a weird look. "And you are . . . ?"

"I'm, um, Kellie. My name is Kellie."

"Honey, I'll be back. I need to pick up your grandmother's prescription," a woman announced as she came around the corner. "Oh, hello," she said upon seeing Kellie, then looked at her husband for an explanation.

"This lady is looking for Grandpa. I don't know why yet. I got as far as learning that her name is Kellie."

His wife looked at him strangely. "*O-kay.*" She turned back to Kellie. "Nice to meet you, dear, but I have an errand to run. Now, if you'll excuse me . . ."

Kellie moved aside so the woman could leave. The young girl had resumed playing her dance game as soon as her dad came to the door. The music seemed louder than it had when Kellie first arrived. Maybe the girl was trying to drown them out. The man watched his wife back out of the driveway in an SUV that Kellie noticed had a Missouri license plate.

"What part of Missouri do you live in?" Kellie asked.

"Excuse me, I don't mean to be offensive, but you reek of alcohol. Are you okay? Can I help you in some way?"

"Don't try to sweet-talk me, mister, and change the subject." Kellie pointed a finger at him. "I asked you a question."

"You ask a lot of questions, but I still don't know why

you're here. Let's start there. Please tell me what you want with my deceased grandfather."

She hadn't thought about the possibility that Mr. Ackerman was no longer living or the fact that if he were still alive, he'd be afflicted with Alzheimer's. "Oh, I didn't know," Kellie responded, wanting to kick herself for not thinking things through thoroughly before coming.

"Interesting . . ." He opened the screen door and stepped in front of her. Kellie moved back a few steps to create extra distance. "He's actually been dead about a year. Not that it's your business, but my wife and I are here to help my grandmother pack up and move to Missouri with us."

"Is your father available? Maybe I can speak with him . . . or perhaps your grandmother?"

He smirked. "My, my, you seem to want to talk to everyone in my family but me. I'm Mason, by the way." He held out his hand, though Kellie refused to shake it. "My grandmother isn't up to speaking at the moment. I hate to be the bearer of bad news, but I'm the only male Ackerman still alive. My dad and brother died many years ago in a car accident. You're pretty much stuck speaking with me, but I have to tell you that I'm about three seconds from calling the police. Your instability is concerning me."

The last thing Kellie needed was another run-in with the Whitehall PD, but her liquid courage fueled her and she found herself confronting him. "Don't threaten to call the police on me. I should be calling them on you! I know who you are."

"Well, of course you do. I just told you my name."

"I know what you did to my brother twenty years ago. I was there." She took pleasure from seeing his smugness fade. "I also know what you did to Mark Jackson last week and a little boy named Ian Valtrose in Missouri. I'm sure there are others."

Mason narrowed his eyes. "Lady, I don't know what you *think* you know, but if I were you, I'd be careful about making such accusations. Someone is liable to get hurt." He looked back at his daughter who was dancing away. "Besides . . ." he turned to Kellie with renewed arrogance, "if there was proof of a connection with any of these people you mentioned, the police would be here, not you. So, Kellie, if that's really your name, I think it's best if you leave now. You obviously have some other issues and I have lost interest in this conversation. You have until the count of ten to get off my grandmother's property or I *will* call the police." He pulled his cell phone from his pocket.

As Mason began counting, Kellie took a step backward, afraid to turn away from him in case he was indeed a killer. Even if he was, it wasn't likely that the man would harm her in front of his daughter, but she didn't want to take any chances. If he was the killer, he had snatched at least three boys from parks in broad daylight. She was sure he'd had help in Jeffrey's case. Maybe his brother? If what Mason said about his brother and father being dead was true, then his brother could never be questioned.

When Kellie reached the edge of the driveway, Mason was on number seven. She felt she was a safe enough distance away from him that she could turn around and get to her car. Once inside, she felt foolish. That man wasn't her brother's killer. She owed him a great deal of gratitude for entertaining her for as long as he had, and for saving her from another embarrassing arrest. Kellie would not tell Mr. Barnes about this incident under any circumstances. She would also send Mason an apology card like she'd done the others. No longer angry, but ashamed, Kellie looked up at Mason one last time, smiling apologetically. He smiled in return, and then gave her the finger, just as her brother's killer had done twenty years earlier.

When Kellie was safely in her own driveway, she pulled out the flask and took several swigs, some of the liquor spilling because she was shaking so much. Back inside the house, she decided that the best thing to do would be to call Mr. Barnes immediately . . . after she poured a drink.

"*This is Tim. Please leave your name, number, and a brief message after the beep. I will return your call as soon as possible.*" This was the third time Kellie had called Mr. Barnes that evening since her confrontation with Mason Ackerman, but now she couldn't leave a message because the voice mail was full.

"Ugh!" she screamed, wanting to throw the phone. Instead, she took another drink and kept trying. Eventually, she fell asleep.

A few hours later, she woke up and saw she'd missed a call from Mr. Barnes. She played his message.

"*Hey, Kellie, I see you've been trying to reach me. I won't be available for the rest of the evening, so I'll give you a call tomorrow. I hope everything is okay.*"

"No! Everything is not okay!" she yelled in response. Frustrated, Kellie had no choice but to accept the fact that she'd have to speak with him tomorrow. She was going to call him first thing in the morning. It was getting late and she needed to sleep off this lingering headache brought on by the stress of today's events. As she climbed into bed, she thought about how she hadn't bought into the whole religious thing since she was a child. Psalm 23:4 was probably the only Scripture she really knew, and that's because it was on her wall. Nevertheless, she found herself praying aloud. "God, Mason

Ackerman killed my brother and those other two boys. I know it. Please don't let him get away with this."

She thought of something someone said on one of the murder mystery shows she watched. A man had spent thirteen years locked up for a crime he didn't commit. DNA evidence eventually freed him. When asked if he was angry about his wrongful imprisonment, the guy said, "No." He believed that prison had been the best thing for him. Although he didn't commit the crime for which he had been accused, the guy noted that he was headed down a destructive path and likely would have ended up incarcerated anyhow. "In the darkest season of my life, I found light," the man stated, referring to his salvation.

At the time, Kellie was astonished by the depth of his faith. At one point, her parents had professed to be Christians, but somehow both lost their way. *Why didn't their faith sustain them?* she wondered. As a child, Kellie, too, at one time was a believer, but life had choked any potential that her childlike faith had of growing. Like the man in the documentary, she had been imprisoned, albeit metaphorically, for a crime she hadn't committed. Maybe she, too, could find light amid such a dark life story. She wanted to give it a shot. As she settled into bed, she looked at the two bottles on her nightstand. Oddly, despite all the craziness of the day and the certainty that Mason Ackerman was a killer, Kellie had a sense of peace. At least for the moment, she didn't need any help drifting off to sleep.

One one thousand, two one thousand, three one thousand—

Kellie was abruptly awakened. Something was wrong. She couldn't breathe. Pain shot through her body as she gasped for air. Someone was choking her. She tried to move her arms, but her assailant had them pinned underneath his body and he was literally squeezing the life out of her. As her eyes adjusted to the darkness, she saw the outline of her attacker's face. It was Mason Ackerman.

How did he know where to find me? As quickly as the question sprang up, she devised a likely answer. When she confronted him, she said that Jeffrey was her brother and she had foolishly given him her real name. Whitehall was so small that he could have found her address with the simplest of Internet searches. Maybe he even drove around the community and saw her car in the driveway. It didn't matter. He was here now, strangling her like he'd done to Jeffrey, Mark Jackson, the boy in Missouri, and who knows how many others.

Kellie looked past the killer to the inscription on her wall. Though Mason was taking her life, she was not afraid. She was at peace, only disappointed that she hadn't been able to connect with Mr. Barnes. She prayed that he would not give up until he found her killer. Mason Ackerman needed to be stopped. She hoped that she would be his last victim.

As Kellie sank further and further from consciousness, she saw the malevolent look in Mason's eyes. She had only one final thought as she faded away. *Yea, though I walk through the valley of the shadow of death, I will fear no evil.*

ALL THAT BURNS THE MIND

BY JULIA KELLER

Ohio State University

I don't think about him much anymore. When I do, his face only stays with me for a few seconds. A brief flash, a moment of uncomfortable reminiscence, and then—*whoosh*, he's gone again. These days, I only remember Greg Barris when, say, I'm sitting in traffic, or when I'm early for a dentist appointment and the magazines in the waiting room all seem to be six-year-old copies of *Golf Digest*.

Let's put it this way: I don't obsess. Perhaps I should, given all that happened, but I don't. I'm not the obsessing type.

My wife often complains about that very lack in me—about my inability to be carried away by anything, be it love or hate or exhilaration or curiosity. She met me several years after I'd left Ohio State, and my emotional poise has always baffled her. Sometimes, albeit briefly, it even seems to enrage her, but then she realizes the unfairness of that—it's an inborn trait, she believes, something I can't control—and she backs off.

The truth is, my detachment is willed. It's purely strategic. It's protection. One slip, one stumble, and everything falls away—the meticulously constructed edifice of my life, that seamless, misleading veneer. One unguarded moment and I plunge into the whirlpool of the past, the churning maelstrom that would instantly tear me to pieces.

Not because of guilt—God no. Because of the wasted effort,

the attempt to save something that didn't end up mattering in the least. The infuriatingly pointless risk.

I met Melissa eight years ago, on the first day of the first class I taught at Ohio State. Freshman English. Room 324, Denney Hall. Mondays, Wednesdays, and Fridays at ten a.m.

Denney was undoubtedly the ugliest structure on the entire campus, a dull, stolid lump that put one in mind of an armor-clad, square-cornered meatloaf. Meatloaf is the Great Midwestern go-to meal, which is why it's the perfect metaphor here—because Ohio State is the Great Midwestern go-to school, an ideal destination for that massive blur of eighteen-year-olds who have yet to reveal any distinguishing characteristics. The eggheads go to Michigan or Northwestern. The cheeseheads go to Wisconsin. The math brainiacs, the kids who wind up as engineers entrusted with the construction of safe bridges and sturdy roads and reliable municipal sewage treatment plants, go to Purdue. The party boys and girls, the frat guys and sorority types, the ones who are as strenuously devoted to the chore of staying drunk, stoned, and stupefied by orgasms during all four years of their college experience as Purdue students are to calculating angles and stress loads, go to Michigan State. The leftovers go to places like Indiana and Illinois and Penn State.

But Ohio State is the quintessential Midwestern institution. It's big and bland and wholesome, and it feels as if it were pried out of a baking dish and plopped onto that land-grant largesse just as the aforementioned meatloaf is offloaded onto a serving platter. Its edges are crispy and browned. Its center is soft and mealy.

I was always struck by the perverse irony of Denney Hall. Think of it: a building that houses the most giddily romantic and ludicrously impractical of academic disciplines—English literature—was itself ordinary and serviceable and pedestrian. Perhaps the university planners were afraid that if they located literary studies in a place more in keeping with its higgledy-piggledy, eccentric nature—if its headquarters were, say, a magnificently daffy edifice with flying buttresses and wild flourishes of finials and leering gargoyles, a concoction more at home at Hogwarts than the Big Ten—the cumulative enchantment would have been too much for that deliberately vapid campus to bear. The whole building might've flown off like an untethered balloon in a sudden updraft, bound for the sparkling ramparts of other, grander dimensions.

As it was, there was no danger of any dimension-slipping. And no sparkles. Denney Hall wasn't like that. It was rooted firmly in the good brown soil of the middlebrow Midwest. The subject matter with which its denizens were forced to grapple might be Wordsworth and Woolf, and Shakespeare and Shelley, and Cather and Plath, but—based on Denney's unrepentant blandness—it could just as easily have been ceramic engineering.

The students automatically called me "professor," but I wasn't one. Not officially. I was a graduate student, pursuing a doctoral degree in English literature, and I was also a TA—a teaching associate, a position enabling a species of temporary employment so catastrophically underpaid that it was barely distinguishable from unemployment. Each TA was assigned to teach a section of freshman English, so as to spare tenured professors the gruesome, soul-pummeling duty of dealing with mush-brained undergraduates.

As I surveyed my class on that first day, I spotted the young man I'd come later to learn was Greg Barris. Last row, last seat on the left.

He chose that spot, he was to tell me during our first private conversation, in order to render himself fractionally less likely to be called upon to answer a question. The problem wasn't his inability to answer—he was quite brilliant—but his shyness, which was pathologically intense. He hated being looked at. It made him blush and tremble.

Greg's reluctance to be scrutinized was understandable. For he was—how to put this politely?—ugly. Spectacularly, surpassingly unattractive. To begin with, he was tall and skinny, a vertical worm. His face—narrow, sallow, and sunken—was starred with furious-looking pimples that, like tiny versions of Vesuvius, seemed to have erupted just seconds before, spewing pus that had instantly cooled and crusted. His nose was a greasy sack punctured by two overlarge and mismatched nostrils. His hair was a whitish squiggle of frizz. He had pig's eyes—small and pink. And no makeover could have rectified the situation. Nature itself had done him in.

Just seconds after I first noticed Greg, I saw the woman I would come to know as Melissa Thalberg. Two rows in front of him, in the middle.

She was an extraordinarily beautiful young woman. Allow me a moment of rhetorical rhapsody: her copious blond hair flounced in golden luxuriance across her petite shoulders, her breasts pushed with naughty abandon against her tight T-shirt, and her ass—oh my Jesus!—moved inside her snug jeans like two exquisite little baubles that constantly invited a delicate and protracted caress, a fancy that occurred to me a few minutes later as I watched her exit that first class, and I was granted an unobstructed view of her angelic bottom.

Thus it was that within the opening minutes of the very first class I ever taught, the two extremes of human physiognomic destiny presented themselves for my inspection: one repugnant, one irresistible.

I began my lecture.

"*Had we but world enough and time, This coyness, lady, were no crime.* Anybody know who wrote that?"

Silence. Of course nobody knew. They were freshmen, and they'd never heard of Andrew Marvell, much less possessed the ability to recognize a line from one of his poems.

"My name's Jason Winfield, by the way," I continued. I had a short piece of chalk in my right hand, and I jiggled it in my cupped palm, the way people do with spare change when they're standing and chatting. I wanted to seem nonchalant. Confident. Self-assured. I was wearing hiking boots, chinos, and a rumpled V-neck sweater—the unofficial uniform (autumn edition) of the Hip Professor. I was only a few years older than they were—twenty-five to their eighteen or nineteen. "And this is freshman English."

There was no alteration in the successive rows of bored expressions, not so much as a ripple of even the mildest, most transient interest. Indeed, I was aware of a replication of slack jaws across the rows; the class reminded me of a roomful of reptiles who had recently unhinged their jaws in order to swallow rodents and other small prey.

A tentative hand was lifted. First row, fourth from the left. A young man.

"Yes?"

"Yeah—uh—you gonna keep us the whole time today? I mean, sometimes—on the first day and all—I heard that we don't, like, have a regular class. We get to go early. So I wondered. Because that's what I heard." Several other students nodded, backing up his assertion.

Not even a full minute into the semester and they were already trying to limit their exposure to potentially life-enhancing literature.

"We'll see," I replied.

The interlocutor sank back in his seat like a deflated soufflé, disappointed that I hadn't automatically promised a shortened class. Truth was, today's session would indeed be brief; there was little to do beyond calling the roll, passing out the syllabus, making the assignment for the next class. But I'd be damned if I was going to reward the galling effrontery of First-Row-and-Fourth-from-the-Left.

"The writer," I went on, "was Andrew Marvell." A few of the students dutifully began writing in their notebooks. That pleased me. "He was a British poet. He lived from 1621 to 1678. Those are the first lines of his most famous poem. It's called 'To His Coy Mistress.' So—what do you think he was getting at when he wrote that?"

Silence. Well, not *total* silence: there was a bit of foot-shuffling, a few random coughs. Somebody cracked a knuckle.

"Anybody want to take a guess?"

No one did. They looked bored, but I was not dismayed. In short order, I knew, they would snap to attention. They would see how cool I was. How unlike the stuffy old English professor they'd thought they would be having this semester, the tweed-wrapped, crinkle-skinned, half-deaf dinosaur they were expecting.

I offered the class my most fetching grin: "He's trying to get a woman into bed." Startled laughter. I reveled in it. "Yeah," I shamelessly hammed it up, "he's, like, *Look here, sweet cheeks. Life's short. Don't play hard to get. C'mon—let's do this. Whaddaya say?*"

More laughter. They were paying attention *now*, by God!

"Marvell did that in a lot of his poems. Listen to this one. It's called 'The Match.'" I cleared my throat in a portentous, here-comes-the-next-Gettysburg-Address sort of way, mocking my own solemnity, and that drew a decent, if slightly less hearty, amount of laughter. I recited: *"But likeness soon together drew, What she did separate lay; Of which one perfect Beauty grew, And that was Celia.* And a few verses later, here we go: *He kept the several Cells repleat, With Nitre thrice refin'd; The Naptha's and the Sulphurs heat, And all that burns the Mind."*

They were confused. Where was the sex part?

"Trust me," I said. I talked out of the side of my mouth, like a bookie offering private advice on a canny bet: "He's horny as hell." The laughter returned to its original level. *I'm a friggin' genius*, I thought. *They love me.* "So you're asking yourself what any of this has to do with freshman English. Well—lots. Words can be manipulated. Shaped to whatever purpose we wish. Marvell's poems are great examples of that." Time to bring it all home: "In this class, we'll be using words to explore who we are, what we want, and why we do what we do. So for our first assignment, I want you to write an essay about a significant moment in your life. Three pages, double-spaced. Printed out on one side of the page only. Due Wednesday. Any questions?"

Silence. A few of the gaping jaws had closed, anticipating the end of class and release from benign captivity.

"If you're having any problems with your essay," I added, "my office is right here in Denney Hall. Office hours are on the syllabus."

I set the chalk in the small aluminum tray that ran the length of the blackboard. I dusted off my palms.

"See you Wednesday."

* * *

By the time I met my wife Claire, my teaching days were long over.

For three years after obtaining my PhD I'd searched—far and wide, as the saying goes, and with increasing despair—for a permanent academic position. Finally, I had to give up. I took a job in the "communications" department of an insurance company in downtown Columbus. Claire sat in the next cubicle.

For her, "communications" did not need to be sneeringly quarantined by quotation marks. She was a few years younger than me, and she'd actually majored in that subject. Corporate communications was what she'd always wanted to do: writing press releases; advising titans of industry on precisely how to phrase their slippery obfuscations and creative denials (my words, not Claire's); responding to public crises with reassuring blather about honesty and transparency. For her, communications did not represent the abject insult that it did for me—because she, unlike me, had never yearned to live an entirely different kind of life. A life of literary scholarship and university teaching. A life spent in quiet study and deep reflection, surrounded by towering stacks of leather-bound books brimming with the world's wisdom and beauty.

Well, screw that.

At virtually the same moment that I received my doctoral degree from Ohio State, the bottom dropped out of the job market. My fellow TAs and I applied to every university that held out even a tiny sprig of hope of potential employment. We humbled ourselves, writing cover letters that were cringingly obsequious: *Dear Madam Chairperson—It has been my dearest lifelong wish to teach at South Bumfuck University in Bumfuck, Nowheresville.*

But nothing worked. Not even crass groveling.

Frankly, I was damned lucky to get the communications job. Otherwise, the next step for me would have been learning how to ask, "Do you want fries with that?" dozens of times per shift without putting a bitter little snarl at the end of the query.

Claire quit her job a few years ago to raise the kids. Twin girls, Rebecca and Samantha. Trust me: it's exceedingly difficult to get by these days on a single paycheck. We live in a scruffy Columbus neighborhood of crumbling homes and patchy lawns—a situation which is, you'll concede, rather ironic. When you compromise on your dreams as profoundly as I did, when you do things you never thought you'd do—naturally you expect to receive a bit more in the bargain as recompense.

During my courtship of Claire, I didn't tell her right away that I'd known Greg Barris. His name was still remembered in Columbus, especially because of what happened before the trial even started. I finally mentioned it on our third date. And she was stunned.

"He was in your *class*? You were his *teacher*?"

"Yeah."

I'd taken her to a Clippers game on a late-summer evening. Because rain was in the forecast, Huntington Park was nearly deserted. Something made me decide to bring up his name. When I did, she stared at me, her brown eyes unblinking, her mouth open a trifle wider than was strictly advantageous to her appearance. Claire is attractive. I mean, she's no Melissa—but let's put it this way: I'm not embarrassed at having ended up with her.

"What was he like?" she pressed me. "I mean—was there any hint that . . . ?" She let her voice trail off.

"That he was a murderer? Um—no."

A nervous laugh. "Right. I get that." She shivered. "I followed that case. Gave me the creeps." She frowned. "Wait. Your name wasn't in any of the news stories."

"I struck a deal with the cops. They kept me out of it."

"What a monster." She shivered again. "Strangling her that way. And leaving her in her dorm room for the roommate to find." She shook her head. "And you *knew* him."

"Not for long. Just a couple of months. Then he was gone. Arrested. It all happened pretty quick."

"The girlfriend's name. I can't remember. Was it Mindy something? Or Mariah?"

I waited, pretending to rack my brain. "Melissa."

"That's it. Melissa."

"She was in my class too. That's where they met."

"*Jesus.*" A frown. "I wonder how her parents ever came to terms with her death. She was—what, eighteen? Nineteen? Her whole life was ahead of her."

"Everybody's whole life is ahead of them." I snapped the words. "Where else would it be—behind them?"

Claire gave me a look.

"I keep forgetting," she said.

"What—the fact that I was an English professor? And that the precise use of language is important to me?"

"No. The fact that you can be a jerk sometimes."

But she ended up marrying me, which means that she could do the compromise thing too.

The seduction was relatively simple.

Melissa came to my office the day after that introductory class, seeking help with her essay. She breezed in with the regal confidence that pretty girls all seem to possess as their birthright, and she greeted me with a haughty little nod.

Without further explanation, she handed me what turned out to be the rough draft of her essay.

She perched herself on the edge of the chair across from my desk. That desk was a chunky wooden one—depressingly similar to the half dozen other chunky wooden desks surrounding it—in a corner of the large square room. TAs were not granted the privilege of individual offices. We, along with our desks, were crammed like hogs in a pen into a single room that branched off one of Denney Hall's endless, boring corridors.

It was shortly after six p.m. and the office, for a change, was empty. I read the draft carefully. At one point I looked up, and caught her just as she was moistening her plump upper lip with the tip of her tiny pink tongue. The sight inflamed me. With that one small gesture, she unraveled any defenses I might have mustered to resist her.

Reluctantly I returned my eyes to the essay. I finished reading. I placed it on the desk, and then I sat back and steepled my fingertips in my best professorial fashion.

"So what do you think?" she asked. Her voice had a sort of purr to it, a serrated, sexy edge.

"I think," I replied, "that we should go get a drink. We can discuss your work in more detail. But for now—it's good, Ms. Thalberg. It's really, really good. I'm quite impressed."

An hour later, having hurriedly departed from one of those dark, ubiquitous bars along High Street after only a few sips of our drinks (Tanqueray and tonic for me, Bud Light for her), we stood facing each other in the living room of my small, squalid, third-floor apartment on East Eleventh Avenue. Our shirts were the first items to go, flung aside, landing wherever. Quickly and deftly, I lifted the strap of her bra from her right shoulder, and then I lifted the other strap from her left, while she unbuckled my belt. Our kisses had escalated from tender and experimental to tumultuous.

I reached around her to unfasten her bra, whereupon her breasts tumbled toward me as if they'd been waiting impatiently to do just that. I murmured something vaguely Marvellian, kissing her as she moaned appropriately.

I knew very well that intimate relationships between teachers and students were forbidden, but—*please*. If the administration didn't want TAs to partake of the delicacies on offer, then it should have paid us a decent wage. As it was, sex with students was an excellent way to make up for the shortfall in our salaries. I put it in the same category as tuition reimbursement: something to paper over the gap. It was nobody's business but mine.

And so that was how my relationship with Melissa Thalberg began—in thunder and chaos and the mad fury of desire. The excitement was supplied by the risk I was taking: if the dean found out, I'd lose my job.

Yet even that danger was not enough to keep it interesting. Within mere weeks our relationship had devolved (at least for me) into the staleness and sourness that wait at the end of all human interactions. Sensing my disillusionment, Melissa became petulant, demanding. She asked me—after one of our increasingly dreary couplings—why I never read poetry aloud to her anymore. My coy mistress had become a whiny bore.

Oh—and what of her essay, the rough draft of which I praised so lavishly during her first visit to my office?

It was shit. Pure drivel.

But you'd already guessed that, hadn't you?

A month and a half into the semester, Melissa had officially become a problem. Her presence in my life—and in my apartment—meant I was getting very little work done on my dissertation ("Andrew Marvell and the Politics of Subterfuge: An Explication of 'To His Coy Mistress' as a Ruminative Rebuke of Oliver Cromwell's Ecclesiastical Ambitions"). And I missed it. I was eager to prove my thesis that Marvell employed words to slyly bend people to his will, manipulating them with style and verve instead of crude force. Any bully could make somebody do something they didn't want to do, using threats and fisticuffs; it took an artist, a poet, to get his way by means of eloquence and wit.

On the weekends, Melissa refused to return to her dorm room. She would only go there if I accompanied her, and that could only happen if her roommate, Paula Something-or-Other, was out of town. I had to remain hidden from other students in the dorm too, for obvious reasons, which is why we spent far more time at my place than hers. If someone *did* spot us together, the fact that I could, in the right light, pass for an undergraduate definitely worked to our benefit.

When her roommate inquired about her frequent overnight absences, Melissa would simply raise an eyebrow and smile lasciviously. She giggled when she told me that.

After we made love, she enjoyed traipsing around my apartment naked and unkempt, her hair a tattered, flyaway mess on account of her habit of squirming determinedly amid the bedsheets while issuing forth kittenish cries of delight that might very well have been feigned. I didn't care anymore about their authenticity. All I cared about now, frankly, was that she not plop herself down on my sofa during her nude postcoital prowls; stains were notoriously difficult to remove from the cheap fabric.

Worse still, her essays never improved. The topics she chose to write about were silly. Her dangling modifiers were downright comical. Sentence fragments and comma splices and clichés littered the pages. But I doggedly kept on praising her work—in the beginning because that praise always put her in a pliable mood. Now it was too late to fix things, too late to go back and state the truth: *You're a lousy writer*.

And then there was Greg Barris.

Intelligence-wise, as well as appearance-wise, he was the anti-Melissa. His sentences sparkled. His metaphors were clever and illuminating. His essays were utterly brilliant. Scintillatingly original.

From his work I learned about his background: blinkered childhood in some grubby Cleveland suburb; raised by a single father whose behavior toward Greg bounced between neglectful and abusive; and then—Oh Happy Day—a full scholarship to Ohio State, based on standardized test scores so stratospherically high that they induced a double-take, and on a truly incandescent talent that foretold of great things to come, now that he'd snapped the shackles of his past.

Shortly before Thanksgiving break, I asked Greg to come to my office. He didn't really require a specific invitation; he usually stopped by anyway, with some frequency, to talk about his literary ambitions.

But this time, I needed to make sure he came. I selected an hour when my fellow TAs were unlikely to be present.

"Hey, Professor," Greg said. He unhooked the overstuffed backpack from his shoulder and let it clunk on the floor. He wriggled his bony backside into the chair across from my desk. As always, he looked as if he'd gone years without a meal. He resembled a wire sculpture in an avant-garde museum, all joint and sinew and sharp right angles.

"Hey," I replied. "So I read your outline for your next essay. It's fine, and you can go ahead and write that one. But in the meantime, I have another idea for you to consider."

Unbeknownst to Greg, his arrival had interrupted my reverie about a savage argument I'd had with Melissa that morning in my apartment. I had tried to break up with her. My announcement to that effect was not met with the calm maturity and philosophical acceptance for which I had hoped.

In fact, she'd erupted in a wild fury. First, she flung the contents of her bowl of Fruity Pebbles at me. Then she stood up. I stood up too. She rushed forward, doing a tom-tom with her fists against my chest—my T-shirt was sopping with milk and cereal, so her blows produced little smacking sounds, like a kid tromping through a puddle—while she repeated the phrase, "You fucking fucker," her verbal speech being just as unimaginative as the written variety. She threatened to go to the dean and expose our relationship.

I finally managed to snatch her fists, gaze deeply and soulfully into her eyes, and gently intone, "I'm so, *so* sorry. I love you, honey. I don't really want to break up. I was just—just scared. Of how much I'm in love with you." She accepted my apology with a triumphant little sniffle.

We wouldn't be able to get together that night—she had an eight a.m. class the next morning—but we could, I proposed, have a few drinks in that blessedly dark bar, the scene of our first hurried kiss.

Now here was Greg, his face twisted into a puzzled frown, perplexed by what I'd said about his essay.

I double-tapped my temple with an index finger. "Let's really test our imaginations. Let's try something—something *daring*. Let's shift the narrative voice. Write from a place of danger. We'll do it together."

He leaned forward, ravenous for just this kind of collaboration. He had a superb mind and a colossal, astonishing talent.

But he didn't have the confidence to go with his gifts. He didn't have any friends, he'd told me, and he spent his time away from his classes alone. Always, always alone.

"*Details*, Greg," I declared. "Details are what make a great piece of writing. Gooey abstractions are worthless."

"Right. I get that." His eager, earnest, ugly face looked even redder and more pimple-ridged than usual.

"And mushy generalities are a positive menace."

"Right. Right." He was nodding emphatically now. The frizzle of hair wavered and shifted.

"You've got to be specific."

"Yes." More nodding, more frizzle-shifting.

"So grab that laptop out of your backpack," I said, with mounting enthusiasm, "and scoot your chair around here. I think we're going to make a great team."

When we'd finished and I'd printed out his essay, I asked him if I could keep it for a few days. At some point, I said, I might like to share it with the other students in the class. Show them how it's done.

That pleased him. I could tell. His little pink eyes glittered with pride and satisfaction.

At approximately three thirty a.m. the next morning, Melissa's roommate, returning from a night of revelry, stumbled in through the perpetually unlocked door of their dorm room on the tenth floor of Taylor Tower. Paula Purvis, as was her habit, didn't turn on the light. But she noticed, in the velvety darkness, a lump on the floor jammed up next to Melissa's bed.

At first she assumed it was a pile of dirty laundry, a frequent feature in the disheveled room. But the shape—long and low, with a bump at one end—made her move a little closer. After a cursory toe-probe brought no response, she leaned over.

What she discovered in her subsequent examination was enough to provoke a series of short sharp screams and a geyser of projectile vomiting from the hapless Paula. Even in the darkness, she could tell what it was.

That afternoon, Detective Dan Runyon of the Columbus Division of Police relayed the essence of Paula's ordeal to me. He'd come to my office to give me the shocking news, news that had yet to be made public:

Melissa Thalberg was dead. She had been found in her dorm room, the victim of what looked to be manual strangulation. No immediate suspects. The Columbus cops were assisting the campus police with the investigation.

"Oh my God," I murmured. "She wasn't in class this morning. But with freshmen, absences are pretty typical, so I didn't think . . . I never imagined . . ." I couldn't go on.

Runyon allowed me a moment to compose myself. He was a hulking man, not obese but well on his way, in a not-new gray suit. He was a walking cliché, a detective from a 1940s crime film, endowed with a gravelly voice and a head the approximate size and color of a cinder block. He'd turned down my offer of a chair. Instead he stood in front of my desk the same way my students did, with his meaty hands dangling at his sides, and explained that he was here because they were contacting all of her professors.

I nodded. I nodded in the way that someone numb with grief would nod: stiffly, slowly.

"She hadn't been . . . ?" I let the sentence trail off. He'd understand what I was asking.

"No. No evidence of sexual assault."

"Thank God."

"We're talking to everybody who knew her, no matter how slightly," Runyon went on. "Teachers, classmates, friends, whatever. Is there anything—anything at all—that you think might help us find out who did this? Something she said? Another student she argued with?"

I waited. I took a long, deep, solemn breath. I looked down at the desktop. My attitude could have been captioned: *He's holding something back.*

"Professor?"

I made no reply.

"Professor?" he repeated.

"I—I really can't."

His voice turned harsh in a hurry. "This is a homicide investigation, sir."

I waited. And then I pulled open the top right-hand drawer of my desk. I reached inside. With a great show of reluctance, I handed him a three-page, double-spaced document. It had been there since Greg's departure the day before.

"What's this?" he said.

"It's an essay I was given this morning by a student who—how can I put this?—had a serious crush on Melissa Thalberg. It's been obvious since the start of the semester. Of course, she rejected him completely. She was *way* out of his league." Sad frown. My pain was clear. "Greg is a talented writer. He sometimes—well, he sometimes shows off for me. I'm his teacher and he wants my approval. That's the only way I can explain why he stuck around after class and handed it to me. He told me it was fictional, but—but it's more than a little disturbing. And given the news about what happened to that poor young woman, I feel I have to . . ." I dropped my face into my cupped hands, clearly overcome with emotion.

* * *

A week after his arraignment, Greg Barris hung himself in his jail cell. Hopeless people tend to do that sort of thing.

The claim of innocence that he'd frantically related to his public defender was based upon a fantastical scenario: His English professor, he said, had persuaded him to concoct a murder scheme, written in the voice of a slickly amoral killer. It wasn't a confession of what he'd done; it was a blueprint for what a killer *might* do.

It was all just a literary exercise.

Greg insisted that he'd barely noticed Melissa Thalberg. Nor exchanged so much as a single word with her. Nor ever set foot inside Taylor Tower. The public defender—to be fair, she was overworked and underpaid—dismissed his bizarre story out of hand, never bothering to check tedious details such as the date stamp for the essay on Greg's computer, which would have proven that it was written before the murder. And Greg was too stunned, too upset, too incoherent with desperation, to suggest such a thing himself.

He had no alibi. No one to vouch for him.

Damningly, the details in his essay lined up perfectly with the circumstances of Melissa's death, even though her name was never mentioned:

> *I followed her back to her dorm room. I slipped into the front entrance behind her, so as to leave no record of an additional key-card entry. I wore gloves, of course. She'd had a lot to drink, and so subduing her was easy. I strangled her with the red power cord of her laptop, looping it around her throat four times. Then I wrapped her body in the blanket from her bed—it was olive green, with little tassels along the hem. I left her on the floor next to the bed. Oh—and before I wrapped her up, I grabbed a Sharpie*

from her desktop and wrote on her chest in all caps: SLUT.
Because that's what she was.

Essential facts of the case had been kept confidential by the police: Melissa's blood alcohol level was .15. The power cord for her laptop was red—not black, not tan, not white, but red. It had been wound around her neck exactly four times. Her bedspread was olive green, with tassels along the hem. And the word written on her chest with the black Sharpie was *SLUT.*

In all caps.

Oh, those damning details. Greg's essay was chock-full of them, brimming with information that only someone who'd been in that dorm room could've known: the precise configuration of the IKEA shelving. The concert posters on the wall—Drake and Taylor Swift. And the position of the body inside the bedspread: she was lying on her right side, arms crossed. One shoe on, one off. The shoes were a pair of knock-off Jimmy Choo pumps. Teal, as it happened.

It was damned difficult to get that shoe off her foot, especially with rigor rapidly setting in. But Greg had been carefully nudged toward including the detail, and it was, I thought, a nice touch.

"The kid was guilty as hell," Runyon declared. "I mean, come on—if he didn't do it, where'd he get all the specifics?"

The detective had stopped by my office again, the day after Greg's suicide, to make sure I was okay. He didn't want me to blame myself.

I shook my head. I was clearly still troubled. Haltingly, I said, "That essay—giving it to me—must've been a cry for help. If only I'd been able to talk to him ahead of time or—"

"He was way past anybody's help." Runyon's clumsy attempt at reassurance was downright touching.

He had more to say: he wanted me to know that Greg's ludicrous accusations would never be made public. The impulse to blame somebody else, the grasping at straws, was typical behavior, he explained. Entirely predictable.

And then the detective gave me the benefit of his sage wisdom, delivered with just the sort of eloquence I'd expect from a man of his caliber: "People are shit, Professor. No doubt about it."

I think Andrew Marvell would have understood. Scratch that: I *know* he would have. Life is a fleeting thing. Passion is a brand that burns the mind but then quickly cools. And so we commandeer these fragile, glittering scraps—we call them words—to ferry us across the dark rivers of our dreams.

But in the end, of course, everybody drowns.

LONG EARS

BY KHALID MOALIM

North Side

She stirs sugar into tea served by Abdi's youngest son. Hunched over the small round table, she listens to Abdi's explanation for why the mall owner should be more afraid of Allah because then he wouldn't bump their rental fees up. She knows she should encourage the sewing shop owner to follow his dreams to do something else, but she can't afford to lose him. Abdi's a talented wallflower. Her most consistent source of information. What's happening in the community. Who's doing what and where. She relaxes at the smell of incense drifting down the corridor from a newly lit *dabqaad*. Her name is Halima, but she knows most people call her *Dhegaha Dheer*. "Long Ears."

Hearing a sound, she turns and watches with interest as Shuri, hijab loose and jeans tight, walks past with a tall black American man by her side, their fingers interlaced. Dhegaha Dheer sips her tea, rises, and quietly follows the pair down the corridor to the store where Shuri's father works.

Inside the dress shop is Shuri's father, Aafi, on a stepladder using a metal pick stick to ease the strain on his shoulders as he rearranges garments sprawled across the display wall. Some have gold lacing around the waist; others have dazzling silver threads on the bottom half. Aafi is short in frame, but the community sees him as much taller. As a man to go to for advice on family, faith, and culture. Dhegaha Dheer understands that Aafi is a man with grit. It radiates off him, as if you know his skin is worn and calloused before you shake his hand. She watches as Shuri leans over her mother's wheelchair and kisses her on the forehead. Dhegaha Dheer runs her fingers down the purple-striped *guntiino* on the mannequin outside the shop door as she sees a shocked Aafi try to figure out who the man is with his daughter.

"Why are you holding hands?" Aafi says softly.

Shuri tries to respond, but can't seem to find the words. All the determination she walked into the shop with seems to have disappeared.

"Who is he?" Aafi repeats, raising his voice.

"I'm Malcolm. Shuri's fiancé," the black man says.

Shuri finally finds her own voice: "I love him, *Aabo.*"

"You are not marrying this man," Aafi says, tending to his wife, lifting her blouse to examine the feeding tube sticking out from her stomach. Everyone in the mall knows how attentive he is to her every need, how he interprets each groan she makes as hunger, thirst, an ache.

Shuri glances at her mother. "*Hooyo* would want me to marry Malcolm," she says, raising her own voice.

Aafi strides across the shop and slaps Shuri across her face, sending her glasses flying to the floor. Dhegaha Dheer knows he will regret this. Knows that he last hit Shuri when she was six or seven at a refugee camp in Kenya, but stopped because of the horror stories he heard of Child Services in America. Knows of his complaints about the lack of discipline parents are allowed in this country.

Noticing the small gathering of patrons outside his shop, Aafi pushes the door shut. Not wanting word to spread about Shuri. It would tear down his reputation as a well-respected man among the Somali community. He is a trusted businessman driven by his religion, but Dhegaha Dheer knows that at times his faith is muddled by his cultural beliefs.

Dhegaha Dheer inches closer to the door. She can't miss this. There's been a drought of whispers her way lately. Shuri and Malcolm are the oil to restart her rusty rumor mill. She hears Malcolm defending himself as a man of God. Aafi shouting his disapproval that he's not Muslim. Shuri saying something about Hassan, though Dhegaha Dheer can't make out what exactly. A minute later she backs up quickly as Shuri, fire in her eyes, rushes out, Malcolm behind her. Aafi comes to the doorway and watches them without speaking until they disappear out of the mall.

They met only a week into Shuri's job as a receptionist at the Wexner Medical Center at Ohio State. Of course Halima knows this. Many whisper in her ears. There is a reason she is called Dhegaha Dheer.

Shuri clocks in around seven a.m. and goes through her daily shift: change into her scrubs in the locker room, get briefed by the employee she is relieving, tidy up the day-care room, greet some of the long-staying patients in the cancer wing—because she knows they like a hello—then grab herself some coffee before settling at her desk.

It was on a Friday when they met. Her heart rate accelerated, a pool of sweat formed under her hijab.

"*Subax wanaagsan*," Malcolm uttered, greeting Shuri in Somali, with his awkwardly handsome smile. *Good morning.* He's a good-looking doctor. His dreadlocks hang below his shoulders. His face is long, his cheekbones high, his nose wide, and his skin smooth. He extends his hand, wrapping her small sweaty one in his strong grip.

"*Subax wanaagsan*," she stuttered back. This was, she

believed in that moment, the start of her life. Just like any twentysomething college junior, she envisioned the whole thing in a few seconds of wild imagining. The large wedding, the three kids, and the very hot sex—all in a snap of a finger.

They walked back to the cancer wing with coffee. He asked about her studies. Shy at first, she soon bragged about graduating in three years. She went on about how she was now working to save up while taking a gap year before medical school. He was obviously impressed, but also smitten, and didn't seem to mind what must be a decade's difference in their age. They went on their first date that very night, a Somali restaurant he'd been to but she hadn't. That's when she was sure she'd met the right one.

Shuri felt free. So free that she did not care about being seen in public with a man. A black American man. Of course she knew her father would never approve. But her mother . . . If only she could share the freedom she felt with her. But it wasn't to be. Her mother's voice, the one that pushed her toward such freedom, was lost now. Taken by the icy roads that night so many months ago. Roads that caused her parents' car to swerve into oncoming traffic. Roads that left her father with minor scratches on the forehead but her mother silent, sitting in a wheelchair with thick wheels to accommodate her heavyset body. Eating and breathing through tubes.

Dhegaha Dheer is walking back to her table with her tea when she sees Hassan passing Abdi's sewing shop. He's short but wiry, loud but awkwardly charming. His father and Aafi were childhood best friends, to the point where Hassan was practically a cousin to Shuri. Dhegaha Dheer signals to Hassan, whispers to him that Shuri brought a black American man to her father. She points to the door and watches as

Hassan chases after the couple. Dhegaha Dheer follows, observing through the glass door as Hassan faces the woman he was promised in marriage. Watches Hassan extend his hand to Malcolm. Their grip is everlastingly competitive. One suffocating squeeze after another. The obvious strong hand belongs to Malcolm, but it is not enough for Hassan to stand down. Dhegaha Dheer knows Hassan won't choose to believe what she's told him about Shuri and Malcolm, because everyone knows he's the one Shuri is to marry. Aafi told him so. At family gatherings and in the mall and at the masjid.

"You guys must be classmates," she hears Hassan say.

"We're not, actually."

"Are you her professor?"

"He's my fiancé," Shuri says, pulling Malcolm away.

When Hassan reenters the mall, Dhegaha Dheer tells him to talk to Aafi because there must be an explanation. Something must be done. Otherwise the family will be shame-ridden, himself included.

"But she doesn't want me," Hassan says.

"She doesn't know she wants you. There's a difference."

"Not that I see."

"You have plans for your barbershop. The car you're going to buy."

"Yes . . ."

"And perhaps there's something about the black American she doesn't see yet."

"Like what?"

"You need to have patience, Hassan."

Many whisper to Dhegaha Dheer. Even Shuri, too innocent to see the dangers in such confidences. But too eager to tell someone of the taboos she is smashing with Malcolm. Of the way, later that evening, the couple took turns pleasing one another in Shuri's bed. How Malcolm kisses her on the lips, makes his way to her neck, moves his hand down, down to where her legs meet. The pleasure of his weight on top of her, the release that comes to her as they rock atop the gray linen sheets.

They stay in bed, holding each other, half covered, cuddling.

"Another round?" Shuri giggles after a while. "I need to sweat more to fit into this dress for the party."

"Another round? You have no idea," Malcolm says, hand trailing down her leg. "But there's something I need to figure out first."

"What?" she asks nervously.

"Your father. What's his problem with me?"

"Don't mind him. He can't stop me from being with you," Shuri says, raising herself to kiss him.

"No—wait. What is it that he doesn't like about me? I mean, I'm a great guy, aren't I? I'm a doctor. My credit is through the roof."

"It's just that he's from a different culture and a different generation. It's not you, babe."

"Then why keep referring to me as *that black man*?"

Shuri wants to say more, but she's afraid Malcolm won't understand. Won't understand the rigid unexplored relationship between Africans and black Americans. "Because you're not Muslim and, ironically, because you're black," she finally says, her voice shaky.

"Because I'm black? We're all black. How does a black man hate another black man for being black?"

Shuri sits up on the bed. "The thing is . . . for my father, the notion of being black didn't exist for him growing up. It was more about what clan you belong to. So he blames black

Americans for the discrimination and disadvantages he's faced in America."

"Okay . . ."

"But he's completely wrong," Shuri says quickly.

"He is wrong. He's racist."

"Don't say that. He's not a racist. He wasn't taught about black history in America and what you endured in the past."

"Maybe he'd like me better if I gave him history lessons," Malcolm replies with a smirk.

"You're so funny," she says as she jumps atop him, reaching her hand to find him again.

The next day Aafi arrives at Shuri's apartment, a few blocks from Hang Over Easy and Thompson Library. Close to the center of campus. The story of his visit doesn't take long to reach Dhegaha Dheer. She makes sure it does. Gossip is her drink; rumor her food. The apartment is a tightly maintained space. Very clean and meticulously kept. It's as though things are placed exactly where they should be and are never moved. Curtains the same colorful green ones displayed at her parents' shop. The duality of Shuri's identity seen in the religious verses on the walls and the record player and hip-hop vinyl collection in the living room under the TV stand. She keeps her space nice because she had to fight for it, opposing her parents' wishes to not move away from the family home. It's Aafi's first visit. He was so against her moving out that he spent his own money to hire movers for her. This way he wouldn't have to see it.

Shuri knows why he's come to visit her. She braces for the worst. Aafi is a constant lesson machine. The whole community knows he once took her to the sentencing of their next-door neighbor who was convicted of murder. They had no business being there, but for Aafi it was an opportunity to instill fear in his daughter. To this day Shuri can't stand watching court shows because of the memory of the chains wrapped around the man's ankles, the way they jangled as he walked into the courtroom.

But he doesn't bring up any shame-ridden stories. For the first time in a long time, ever since her mother's accident, they sit together drinking tea calmly.

But only for a brief moment.

"Look at all the things we've done for you. You're blessed," Aafi says.

"And I appreciate that, *Aabo*. But marrying me to someone I don't love is not a blessing. I love Malcolm. He's my blessing."

"This will ruin us, *Aabo*. What do you think people will say about us? About your mother?"

"Stop caring so much about what people think of us. You're my father. Don't you want me to be happy?"

"Of course, *Aabo*. That's all your mother and I want for you," Aafi says. "Your sweet mother. I wish she was here with us right now. She'd know what to do."

"She's still here with us, *Aabo*. She's not gone," Shuri says, placing a comforting hand on his shoulder.

"Marry Hassan. Stay and help me care for her. I've already hurt her enough with the car accident. She can't take any more."

"I'm not hurting anyone by being happy. *Hooyo* wants me to be happy."

"Happy is not going against our faith. It's not going against your father. And definitely not going against your mother."

"Stop bringing up *Hooyo* and using her against me. You hurt her. I didn't. You should have been driving safer that night. *Hooyo* wants me to marry Malcolm because he's the furthest thing away from being you."

Stung, Aafi stands up, walks to the door, slips his over-worked feet into his open-toe sandals. "You marry that black man and we are nothing to each other."

Dhegaha Dheer sips her tea the next day, sitting at her table at the mall. Abdi leaves his shop, approaches her, eager to tell her something. She waves him over, but hardly listens. She's heard the story at least ten times already today.

Knowing Malcolm worked at the hospital, Hassan caught the number 1 downtown, then hopped on the number 16 to campus. He wasn't sure what he had in mind, exactly, or even how to find the doctor. But luck was with him. He was walking toward the hospital doors near 12th and Neil, late in the afternoon, when he saw the black American step out, his tie loose and his sleeves rolled up. A woman followed him. Black American like him. Hassan fell back, listening from a distance, and could tell the woman was angry.

"Five years with me," he heard her say. "Five fucking years. You wanna throw that away?"

"Erica, please. You have to—"

"I don't have to do anything, Malcolm. This is on you."

"I'm sorry you heard it from someone else. I was going to tell you."

"I can't believe you're doing this to me. To us."

"Move on, Erica. We've been broken up for over a year. Move the hell on."

Hassan watched as they arrived at the entrance to a parking garage. Malcolm tried to open the door, but stopped as he heard Erica start to cry. He turned back to console her with a hug. She grabbed his face, forcing their lips together.

They stood together for a long minute until Malcolm finally, slowly pushed himself away from her. He whispered something in her ear, and the woman nodded. Another minute later they parted and Malcolm stepped into the garage. Hassan followed once he was sure the doctor was alone.

"You!"

Malcolm turned, surprise in his eyes as he recognized Hassan. "What are you doing here?"

"I'm going to tell Shuri you're cheating on her."

"What are you talking about?"

"I saw you kiss that woman."

"Were you spying on me?"

"You don't deserve Shuri," Hassan said. "She should be with *me*."

"Listen, man. You don't know what you saw. And you need to leave me and Shuri alone."

"Or what?"

"Don't test me, man."

Hassan rushed forward at that moment and grabbed Malcolm by the shoulders, shoving him toward a wall. Shocked, Malcolm tried to push him away. In the confusion Hassan stumbled, falling onto the garage's asphalt.

"Get real," Malcolm said, looking down at him. "This is over for you."

Moments after Abdi departs her table, Dhegaha Dheer watches as Hassan rushes into the mall, scurrying off to Aafi's shop. Curious, she follows. She knows he can't wait to tell Aafi what he's learned about Malcolm. Malcolm and Erica. She watches as he looks through the shared bathroom, the café, and the shop next door where Aafi usually socializes and listens to BBC Somalia on the radio. He's nowhere to be found.

Dhegaha Dheer says, "*Adeer* is at physical therapy with his wife."

"I forgot. Always Thursdays."

"How are things coming along with Shuri?"

"She's going to be my wife soon."

"I see. You took care of it."

"Yes . . ."

"Make sure you finish it."

Hassan pulls out his phone and dials Aafi, only to be greeted by voice mail. He hangs up and dials again.

"*Adeer*," he says, "give me a call back when you get this message. I saw Malcolm and there's something about him that I need to tell you." He glances over at Dhegaha Dheer for a good moment. "Actually, meet me at the new apartment complex on King Avenue." He recites an address. "Salam."

Inside the shop, with Dhegaha Dheer fluttering outside, unseen, Hassan flips through a photo album hanging on the edge under the register. Family photos. He takes a moment to appreciate one in particular. It's of him and Shuri. Cake smudged all over their faces and their arms wrapped around one another. Young and happy. As he continues to shuffle through the album, he comes to a set of documents. Legal documents, he sees, looking closer. Documents with Aafi's name written all over them.

That night, Abdi shows up to his shift at the downtown Marriott on Spring Street where he works as a janitor. To his surprise, there's Shuri, in a black dress that stops above her knees and wearing her hijab turban-style. Wrapped up in Malcolm's arms. Abdi makes sure it gets back to Dhegaha Dheer, sending a text before changing the liners in the large silver trash cans, his face hidden by a sand-yellow cleaning mask.

The happy couple are surrounded by family and friends to celebrate their engagement. More friends for Shuri than family. Friends that are more like her, caught between the vortex of what they want and their cultural obligations. But they're there supporting one of their own.

"This is Shuri," Malcolm tells the crowd. "My beautiful fiancée."

"It's great to finally meet you, darling," Malcolm's mother says.

It's the first time that Shuri has met Malcolm's parents. Their home in Georgia far away. A doctor and a retired US Army general.

"We've heard so much about you," Malcolm's father says.

"I can't stop talking about you, can I?" Malcolm says, holding Shuri tight.

"I'm sorry your parents aren't here," Malcolm's mother says.

With no hesitation, and her grasp on Malcolm firm, Shuri says, "Yes. Their flight was delayed."

"You should have said something, Malcolm," his mother says. "I'm sure it would be no trouble to push to tomorrow night. They shouldn't miss the big occasion."

Shuri knows Malcolm dislikes lying to his parents, but she continues anyway: "No, no. It's completely fine. They're okay with it. We see them tomorrow."

Everyone at the party wants a piece of the couple, selfishly. Photos to post on social media to show off the night. Photos that Dhegaha Dheer stares at greedily.

Around the same time, Hassan is standing in front of a brown door inside an apartment complex. He tries the knob, but it's locked. He texts Long Ears, asks for help. She offers a suggestion.

He looks to his sides. No one. He then checks under the door-mat. How amateurish and predictable, he thinks to himself, palming Malcolm's spare key. He lets himself in.

The living room a mess. Dirty clothes, dishes, cups, half-empty beer cans. Who would live like this? There's barely room to navigate without having to step over something. Hassan recognizes a yellow blouse in the mess that swells his chest with jealousy. He knows it belongs to the girl he wishes would leave it at his apartment instead.

He backs out, shuts the door without locking it, deciding to wait in the hallway. He pulls the legal file from his backpack once more, to confirm that what he read before is still a fact. He's reading as Aafi exits the elevator toward him.

"Whose apartment is this?"

"It's Malcolm's," Hassan says.

"Why are we here?"

"Because he's cheating on Shuri."

"Good job, *Adeer*."

"She doesn't deserve this."

"You're right. Shuri deserves you, Hassan. Not that terrible black man."

"No. Not any of this. Not Malcolm. Not you," he says, extending the documents to Aafi. "You were drunk the night of the accident."

"I was not drunk," Aafi replies, thumbing through the papers as if he's never seen them before.

"It says it right here. You were driving while impaired. You were drunk and you hurt your wife. Shuri's mother."

"I wasn't drunk. I had khat earlier that day with Abdi, but I'd come down by the time I was driving. I wasn't drunk, *Adeer*."

"Does Shuri know what you've done?"

Aafi looks once more at the documents, then lowers his head. No motion. No words. Hassan watches his face, sees the guilt left by the night of the accident and the loss of his wife, mentally and physically.

"Shuri is the love of your life," Aafi says. "Don't destroy your chances with her by this nonsense."

"Her love for me will remain because the truth is the only way. You taught me that, remember?"

"What if the truth tears your family apart?"

"Not if it comes from you," Hassan says. "I did enough by getting dirt on Malcolm. Telling Shuri the truth about her mother is the least you could do."

"You don't understand," Aafi says.

"I do understand." Hassan wipes away tears. "My father could have had a better life, but khat kept him stagnant. For you to do this . . . I love your daughter. So very much. I can't sit on this. I'm telling her."

"You won't do such a thing."

"I will—" Hassan says, but his words are cut short. Aafi seizes his neck between his hands. His breathing thickens by the second. His own hands pulling on Aafi's arms to free himself weaken and drop slowly to his sides until there's no air flowing out of him. *Dhegaha Dheer was right*, he thinks before crumpling to the floor. *Aafi is a man of grit.*

Aafi shakes Hassan to wake him up. When he can't, he drags the body inside Malcolm's apartment as he weeps uncontrollably.

"*Ya* Allah, forgive me."

Not long after, he leads Dhegaha Dheer, the only person he trusts, inside the apartment. She knew that getting a call from Aafi this time of night meant something big, but nothing like this. Nothing like seeing Hassan's body laid out awkwardly on the floor of Shuri's fiancé's apartment.

"I didn't want to do this. This wasn't supposed to happen," Aafi says, not able to control his unsteady hands.

"Go to the Marriott on Spring Street. You'll find your daughter. Leave this to me." Nodding, she shoves him out the door.

Aafi follows Abdi through the large double doors, making his way into the lively party. Aafi is unsettled by Shuri's intimate swaying with Malcolm, but he collects himself.

"Shuri," Aafi calls out in the middle of the dance floor.

"*Aabo*," Shuri responds, shocked, "what are you doing here?"

"Shuri?" Malcolm says, staring.

"I'm really sorry for this," she whispers, before turning to her father. "*Aabo*, I can't believe you're doing this."

"I'm here to see you be happy, *Aabo*."

"What do you mean?"

"I'm your *aabo*. I want you to be happy. If that means you want to marry this wonderful man, then so be it."

"Thank you, sir. I promise to take care of her," Malcolm says.

Shuri's face drowns with tears. She embraces her father.

Shuri brushes her teeth, dancing around with a large grin across her face to the music in her head from the engagement party. The revelry continued a little past midnight. She came home alone, leaving her fiancé to drop off his parents at their hotel and to grab a change of clothes for himself from his apartment.

The thought of her mother brings the happiness she feels to a screeching halt. Shuri knows her mother would have danced freely at the party, even as her father would have watched, disapproving, from a corner.

Shuri's cell phone vibrates while she throws her pillows on top of one another.

"Hey, babe," she says, "I'm heading to bed. Left the door unlocked for you."

"I need you to come to my apartment right now."

"Now? I'm so tired."

"Shuri. *It's Hassan.* His body is in my fucking living room. He's *dead.* I don't know what to do. Oh my God. What should I do? I'm calling the cops. Come right now."

There's a long pause. They listen to each other breathe down the phone line.

"Don't do anything. I'll be right there," she says.

A disheveled Shuri, hair loose, still wearing slippers, is met with yellow tape preventing her from entering the complex. She pleads to the officers to let her in because her fiancé is inside. She tries a coroner, busy gathering information with clipboard in hand. The investigators who are talking different possibilities. No one responds. Columbus police cruisers line the block, and a small group of reporters and cameramen camp out in their designated area.

Dhegaha Dheer approaches Shuri and points to a cruiser. Shuri sees Malcolm, seated in the back, hands cuffed, his wide eyes filled with fear.

"Oh my God, Malcolm," Shuri says, tripping over herself to reach him.

"He was following me the other day!" Malcolm shouts.

"Who was following you?"

"Hassan. I didn't do it. You gotta believe me."

"I know, babe. I know. I believe you," she says, placing her hands on the car window, badly wanting to touch him.

"Ma'am, move away from the vehicle," an officer says.

She turns, eyes wild. "You have the wrong person. That's my fiancé. He didn't do anything."

"Ma'am, I need you to move away from the vehicle," the officer repeats, taking her arm.

Shuri pulls free. As she walks away she notices Dhegaha Dheer pointing in her direction as she talks animatedly with investigators. *What could she be telling them?* Shuri asks herself. Dhegaha Dheer must know something. She's all-knowing, after all. Perhaps she might know why her father suddenly allowed her to marry Malcolm. *Does he know Hassan is dead?* She massages her temples, as if waking up from a horrendous dream.

Finished with her story, Dhegaha Dheer walks to Shuri. Folds her into her arms. She knows everything Shuri is thinking. Knows that Shuri feels it in her bones that Malcolm did not kill Hassan. She also knows it's wiser for Shuri not to find out about what her father did to her mother. Many people whisper the truth to Long Ears. It's up to her what truths she tells to the world.

A month later, Dhegaha Dheer sips her tea, hunched over a round table, in front of a small crowd of mall goers. She listens, sated, to the rush of gossip they give her, all of them so attentive.

"She's testifying against her father? About what really happened the night of the accident? What a shame," one says.

"What about the black man? What happened to him?" another asks.

"He's going away for a long time," answers another.

"She had two men who loved her. Now she has none."

"She lost her mother, and now will lose her family."

"What will happen to her?"

"No man wants to go near her," Dhegaha Dheer says.

"How can you know this?"

The gathered crowd goes silent, leaning in toward Long Ears.

"It is what I have heard," she says.

FOREIGN STUDY

BY NANCY ZAFRIS

West Broad Street

Z ach Wang stepped into the grocery named Garcia's to ask directions to Ohio State University. An hour earlier an Uber had taken him from the airport to a grand stone courthouse where the driver said foreign students had to officially check in. The driver parked in front of the courthouse and twisted around in his seat to face Zach in the rear. Eye to eye. Tiny stars flew out of the Uber driver's shirt collar. Mostly blue stars with a couple of red. The silence was long while Zach studied the tattooed neck. He smelled peppermint from the lozenge clicking in the driver's mouth.

"Okay, thank you," Zach said.

The open palm of the Uber driver slid over the top of the seat.

"I pay," Zach said. "I pay." He held up his iPhone.

The Uber driver shook his head. "Yeah. That." The peppermint lozenge materialized between his teeth as his tongue rolled it in somersaults. "That ain't gonna work, dude." The open palm remained outstretched until Zach placed a twenty-dollar bill upon it. His mother had warned him to have these bills at the ready, the way she always did with her yuan and the little bribes necessary for their widowed landlady.

On the steps of the courthouse he met a man who said he was a federal judge who explained that he could officially check in Zach and save Zach the trouble. He pointed to the police station across the street with a long-suffering sigh. "It'll take you all day if you try to do it yourself. I can get it done in ten minutes." He addressed Zach as "Mr. Wang" and followed it with a ceremonial bow. Zach gave the federal judge twenty dollars for checking him in. He followed the judge's directions to head down Marconi Boulevard to Broad Street and turn right. Soon Zach had left the downtown river behind and he passed the children's science museum where he noticed a pretty mother with a stroller and two toddlers. The museum with its big multicolored sign of lowercase letters buoyed his spirits. He smiled. A science museum would be close to the university. The federal judge had told him to continue beyond the museum, past a maze of new construction sites, to keep going and he couldn't miss it.

He walked and walked and walked before the sun finally discovered a cloud. He was without sunglasses and kept having to shield his eyes. It was impossible in the glare to view his surroundings clearly and distinguish what the horizon held. Now in the welcome cloudiness he blinked away the sunspots from his eyes. He could not see a university on the horizon. He could see, however, that the buildings had diminished into smaller and skimpier storefronts. Some had hand-painted signs and sandwich boards with crooked lettering that switched between upper and lower case. Some were nice, like the fresh-looking coffee shop across the street. A lighthearted marquee displayed the place's name in upside-down font. He twisted his head to read it: *BOTTOMS UP*. He had never heard that phrase, but yes, he could figure it out. You drink coffee, you throw your head back, the bottom of the cup goes up. Wonderful!

Without the sun the hot air grew thicker and grungier. Yet he smiled again. It seemed the American sky had taken pity on him and brought along a bit of his homeland. It had suddenly become a hazy day just like where he had grown up in Tianjin and he watched without alarm as this new American sky grew dark with pollution. Somewhere inside his backpack was a face mask, but he wasn't about to unpack and scatter his stuff right there on the street, in front of this little grocery that a scrawled sign called *Garcia's*.

Even without the sun, the summer heat intensified. The humidity crawled inside him. He burst into a dripping sweat. His backpack had grown heavy as sand. And then heavier— heavy as wet sand now, wet and getting wetter. When he bent over to catch his breath, lights popped at his temples. His mouth ached for water. He could not move his feet to cross the street to the coffee shop. He dropped the backpack on the sidewalk and staggered through the narrow doorway of Garcia's.

The grocery was clammy and dark. His brain knew he wasn't at the university, but his body could do nothing about it. It didn't even feel like he was in America, not that he would exactly know. He began to suspect that the federal judge who had given him directions wasn't a federal judge at all, even though he had resembled Confucius with hooded eyes, thick white hair, and a white beard. The beard was too messy, the hair too long, and the eyes poisoned. His mother would have shooed the man away with a hiss.

Garcia's grocery. The apostrophe told him Garcia was a person's name. In his head he pronounced it *Garsha*, the way *Marcia* was pronounced. Marcia was the name taken by a Chinese girl in his class at Nankai University. They had learned in class that *cia* was pronounced as *sha*, and *ch* as in *Zach* was pronounced like *k*. Marcia was already through two semesters at Purdue University. Purdue was in Indiana, right next door to Ohio. She told him to visit after he arrived. *Drop by*, she'd written in English, as casual as any American.

"Hello," Zach said to the young man behind the grocery counter. As soon as he spoke, two other men appeared. They were just there. He hadn't seen them arrive or come out from behind grocery items, many of which were brightly colored. Candy, he realized. He was looking at candy. And near the candy were blue and red slush machines, stirring in their transparent vats.

The young man wore a vibrant pink T-shirt that was much too big for him. The T-shirt said, *DON'T LAUGH, IT BE-LONGS TO YOUR GIRLFRIEND*. The two men who joined him were older and softer. Softer but bigger. They might have done something once. They might have been strong. Now they looked as though they had been living in the candy aisle the past few years.

"May I have it, please?" Zach pointed to the colorful ice. Already his mouth was open, his tongue reaching to taste it. He didn't think he could wait ten more seconds.

No one spoke. Zach fished out his wallet and pulled out a twenty. The young man grabbed at it. Zach held on and pointed to the slush machine.

The young man tugged harder. The twenty-dollar bill sprung loose. "Self-serve," the young man told him. He waved Zach to the machine. The three men watched him work it out on his own. Zach selected the biggest cup he could find. He messed with the spigot until the red melted ice poured out. And then he gulped at it—bottoms up! bottoms up!—until he spasmed over with a sharp groan and cradled his head. He tried holding his breath, he tried gargling, he tried gasping in and out. He clutched his head and pulled at hanks of hair un-til the pain from the brain freeze finally subsided. He stood up and looked around. Three men with body odor looking at him in a dark room with candy. This is where he was. He could not be in America. This could not be it.

"Are you Mr. Garsha?" Zach asked the young man in the pink T-shirt.

The three men burst out laughing. They spoke so rapidly to each other, Zach understood not a word. He had been very happy to speak with the Uber driver and the federal judge, so happy that he had understood everything they'd said.

"I would like to speak to the owner," he told the young man.

The men laughed harder.

"I must go to the university."

Already outside his backpack had been spotted. Two boys without shirts were trying to steal it. Zach set down his slushy and ran out, stumbling over some heavy bags stacked on the grocery floor. He noted vaguely the word stamped on the bags—*arroz*—as he picked up one of the fifteen-pounders and ran outside after the two boys. The boys should have been too young to sweat, but they were sweating like grown men. Their naked backs streamed rivulets. Each boy shared an end of the backpack as they tried to conquer its oppressive weight. When they turned to see Zach chasing after them with a bag of rice, they too began to laugh like the men inside the grocery. Zach heaved the bag of rice at them. It missed the boys but went right in between them and landed ahead on the sidewalk where it burst into a sea of white. One of the boys slipped on the grains, whipped into the air, and landed on his back. The other boy skated through the grains and took off. Zach was too tired to pick up the backpack again. He dragged it along the sidewalk, yanking it like a child having a tantrum back to Garcia's grocery. The young man in the pink T-shirt stood watching from the narrow doorway. The other two men watched out the window, their faces pressed against a grimy neon sign that advertised *Checks Cashed*.

Zach stood in front of the young man who blocked the doorway.

"How much for rice?" Zach asked.

The young man held out his hand until Zach put another twenty in it. The young man continued to block the doorway. Zach tried not to look desperate as he motioned toward the counter where his red slushy sat.

One of the older men brought it to him. "You need a lift, right?" the guy asked. A line of dirt from the sign's neon tube, straight as a ruler, stretched across his forehead.

When Zach didn't answer, the man made steering wheel motions. "We're going up to Hollywood. We can take you for twenty bucks."

"Hollywood!" Zach exclaimed. He shivered a dismissal.

"Right up the street," the man said. "It's like Chinatown."

"No thank you."

"Lots of Chinese in there."

"Yeah," the other man said.

Zach looked to the young man. "I don't know," the young man said. "I'm not allowed in."

At the top of a rise, the mammoth signage for Hollywood rose up like a giant bruised thumb.

The men parked their car, which had smelled very bad as Zach sat quietly during the fifteen-minute drive. He was ashamed he could not understand any of their chatter until he realized the English they were speaking to each other was Spanish.

"Are we at university?" Zach asked.

"Hilltop. And this is the top of the hill. Final stop." The man held out his hand for payment.

Zach lifted his backpack and strapped it on. The two men, soft and big, paused to enjoy Zach's confusion before pocketing the twenty dollars and stranding him in the parking lot. The Hollywood seemed to be a gigantic welcome center dressed in the flaming colors of bruises and bloody injury. When Zach finally walked in, summoning his courage behind a group of elderly ladies, he discovered it was a casino. At that moment he didn't care what it was, because it was mercifully, generously air-conditioned. The icy air returned him to life. He stood breathing for several long moments, his eyes closed in rapture.

A man swimming inside a mustard jacket greeted the guests as they entered. The ill-fitting jacket made the man look ravaged by disease. He nodded at each elderly lady passing through the golden ropes, but appeared too tired to speak. His feeble hand waved Zach to a stop. He motioned to the backpack. Zach undid the belt, unshouldered the pack, and dropped it to the burgundy carpet. The man waved over another person. A woman with a walkie-talkie Velcroed to her chest came over and looked down at Zach's backpack. She nudged it with her toe. The black clump that held his life didn't budge. She spoke into her shoulder before waving over a worker exiting a restroom with a broom and mop cart. The worker lifted the heavy bundle, balanced it atop the mop cart, and wheeled it to a cloakroom.

Zach sat down at one of the slot machines to rest and enjoy the cold air. The machine in front of him was fancy. It displayed a movie video of a girl in braids, a scarecrow, a tin man, and a lion. It seemed very familiar. He knew this story, he was quite certain. The video showed the arrival of a terrifying tornado and then the girl in braids and her little dog swirled inside of it. Yes, he knew this. It was on the tip of his tongue. "Pigtails," he said to himself, happy that he knew this word.

From his seat, he could spot a couple of food service venues. One of them was painted in lantern red, which probably signaled Chinese food. Zach squinted. He could make out the words *Zen Noodle*.

First thing, he would eat. He realized he was very hungry. Then he would make his way to the blackjack and pai gow tables and look for one of his own, a comrade who spoke Mandarin and could explain to him where he was and help him find where he needed to go.

Zach read the menu while he stood in line at Zen Noodle. When his turn came, he was only halfway through reading it. The cashier opened her eyes wide at him as if to say, *What are you waiting for?* She might not open her mouth to say the rude words, but her bold eyes were daring him to take just one second longer. Zach jerked under her gaze. He read out loud the current menu item he was struggling over: "Mongolian beef." To whatever questions she asked him next, he said yes. She handed him a receipt and tugged her head toward a waiting area. She wore a scarf that covered all of her hair. It was red and had the words *Zen Noodle* written on it. She was overweight in a way that he had already seen several times in the casino, women with unflattering arms that exited the confines of short sleeves.

At one of the snack tables he glimpsed two Asian faces. Small women who ate quickly. He would try them out, first in English, then in Mandarin.

Before he could step toward them, he was tapped on the shoulder. He turned to face the woman supervisor with the walkie-talkie, the one who had looked down upon his heavy backpack with the most unpleasant of expressions.

"We need to see your driver's license," she said.

"I don't drive," Zach said. "I don't have driver's license."

"Then you have to leave." She pointed somewhere, in the air somewhere, toward a sign somewhere.

"Oh," Zach said. "I'm very hungry. Very hungry."

"Let's go," she told him.

He sat outside the entrance, using his backpack for a cushion, until the casino security guard told him to move. He strained to heave the backpack over his shoulders, buckling it once again over his hips as he wove among the cars. He followed arriving cars to their parking spots and waited for someone Asian-looking to step out. But the casino guests were old women in groups of three, or an old woman pushing an old man in a wheelchair, or isolated single men who looked harsh and unshaven. Or guys who looked like the two men from Garcia's grocery. Men who laughed and took his money. Or men who didn't laugh and took his money.

A car pulled up beside him, an old gold car with rust eating the wheel wells. The cashier with the big arms and admonishing eyes sat behind the wheel. The *Zen Noodle* scarf was gone. Her coarse hair was mostly flattened against her scalp although a few stiff strands popped straight up.

"I got your lunch, baby. Come on and get it." She held out a Styrofoam plate clicked shut. He leaned through the passenger window to reach for it. "Just got off work," she said. "Now that wasn't right, what they did. Now how old are you?"

"I am twenty-six years old."

It was the third time in an hour than an American had laughed in his face.

"Now see," she laughed, "why you don't just show 'em your driver's license?"

"I don't drive."

"What's your name, baby?"

"My name is Zach."

"Your name ain't no Zach."

"My Chinese name is Wang Xiu Ying."

"Okay, Ying Ying Yong, you got a passport, don't you?"

"Yes, I have a passport."

"Why you don't show 'em your passport?"

"I don't drive," he said.

"It's not against the law not to drive," she said. "But being under twenty-one is. You gotta be twenty-one to enter the casino."

"Where is the university?" he asked. "I must go to university."

"The university? That's just down the street, baby. Come on, I'll drop you off. Because it's gonna rain any second. It's gonna *ray ay ayn*."

The cashier's car smelled sweet like flowers. They had driven for only a couple of minutes when she pulled into a vast, deserted parking lot. The long building at the end of the lot fanned out in two wings. The buildings were two stories, constructed out of white stone, and trimmed in turquoise paint and turquoise metal awnings. He stepped out of the car and walked toward the buildings until he could see what they housed. But for the pockets of weeds twisting out of cracks in the parking lot, he might have convinced himself that this indeed was the university.

Closer, he could see a stone etching that read, *Zenith Academy*. Beside it was *Community Dental*, and beside that it said, *Plasma Resource*, and in between were *For Lease* signs on the giant windows.

Zach walked back to the gold car. The cashier was busy eating his Mongolian beef.

"This isn't for PhD."

"You didn't say you were getting a PhD, baby. I thought Zenith Academy was good enough for you."

"I'm getting PhD."

He yanked his backpack out of the car and strapped it on. Each time he had shouldered the bag, it had grown heavier. Now he could barely stand under its load. He leaned over to adjust to the weight when the sirens went off. The sirens blew in from everywhere. They didn't keen to an unbearable pitch and fade out, like a police car passing by. The sirens never took a breath, just kept going in one loud shout.

Two men in underwear shirts and drooping shorts stepped out of an empty *For Lease* office and stared at him. It was true that when he once traveled to Beijing to meet a renowned scholar, the famous man had sprung into the alley in drooping jogging pants and a sleeveless underwear shirt, his sparse body hair worn away by age. But these men in the same underwear were not scholars. They were not famous men.

"Hey, Ying Ying Yong, you get back in here!" the cashier yelled at Zach. "What you think I'm gonna do to you?"

The two men looked dangerous. Their arms were solid blue with tattoos. His heartbeat quickened and then thundered hard when they took a step toward him and waved their arms. His feet scraped backward and his heel caught a tuft of weed. He lost his balance. The backpack did the rest. He found himself faceup in the parking lot, on top of his pack, trapped by his pack. It pulled him back down when he tried to sit up. It was too heavy, too heavily filled with his home and his hopes and the books he would write. For a moment all he desired was to lie there on the hot blacktop and think. He had learned new English words today and that made him happy. *I know pigtails*, he said to himself. *I know Garcia. I know plasma.*

"Is that what you think of me? Get in here!" the cashier screamed.

The sirens screamed along with her voice.

"Is that what you think I am!"

The car was rocking as she bounced in her seat, screaming. The cheap gold of the car turned a rich honey as the sky continued to darken. The rings of rust became bees buzzing about the wheel well. Behind the car, high in the sky, the cloud of dark pollution was swirling into something beyond contamination, something he had never seen before except on the slot machine video. He pitched to and fro on the blacktop, trying to wiggle free from his backpack straps. The two men were gone. The cashier gunned her car and charged off.

He watched her gold car jump a curb and screech toward a plot of concrete units all in a row, all with green metal garage doors. Her car bounced into the only open unit. He could hear the crash of fender. She got out of the car and stood in the garage. She waved to him. It was quiet now. In the new deadly quiet he could hear her screaming. The sirens had stopped. The cars had stopped. There were no other people. No vehicles on the road. No yellow buses. No long white trucks. *I know zenith*, he thought. *I know dude. I know bottoms up.*

The silence gave way to a rumbling as the sky charged toward him. From the storage garage, the cashier continued to wave at him, her large frantic arms larger than anything he had ever seen in his homeland—his homeland, which was coming to retrieve him before he had even arrived.

ABOUT THE CONTRIBUTORS

Kay Gaskill

TOM BARLOW is an Ohio writer whose stories can be found in several anthologies, including *Best American Mystery Stories 2013*, *Dames and Sin*, and *Plan B Omnibus*, and periodicals such as *Pulp Modern, Red Room, Heater, Plots with Guns, Mystery Weekly, Needle, Thuglit, Manslaughter Review, Switchblade*, and *Tough*. He is the author of the novel *I'll Meet You Yesterday* and the short story collection *Odds of Survial*.

DANIEL BEST is a Floridian transplant to Columbus, with degrees from Florida State and Ohio State. He practices law during the day, working as a civil litigator in cases ranging from product and professional liability to insurance, and writes during the night. He got his first taste of mystery by watching movies and documentaries while asking, "What if *this* happened?" Best can often be found killing his darlings during writing sessions at the Grandview Grind coffee shop.

Jason Mailloux

LAURA BICKLE grew up in rural Ohio, reading entirely too many comic books out loud to her favorite Wonder Woman doll. She is the author of the critically acclaimed *Wildlands* contemporary fantasy series. Bickle's work has been included in the ALA's Amelia Bloomer Project 2013 reading list and the State Library of Ohio's Choose to Read Ohio reading list for 2015–16.

CHRIS BOURNEA is a journalist, author, and filmmaker based in Columbus. He is the director of a documentary about the early days of professional wrestling, *Lady Wrestler: The Amazing, Untold Story of African-American Women in the Ring*. With Raymond Lambert, he cowrote the nonfiction book *All Jokes Aside: Standup Comedy Is a Phunny Business*, a history of Lambert's Chicago comedy club.

Elaine Phillips

JULIA KELLER is the author of the Bell Elkins novels, a mystery series set in West Virginia that begins with *A Killing in the Hills*, and includes *Bitter River, Summer of the Dead, Last Ragged Breath, Sorrow Road, Fast Falls the Night, Bone on Bone*, and *The Cold Way Home*. She is also the author of the *Dark Intercept* science fiction trilogy. While at the *Chicago Tribune* she won the 2005 Pulitzer Prize for Feature Writing.

Amanda Barczak

MERCEDES KING is a Columbus native and a founding member of Buckeye Crime Writers. With a degree in criminology from Capital University, she enjoys combining her love of pop culture with history and exploring the depths of deviant behavior. Since her stories often mix fact with fiction and are shaped by not-so-distant decades, she refers to many of her works as modern historicals. In 2016 and 2017, King was a finalist for the Killer Nashville Claymore Award.

Coley & Co.

KRISTEN LEPIONKA is the author of the Roxane Weary mystery series. Her 2017 debut, *The Last Place You Look,* won the Shamus Award for Best First PI Novel and was also nominated for Anthony and Macavity awards. She grew up mostly in a public library and could often be found in the adult mystery section well before she was out of middle school. She is a cofounder of the feminist podcast *Unlikeable Female Characters,* and she lives in Columbus with her partner and two cats.

Cathy J. Martin

LEE MARTIN is the author of the novels *The Bright Forever,* a finalist for the 2006 Pulitzer Prize in Fiction, *River of Heaven,* *Quakertown, Break the Skin,* and *Late One Night.* He has also published three memoirs, *From Our House, Turning Bones,* and *Such a Life,* in addition to two short story collections, *The Least You Need to Know* and, most recently, *The Mutual UFO Network.* He teaches in the MFA program at Ohio State University.

CRAIG MCDONALD has been a finalist for several American and French crime writing awards. His most recent works are *Head Games: The Graphic Novel,* based on his Edgar- and Anthony-nominated 2007 debut novel, and the 2019 novel *Once a World.* A lifelong central Ohio native, he has also launched and edited several weekly newspapers serving German Village. One of his stories was included in *Dublin Noir.*

Michael Ori of Orimedia

KHALID MOALIM is a Los Angeles–based filmmaker and writer from Somalia who immigrated with his family to Minneapolis at age six. He attended Ohio State University where he worked on the *Lantern* and served as a reporter at NPR affiliate station WOSU in Columbus. Moalim has worked on music videos, commercials, television programs, and the award-winning film *Sorry to Bother You.*

YOLONDA TONETTE SANDERS is an Ohio native and author of the Protective Detective series featuring Columbus homicide detective Troy Evans. She also runs Yo Productions, LLC, offering services to writers; founded the Ohio-based Women's Weekend Writeaway; is a cofounder of the yearly Faith and Fellowship Book Festival; and is an editor for Urban Ministries, Inc.

ANDREW WELSH-HUGGINS, an editor and reporter for the Associated Press in Columbus, is the author of nonfiction books on the death penalty and terrorism, and six novels about private eye Andy Hayes, an ex–Ohio State and Cleveland Browns quarterback turned investigator. Welsh-Huggins's short story "The Murderous Type" won the 2017 Al Blanchard Prize for best New England short crime fiction.

ROBIN YOCUM is the author of the Edgar Award–nominated, barnesandnoble.com best seller *A Brilliant Death*. He earned his chops as a crime and investigative reporter for the *Columbus Dispatch* from 1980–91. He has five novels and two nonfiction crime books to his credit. He lives in Galena, Ohio, where he is the president of Yocum Communications, a public relations and marketing consulting firm.

NANCY ZAFRIS, the former fiction editor for the *Kenyon Review*, is the author of the short story collection *The Home Jar*; the novel *The People I Know* (winner of the Flannery O'Connor Award for short fiction as well as the Ohioana Book Award); *Lucky Strike*; and *The Metal Shredders*, a *New York Times* Notable Book of the Year. She has taught at universities in Brno, Czech Republic; Tianjin, China; and Chennai, India.